ASSASSIN'S MAZE

ASSASSIN'S MAGIC
BOOK FOUR

EVERLY FROST

DISCOVER THE EVER REALMS

Seven series. One world.

Suggested Reading Order:

Bright Wicked
Storm Princess
Assassin's Magic
Soul Bitten Shifter
Supernatural Legacy
Dark Magic Shifters
Kingdom of Betrayal

For the warrior in all of us, the days we battle through, the new hope we find, the persistence that keeps us going, and the friendships we form along the way.

CHAPTER ONE

I creep along the alleyway, stepping silently around the trash, my blurred body imperceptible to the human eye.

The moon sits high above me, its light as cold as my heart.

I step out of its rays and into the shadows where I belong.

My fist tightens around my dagger. I didn't bring a gun for this mission and I won't use my killing power. I need information first.

My target leans against the dirty brick wall ahead, his breath frosting in the chill air, sleeves rolled up as if he doesn't care about the cold. I guess shifters run hot like me. Or rather, like I used to.

He picks his teeth before he ruffles through the wad of cash he just stole from the woman lying bleeding on the pavement at his feet. He targets business women, captures and drugs them before leaving them in a semi-public place to die. Their deaths look random, drug-related, but they aren't.

They are bloody messages for anyone who defies Lady Tirelli.

Half an hour ago, at midnight, his victim's daughter beat down the bookshop door begging me to save her mother. She wrote in my ledger in the middle of the night, mere hours after I fought Lady Tirelli herself—a woman whose true name is Amalia Avery, the last Valkyrie Queen.

Amalia told me that I'm dying and left me with a threat: bring the last Keres woman to her or she will rip Slade's soul from his body.

I intend to bring more than the Keres woman.

I intend to bring war.

My fist closes around the shifter's throat a moment before I press my blade against his ribs, angling the weapon so it will slide neatly between them when I want it to. He doesn't react. He can't feel my hand or the blade while I'm blurred.

I grip his throat tighter, firm enough to break his windpipe and snap his neck if he moves. Then I materialize beside him.

He jolts, drops the money, and curses. He tries to wrench out of my hold, but I press harder, forcing his head back against the brick wall.

He winces, curses, and whisper-shouts, "Assassin!"

I snarl at him. "You will tell me the time and location of Lady Tirelli's next weapons delivery."

The shifter's eyes boggle wide. His animal tries to take over, his human pupils constricting into fine points, his jaw partially shifting.

His leopard shines from his yellowing eyes, but I shove a knee against his stomach, pinning him with my body as well as my fist. "If you shift, I won't wait for an answer before I kill you."

The animal halts, the shifter's face reverting back into human form. "I don't know when it's happening."

He is Lady Tirelli's top henchman, next in line after the brothers I killed yesterday. I narrow my eyes at him, digging a fingernail into his neck as emphasis. "You do."

He tries to shake his head but he can't move within my grasp. Without mercy, I pierce his side with the blade, cutting skin but not too deep. He shouts, hits out with his free hand, but I absorb the blow and hold on.

I command him, "Tell me where it is!"

He hits me again. Pain bursts across my cheek, but I don't let go. Hissing beneath his teeth, he stops beating at me, his breathing erratic, panicked now that his blows have had no impact. "You'll kill me anyway."

It's true. I will.

"But I will do it quickly," I say.

He searches my eyes, snarling, "She's dying. The longer you take with me, the closer she is to death."

He means the woman he attacked. He isn't lying. She only has minutes unless I bind her wounds and get her to a hospital. But the mask I wear now is complete, cold, and unyielding.

"What makes you think I care? I want to destroy Lady Tirelli. Tell me about the weapons delivery or I will cut you to pieces slowly, starting with your…"

The blade slides down his thigh, slicing through his jeans.

He twitches. "I'll tell you… if you let me live."

I smile. "That sounds fair enough."

"It's tonight. A white van due into Boston at one a.m. traveling on the Northern Expressway."

"Good," I say. "Now tell me something else: where does she live?"

He rattles off the address, saying, "You'll know it by the rose bushes out the front. It's winter but they bloom anyway."

I wrinkle my nose. Roses. It's the scent Amalia wears to hide the stench of decay that exudes from every part of her body. She, too, is dying and has been for much longer than me. She has kept herself alive by assimilating stolen Keres feathers into her wings, using them to force her soul—her life—to remain in her body.

Without another word, I flip the dagger and drive it into his throat, all the way through his spinal cord. He doesn't have time to register shock.

Removing my dagger and allowing his body to hit the pavement, I rip off his shirt and hurry to the woman lying on the ground, quickly locating her worst wound. The cut to her left wrist is life-threatening.

Wow, he actually tried to make it look like a suicide—right down to the needle jabbed into her other arm, as if she couldn't live with herself because of her supposed drug habit.

Wrapping the wound and tying it off tightly, I pick her up and stride to the end of the alleyway, preparing to blur and release my wings.

"That was cold, Hunter."

Lutz Logan's amber eyes are bright in the moonlight. He chose to stand right where the light shines, making himself fully visible. I guess he knows better than to take me by surprise. More than he already has, that is.

He is hours away from killing Briar. Yesterday, she broke the assassin's code when she killed Fallon. She stopped me from ending Fallon and now she will take the punishment that I would have willingly taken to have seen him die.

Lutz volunteered to carry out Briar's assassination when nobody else would do it. He will accept all of my hatred... and he knows it.

I have to keep moving so I don't think about it. Only violence can numb my mind to the pain of losing her.

"What are you doing here, Lutz?"

He shrugs, rolling his shoulders. "I couldn't sleep. I kept thinking about my life before the Legion. What was so bad about it that I wanted to leave it behind...?"

I don't know anything about him. Not his past or his family—if he has any.

He doesn't give me time to ask, lifting himself off the wall as he says, "I will bring Briar's body to you so you can bury her."

I stiffen. "Damn you, Lutz Logan."

"I'm already damned, Hunter. There's no absolution for me."

He blurs on the spot, disappearing into the moonlight like a ghost.

Pulling the wounded woman close to my chest, I hold her tightly so I can blur and spread my wings, my silver feathers gleaming when I beat them and rise into the air, speeding across Boston.

I land outside the hospital where I told her daughter to wait. The young woman huddles against the wall of the building near the brightly-lit sliding doors, her head in her hands, her shoulders hunched. She cries quietly as she prays. "Please... please..."

I freeze, hearing my own voice begging my mother not to die while she bled out, her fists like iron around my hands, stopping me from plucking out one of my feathers to heal her. She didn't know that removing a feather would kill me. She just knew I shouldn't do it.

I force myself out of the memory, tucking away my wings and crossing the distance before I make myself visible to the human eye again.

"Annabeth?"

Her tear-stained face flies upward, her gaze shooting from me to her mother. "Mom!"

"Your mother is alive, but she needs medical attention right away."

"Thank you!" Annabeth doesn't waste time, spinning on her heel and tugging me toward the door, crying for help as soon as we step inside. "My mom needs help!"

It's risky for me to walk inside carrying the woman. At least I'm dressed in regular clothing—jeans and a cropped leather jacket—so I won't draw attention like I would if I were in a protective suit. Luckily, a couple of medics race toward us without much more than a glance at me.

I tell them: "She has cuts to her wrists and body. The damage to her left wrist is life-threatening. It's not attempted suicide. She was attacked."

Her weight lifts from my arms as they hurry her onto a medical stretcher. One of them says, "Wait here. The police will want to talk to you."

No chance of that. I grab Annabeth's arm before she can follow them. "Tell anyone who needs help defending themselves against Lady Tirelli that my ledger is wide open."

She gives me a nod before she hurries away. By the time she looks back, I'm blurred again. She misses a step, searches the corridor for me, but quickly continues after her mother. I wish my heart was as cold as I pretend it is. I wish I only helped Annabeth for information—to find out about the weapons delivery and where Amalia lives.

I take to the sky and head straight to Amalia's address, circling above the brownstone. The shifter was telling the truth about the roses. Bright red ones bloom on the bushes out the front, their scent heavy and defiant in the midnight air.

I alight on the roof, crouching and expanding my senses. The space inside the home is empty of life. In fact, I sense nothing more than bare walls. Then... my senses tingle. Valkyrie energy reaches out to me—Realm energy. It's a sense of being swallowed into a space I don't control.

I quickly lift off the roof and take to the sky before it hurts me. It must be a security mechanism. The brownstone may be Amalia's visible home but she has created a Realm inside it, which is where she actually lives. I can't get inside unless she chooses to let me. Nobody can. As long as she remains inside, she is untouchable.

Never mind. She has to come out eventually. And she will. Especially after tonight. My days of avoiding the hornet's nest are over. I'm going to tear that nest open, one stab at a time.

I fly north, heading along the Northern Expressway, scanning the horizon and keeping my eyes peeled for the white van. I calculate that if it's due into Boston at one a.m. then it should be right around...

There.

The vehicle speeds along the highway, a white blob clearly identifiable in the dark. I'll need to fly fast to keep up with it but I want to make sure it's the right one.

Still blurred, I dive toward it, keeping up with it for long enough to identify the driver. He is heavily armed and a manifest with a red rose printed on the front rests on the passenger side seat.

More roses. Subtle.

It's all I need to see.

The road is clear in front and behind the vehicle. The van is about to pass through a forest area so there's nothing on either side for it to crash into except a ditch and trees.

I wait another moment for a vehicle coming in the other direction to pass. Then I spear toward the driver's door, harnessing my strength to wrench it open and rip it right off, metal screaming into the night.

The driver shouts and lurches away from me, but I grab hold of him and pull him out. He hangs onto the steering wheel long enough to veer the vehicle off the road, saving me the trouble of diverting it.

A tranquilizer is all it takes to knock him out.

He slumps in my arms as the vehicle hits the nearest tree, its front busting up with an ear-splitting *crunch*.

I deposit the driver safely off the road where he will be easily found before I soar to the vehicle and grab the manifest from the seat, tucking it into my jacket.

Then I race to the back of the vehicle and pull open the doors.

It's filled with wooden crates, each one containing semi-automatic machine guns just like the ones Amalia's thugs used to attack Saber Lane.

I take note of the insignia on the side of the crates: *Draven Industries*. It's the company responsible for supplying most, if not all, of Lady's Tirelli's weapons.

I continue searching through the crates…

C'mon, give me something explosive.

I crank open the final crate and smile at its contents: a

shoulder-launched surface-to-air missile. It's the sort of thing used to take down low-flying aircraft.

Or Valkyrie like Slade and me.

Not today.

I prepare the weapon, step back from the vehicle, adjust my balance to accommodate the missile's weight across my shoulder, and take aim at the weapons inside the van. As soon as I fire this thing, the authorities will rain all hell down on me—not to mention I'll face Amalia's wrath.

A smile breaks across my face as I pull the trigger.

The van bucks, the missile tears through weapons, crates, and the van itself. The explosion is deafening, the heat an intense burn across my skin.

I welcome it.

It might be the last time I feel warm.

CHAPTER TWO

I steal inside the bookshop on Saber Lane, hauling the missile crate with me.

I remain blurred so I don't wake the people on the street. Vlad is still at Tansy's, along with the Guardian. The Legion assassins are staying on Saber Lane too, sleeping on couches and in any available spare beds.

Yesterday, Amalia decimated the Legion, killing half of the assassins who lived in the Realm, and then she sent Gareth and Fallon to attack my home. The fight ended when Tansy used her instinctive magic to create an unbreakable shield over Saber Lane that stops anyone from entering who has ill intentions.

It feels a little ironic that nearly every Master Assassin, including myself, is sheltering on Saber Lane tonight. The only one who isn't is Cain.

I warned him to get his sister out of the city immediately. I couldn't tell him that Amalia is Valkyrie, but I made sure he knew she is more powerful than we expected. Collateral damage means nothing to her.

Cain promised he was having breakfast with his sister this morning and he would prepare her to leave.

My ledger is open on the shop counter where Annabeth wrote in it, the Guardian's sanction glowing softly golden in the dim light.

I already recorded yesterday's missions in it, closing out the Tirelli brothers as complete. Against the entry for Lady Tirelli, I had to write: *Failed*. That single word carries so much weight, like a burden on my shoulders.

Slade is waiting for me in front of the counter, his focus homing in on me as soon as I step foot inside—even though I'm invisible.

We're slowly working out what his bond with me means and how it will affect him. It didn't hurt him when I left an hour ago like bonding hurt me, but it seems to allow him to sense my presence even though my blur is complete.

His presence is powerful to me, the slow smile he gives me making my stomach flip-flop, heat rising to my cheeks.

I nudge the door closed with my foot and deposit the crate next to a glass case containing several ancient books. When I turn back to him, materializing again, his expression falls.

"Hunter!"

"What?" I follow his line of sight to my bloody jacket. Annabeth's mother was bleeding and I'm covered in her blood. I quickly reassure him, "It's not mine. I'm okay."

The relief that rushes across his face kills me. He pulls me to his chest, cradling my head, his heart pounding. "Brandon was watching the hospital. He saw you save Annabeth's mother, but then he lost you."

Brandon Baker was a Novice with us, a steely-eyed man who once told me he would follow me to hell and back. He was always Ridley's choice when it came to keeping tabs on me. I shouldn't be surprised that he followed me tonight.

I growl, "I don't need backup."

"I know, but Ridley doesn't listen."

My father may have taken a while to get used to the idea of having a daughter, but in the last three weeks he has embraced it. It feels like he's trying to make up for his absence all my life. I can't hate him for it, even if it cuts into my independence more than I like.

Slade inclines his head at the crate with a satisfied smile. "It looks like you succeeded."

"I'm taking the fight to Amalia." I pull out the manifest and spread it open on the countertop. "This was the intended delivery address. It has to be Amalia's weapons storage. I'm not sure what else might be hidden there, but I'm hoping money, drugs, more weapons. If we target her supplies, we can cripple her operations. We'll need to move fast before she realizes we've located it."

Slade studies the page before he jabs his finger at the address. "This is where my mission was."

"Which one?"

"The one that nearly killed me. The seven guys I took down were all heavily armed. If this is Amalia's warehouse, then it means they weren't holed up there—they were guarding the place. *Damn…* If I'd known, I would have destroyed the building, too."

I place my hand on his arm. "Well, we know now."

I brush my fingertips across his cheek, easing away the regret in his expression. Just hours ago, Amalia ripped Slade's soul from his body and held him captive until I agreed to bring her the Keres woman.

He died, and neither of us has dealt with the shock of that yet. "You need to get some rest."

He gives me a small smile, stroking the loose hair behind my ear, his fingertips playing across my neck and tugging at the collar of my ruined jacket, making me shiver and draw closer to him. "So do you."

I squeeze my eyes closed with a sigh. "I can't sleep. I can't stop moving, Slade. I don't know how much time I've got and…"

He stops me with a kiss, gentle and warm. His hand closes around mine and his power tingles through me, bringing me alive with its force. "If neither one of us can sleep, then we may as well make the most of being awake."

For a second, I think he's going to kiss me again. I would welcome the distraction, his nearness. The painful reality is that at some point, I won't be able to function anymore. Every moment with him is precious now. I must have given him a smile that said my mind ran straight to my bedroom, because his chest rumbles with soft laughter.

He grins at me. "I wasn't thinking of that, but now I am."

I press my lips to his, capturing his attention. "Then what were you thinking about?"

He speaks softly, slowly, as if he knows it will be painful for me to hear. "William's notes. I think he found something."

I haven't grieved for William yet, haven't allowed myself to cry. His scribbled notes are scattered all over the kitchen table where he left them before Gareth and Fallon attacked yesterday.

William was trying to decipher the words hidden in the identical illustrations that appear in both the Keres Coda and Valkyrie Vade. It is a picture of a woman holding two children, their birth feathers floating in the air beside them.

William thought the woman was Nyx, the mother of death and that she had two baby girls: the first Keres and the first Valkyrie.

Our species weren't enemies then. We became enemies when the Keres Queen bought her freedom from the ringmakers by selling out the Valkyrie. That was when Amalia struck back, stealing Keres feathers to keep herself alive.

The Coda and Vade are safely contained in William's locked safe now, but when Slade and I returned from the ball, I couldn't look at William's notes—all his written thoughts, all the secrets he was trying to uncover. Reading them somehow feels like acknowledging that he will never come back.

Slade rubs my arms and back, giving me a moment to center myself, before he asks, "Will you come upstairs and look at them?'

I nod and step in that direction, climbing the stairs and preparing myself for the sight of the kitchen where William drank tea and studied books.

When we reach it, Slade pulls me into his arms, sliding a chair out from the table. He keeps me close as he takes a seat, gently propping me on his lap and nestling me in the crook of his arm, protective, supporting me in this moment but not making a big deal out of it. "William started writing to you..."

"Oh." I catch my breath and control my emotions, before I lean forward, focusing on the note Slade points at, written in William's curly script:

Hunter,

It's not a riddle. It's a maze…

His handwriting squiggles at the end, as if he was interrupted. He must have been right in the middle of writing when the attack happened. During our last conversation, William told me he had deciphered multiple words in the images but he was trying to piece together what they meant.

He told me what he had already deciphered: *riddle, royalty, adversary, healer,* and references to death and darkness.

Slade points from one note to the next, his strong hand traveling a curve across several papers in turn. "His notes are disjointed and at first I thought they were random, but if you look at them in the right order, there is a message in them for you."

Slade points from note to note, patching together the circled words on each page to read them aloud. His rendition is slow and faltering, but it comes together.

"The maze... hides... the original... birth feathers. The feathers heal... all wounds."

Slade's brow furrows at the next note. It contains many crossed-out words, as if William struggled even more with this one, but Slade persists. *"Only the Keres... can open the maze. Enter the maze... and defeat the...* hmm..." He taps the page. *"Silver royalty?"*

"Valkyrie Queen," I murmur. "Defeat the Valkyrie Queen."

"That's it."

I whisper, "Amalia said that the Keres woman can lead her to a place where she can be healed forever, where she can replace her lost feather with a more powerful one."

Slade nods. "That's why Amalia wants her."

He presses his cheek to mine, his bristles a soft graze against my jaw, demanding my attention. "If the feather can save Amalia, it can save you, too."

CHAPTER THREE

lade's determined voice thrums through me. "We need to find that Keres woman."

Hope is like a knife, sharp and piercing. I want to cling to it, but I'm afraid of it. Hope is fragile whereas *hate*... my anger is what drives me now: my determination to stop Amalia from hurting anyone else.

"Locating the Keres woman is the first hurdle. Convincing her to help me will be harder. We're enemies, Slade."

He presses a gentle kiss to my earlobe like planting a seed of belief in me. "Her mom trusted your mom. That has to count for something. You won't know until you try."

I twist so I can see him, chewing my lip. "You sound like William."

He plants another kiss on my forehead, then one on my cheek, carefully avoiding the stitches across my cheekbone. Amalia cut my face during our fight. Unlike previous occasions, I allowed the Legion doctor to stitch my wound.

Slade says, "I don't have his wisdom, but I will never give up on you."

His lips remain pressed against my cheek. A hint of worry enters his voice. "You're cold, baby."

It's normal for me to run hot, part of my inner power. My inability to retain my body heat is a warning that my power will eventually fail. The fact that I'm cold indicates it's failing faster than either of us wants to admit.

I run my hands through Slade's hair, trying to ease his worry, but the crease of concern remains on his forehead—he has worn it since we returned from the ball.

Amalia and I are both dying because we lost a feather. Both of them went to Slade: her feather powers his assassin's ring, and mine saved his life and changed him irrevocably.

I'm not sorry about either of those things.

I attempt to smile. "I'll warm up."

He is quiet, searching my eyes before he murmurs, "You need to cry. For William."

I shake my head, pressing my face against his neck. "If I start, I won't stop."

"You lost him, and you're about to lose Briar, too."

"I can't be weak in front of anyone," I say. "Not even you."

He cups my undamaged cheek with his hand, drawing back to pin me in his fierce gaze. "You are the most ferocious woman I have ever met. Crying will not diminish you."

I pull my legs toward my chest, barely remaining on his lap. Curling into him, I press my hand to his heart, sensing the deep rhythm and how his heart rate speeds up when I touch him. When I lean in to brush my lips against his, his heart kicks in his chest, a rapid *thud-thud*.

"I would like to be warm now," I whisper.

Slade's ferocity softens into a fire that makes my heart leap. He picks me up and carries me down the hall to my bedroom.

Inside, I'm confronted by the symbols of my life. The dress I wore to the ball is thrown over a chair. The garment is torn, ripped, and bloody. The top drawer in my chest of drawers is partially open, the glass case containing the Keres ring glinting in the lamp light. My protective suit hangs in my closet, my gloves fallen to the floor.

This bedroom belongs to an assassin, not a woman.

A silver glow builds around Slade as he lays me down on the bed and joins me there, stroking the hair from my eyes, planting gentle kisses in a careful row across my forehead, avoiding my wound.

His power sparks and our surroundings change, the walls and furniture shimmering and morphing into a cabin, the warmth from a fireplace filling the air around me. Thick, warm blankets appear around us and cushion our bodies, providing a safe cocoon in which to rest.

Once he is finished creating the Realm, Slade helps me remove my jacket and pulls the blankets around me so that he lies inside them with me. I wait for him to kiss me again, but he doesn't.

He nuzzles his cheek against mine, causing my eyelids to flutter closed.

"There's nobody here but me," he says. "You can feel whatever you need to feel."

I dig deep into the mire that surrounds my heart. To my shock what hits me hardest is not losing William, and it's not the fact that I'm dying. It's the way I felt when Amalia held Slade's soul in her fist and threatened to kill him whenever she wanted. It's the way I felt when the Guardian sanctioned Briar's death.

Powerless.

I will not be powerless like that again.

All my pain comes screaming to the surface. My eyes flash open. I jolt within the blanket, hook my leg around Slade, and push him onto his back, straddling him. My voice is fierce as I capture his gaze. "I won't lose you. Do you hear me?"

"I'm not going anywhere." He smiles up at me, the harsh lines of his face softening. "I'm bound to you."

"That won't stop Amalia."

He wraps his fingers in my hair, stroking down my back, before he lifts up beneath me to kiss me. "You won't lose me. I promise."

His kiss deepens, drawing me closer. He promised me I won't lose him, but I lose myself as he finds the base of my shirt and tugs it from the top of my jeans. His hands slide beneath my clothing and up my back, undoing my bra strap so his fingers can splay tantalizingly across my bare skin, stroking up to my shoulders and down to the small of my back.

I arch into his touch, my heart rate speeding up, his nearness growing more intense as he kisses me fully, tasting my lips and my tongue.

He breaks the contact, giving me a chance to catch my breath, while his gaze caresses me from my eyelashes to my lips and his thumbs stroke my sides, grazing the sensitive curve at the sides of my breasts.

I may be cold and relentless in the outside world, but with Slade... my control and inhibitions barely exist. I lose them both as soon as he maneuvers us into a sitting position to pull off my shirt and bra, his fingertips stroking along my neck and up into my hair, his lips finding all the soft spots beneath my ears and across my shoulders.

Shivers run the length of my spine and an intense ache grows in my center.

I curl my legs around him, wanting more. It doesn't matter how many times I'm with him, I never have enough.

I coax his arms up so I can remove his shirt, my fingertips following its hemline to stroke all the way up his chest, pulling it over his head and kissing his lips while I wrap my legs around him.

I trace the muscles of his back, inhaling his quick breaths as I arch against him, my center pressed against his.

With a groan, he rolls me onto my back, his hungry lips finding my neck, lingering over my breasts, and descending to my stomach.

Finally, my jeans and underwear find their way to the floor and Slade's mouth finds the delicate skin inside my thighs while his thumb grazes my center.

My body is ready, was ready since he laid me down on these blankets, but he takes his time exploring my curves as if he has never touched me before, kissing all my sensitive places from my neck to my toes.

I glower up at him when he deftly avoids my attempts to dispense with his jeans, the intense need in his eyes a deep contradiction to the way he slows us down.

His voice is a husky, barely-controlled whisper. "Every moment with you is one I want to last forever."

Neither of us knows how long I have or whether we will find the feather that can save me. Tears burn at the back of my eyes that he is stretching out these moments with me because he doesn't know if we will have this again, because there are no guarantees.

I relax into it as he continues to explore my body, but every touch makes my head spin and my need rises uncontrollably.

By the time he removes his clothing, casting his jeans and underwear to the side, I'm burning and shivering, and my breathing is out of control. He gives me a satisfied smile as he dispenses with his clothing, his appreciative gaze running over my naked form in a way that feels like a physical touch.

He isn't in any hurry, but I can't wait anymore.

I follow his movements, sitting up before he can turn back to me, running my hands across his chest to grip his shoulders and hook my legs around his hips so that I'm straddling him, taking control.

His lips rise into a smile that makes my heart pound. He adjusts my legs around his hips, giving me permission, his gaze focused on me as I press downward, needing the connection between us, drawing him inside me.

Our bodies fit perfectly; his fingers splay and flex around my waist, and the light in his eyes burns silver. I draw him inside me like I want to be part of him, part of his life, my body burning so hot that I can't think, can only feel as I draw him deeper.

Despite my determination to make this moment last, I lose control and shatter around him with a single movement, my senses exploding so suddenly that it shocks me. I gasp, crying out against his lips, my breath drawing in and out of me suddenly and sharply.

His eyes fly wide. "Hunter..."

I grip his shoulders harder and level my gaze with his, because it is not enough. He immediately senses my need, his hand shifting to support my head, tangling in my hair as our surroundings shift.

I barely register the way he conjures a bed behind me, swiftly positioning me onto it while he keeps our bodies joined.

The firelight flickers over the muscles of his arms and torso, highlighting all the hard lines of his face, even the slight cleft in his chin.

He is no longer in control of his breathing, his chest rising and falling rapidly as he strokes his fingers across my lips, following their path with his mouth, making me moan against his lips.

His body begins to move, every stroke fueling a fire inside me. The intensity in his eyes burns deep as I match his movements, fisting the blankets to brace myself, drowning in the physical connection between us.

Slade's movements become more demanding and I match his rhythm, my breathing increasing again, scorching sensation pushing my senses into overdrive.

He whispers my name, his hands shifting from either side of my head to grip my hips and draw me closer, the intensity in his voice telling me he is close to the edge but he won't let go of his control until I do.

His eyes meet mine, his hand brushes across my lower stomach, skirting my center, and my senses explode, the crash taking me closer to him even as all of me splinters apart, a storm building inside me that rips through me, its force carrying me upward, setting me free to ride the waves.

"Hunter." Slade speaks my name again, but this time it's intense, emotional as he draws me as close as we can get and lets go of his control, spiraling with me.

A long time later, before I finally fall asleep, I whisper against his lips, "I don't need to cry. I need to kill Amalia."

I will destroy her networks, annihilate her supporters, and wipe out her operations. She will regret ever targeting me.

More than anything, she will regret ever hurting the people I love.

CHAPTER FOUR

The early morning sunlight is accusingly bright as I stand in the middle of Saber Lane, feet planted, shoulders thrown back, my heartbeats ticking past at frightening speed.

Slade and I slept for a mere three hours before the new day's light struck through my nightmares and reminded me that today is a day of death.

Lutz Logan promised to bring Briar's body to me. Every second brings me closer to the moment when he will lay her at my feet. My teeth clench and my heart rate finally slows, anger making me colder than the air around me.

Slade is a steady presence at my side, his blue eyes steely gray in the early morning light. He is silent and focused, wearing ink-black clothing, his features set in the hard lines of a Master Assassin.

He ordered the other assassins to stay inside this morning until Briar is returned to me.

Her death is not a show for others to watch.

Then we will bury her with proper respect.

Movement at the front of the street makes my heart skip a beat, but it's Vlad, Tansy, my father, and the Guardian, all four moving quietly, their breath frosting in the chill air. Their coats slap their legs as they walk, the only sound breaking the heavy silence.

They don't speak as they join us, although Vlad lays a big hand on my shoulder, his gray eyes meeting mine for a moment.

He told me that he has to leave today. The way Tansy fixates on the pebbled street tells me she hasn't figured out how to say goodbye to him. She swore there was nothing going on between them but it is clear she doesn't want him to leave. Not when her emotions are still raw after losing William.

Ridley is the last to reach us, stopping directly in front of me. He undertakes a quick assessment of my stitches before he moves to stand on the other side of me.

He knows I won't break down no matter what happens this morning, but the brief touch of his hand on my shoulder tells me that he is here for me.

I clench and unclench my fists, focusing on the deep pit of anger inside me, my determination that nobody else will die because of Amalia.

I stop breathing when Lutz Logan's blurred silhouette races around the distant corner. I brace for what I don't want to see, forcing myself to remain frozen, unfeeling, and clinical.

He will hand her to me. I will take her body and bury her...

Except... Lutz runs toward us, arms pumping.

Empty arms.

I don't know what this means. Did he leave her body behind?

He materializes from his blur halfway down the street. His protective suit gapes open on one side, flashes of crimson blood visible between the flaps.

He rips off his facemask after he skids to a halt, dropping his backpack to the ground and sucking air into his lungs.

Technically, only Slade can demand answers from him, but this is my territory and there's no way I'm waiting for an explanation.

To my shock, I don't ask what happened or where Briar is.

Instead, I exclaim, "Lutz! Are you okay? Are you hurt?"

Damn. I used to hate this guy. I'm not supposed to care.

His gaze jolts to mine, as he appears as surprised as I am by my outburst.

He recovers quickly, his expression softening a little. He takes a moment to pull wide the rips in his suit to check his wound, his forehead creasing as he considers the cut. "I'm okay—it's only superficial. He left me alive when he could have killed me."

Lutz shakes his head, the hard lines returning to his expression as he continues. "He shouldn't have let me walk away."

I ask, "Who? Lutz, what happened?"

"I failed. Briar is alive."

My heart leaps. *She's alive!*

But the deep concern in Lutz's eyes halts my elation. His normally arrogant expression is missing, replaced with tension around his eyes and a clenched jaw.

Slade quickly steps into the conversation, his deep voice resonating through me when he asks, "How, Lutz? Briar has skills, but you're the most efficient assassin in my Legion. You've never failed."

There was a time when Lutz would have made the most of any compliment thrown his way, but he has changed since we joined the Legion.

He barely acknowledges what Slade said, focusing only on his question. "Briar was rescued by a bystander. The fifth rule was broken."

The fifth rule of the assassin's code states that a bystander who prevents an assassination forfeits their own life.

Slade considers the damage to Lutz's suit and the blossoming bruises on his face and the parts of his body that are visible through the rips. "A bystander did that to you?"

"Not just any bystander." Lutz takes a deep breath. "It was Archer Ryan."

My heart skips a beat. Archer Ryan is the son of Patrick Ryan, the mobster whom my mother protected from the time I was a baby until the day she died. It was because of Mom that Patrick rose to the top of the underground—a position that Amalia now holds.

The others shuffle behind me. The Guardian's eyebrows rise in surprise, Vlad exchanges a look with Ridley whose brow is deeply furrowed, and Tansy casts me a worried glance. She knows all about my mother's history. Archer Ryan is a part of Mom's past that I never understood—how Mom could protect such violent gangsters is beyond me.

Slade also appears wary. "I thought Archer Ryan was dead."

I shake my head. "Gone. Not dead. There was always a chance he would come back."

A torrent of questions crowds my mind. *Why now? Why save Briar? What is Archer's motive?*

The tension increases around Lutz's amber eyes. "A ghost didn't do this to me. He fought like a devil, as strong as a magical creature but he has no aura. He's human."

"With all due respect, I'm not surprised," I say. "Archer was trained by the most brutal mobster in the history of Boston's underground. There were whispers that Patrick would routinely beat and hurt Archer to destroy his humanity. Archer Ryan was trained to kill anything with a heartbeat and… apparently… to feel no remorse about it."

"Then why save Briar?" Lutz says. "Why leave me alive?"

He seems almost disgruntled about it, as if it's an insult to him that Archer went easy on him.

"Did he say anything to you?" I ask.

"He told me to get off his turf."

Slade nods beside me. "Then he wants Lutz to be his messenger. Archer is back to claim his territory." A sudden humorless grin breaks across Slade's face. "Amalia won't like that. Archer is a threat to her rule over the underground."

I answer the question in Slade's eyes, saying, "Archer could be an ally. A dangerous one, but having him on our side could make a big difference." I heave a frustrated sigh. "Except that he broke the fifth rule. The consequence is death."

Lutz says, "There's more."

He looks to the Guardian as he speaks, making me turn to allow her into our conversation.

She contemplates Lutz in her quiet and considered way. I've only seen her flustered a handful of times and each time she regained her heart of steel within moments. "Something has made you uneasy, Lutz Logan. What is it?"

Lutz presses his lips together for a moment. "Rowan tracked Archer from the alleyway where we fought. I didn't want to re-engage Archer but I also didn't want to lose him. Rowan called just now to give me an update. Apparently, Archer was last seen with Cain Carter."

Surprise flashes across the Guardian's face. "What was the nature of their interaction?"

"It was unclear. Archer stumbled on the sidewalk and Cain grabbed him before he fell over. I'm not sure why he stumbled. I didn't hurt him—I barely made contact during our fight. It's entirely possible that they just bumped into each other."

"But?" the Guardian asks.

"Rowan got the impression that they know each other. Cain seemed strangely…" Lutz shuffles again, his expression crinkling with discomfort. "He seemed protective of Archer. He made sure that Rowan backed off."

I shake my head. "That isn't possible. Cain wouldn't mix with the likes of Archer Ryan."

Lutz raises an eyebrow at me. "Cain didn't want Briar to die any more than I wanted to kill her."

The Guardian interjects before I can respond. Her question is sharp. "Are you suggesting that Cain asked Archer to intervene in Briar's assassination?"

Lutz shrugs. "Nothing is certain right now."

"You're damn right it's not," I snarl. "Cain wouldn't dishonor the Code like that."

I swallow my anger. Even I hadn't considered stopping Lutz, despite the fact that Briar is a dear friend to me.

But Cain… he knows how much I've lost. The hug he gave me last night nearly sent me into a spiral of tears and grief. He has more compassion than any assassin I've ever met—despite being capable of terrible violence.

Would he break the Code to save me from the pain of losing another friend?

No… Cain can't have had anything to do with it. "Cain is far too smart to be seen with Archer in public. If he orchestrated the interference, we wouldn't know about it."

Lutz gives me a rare smile and a conciliatory nod. "You're right. In fact, Archer started the fight by throwing a cup of coffee at me. If he knew he was coming to a fight, he would have brought his own weapons." His shoulders rise and fall in a slow, reflective shrug. "For the life of me… I got the impression Archer was in the wrong place at the wrong time."

Slade speaks up beside me: "Either way, Archer has proven himself to be a danger to us. He can't become an ally because he has broken the Code. Guardian, I'm bound by the rules. May I have a ruling, please?"

The Guardian's brown eyes flash. "Archer Ryan has broken the fifth rule. He has forfeited his own life. The Legion is sanctioned to carry out his assassination."

"Very well." Slade spins back to Lutz, but he chooses his words carefully. "Normally, this is something I would take care of myself but there are other things I need to do."

His gaze flashes to me for a moment before he continues, "Lutz, get cleaned up and take care of your wounds. I want you to track Archer, find out everything you can about him, and report back to me. I will end him once we have a full picture of his skills and motives."

Lutz appears disquieted. "Me? I lost a fight to Archer. I don't think I'm the best candidate—"

"You are my best assassin. Archer may have beaten you once but he won't succeed again." Slade's order is firm. "You will take care of it."

Lutz's expression turns blank. I consider the brutal assassin with some disquiet.

Twice now, Slade has complimented Lutz and he hasn't reacted with any hint of his former arrogance. He didn't want to assassinate Briar. In fact, he was full of self-loathing that was only overpowered by his unbending duty to the Code.

In that regard, he and Slade are identical. Neither of them will break the Code no matter what it costs them.

Slade may wear pain as a mask.

But Lutz… he wears pain as a shield.

"Yes, Master." Then his expression changes, defiant for the first time. "For what it's worth, I wasn't sorry to let Briar go."

Without another word, he turns on his heel and strides away along the street.

With that, our group disperses. The Guardian places a gentle hand on my arm before she follows Lutz. "I'm glad Briar is okay."

I give her a formal nod despite the sudden overwhelming relief that floods me.

Briar is safe. A failed assassination can't be attempted again. She is truly safe.

Vlad presses a big hand to my shoulder with a broad grin before he turns to Tansy, clears his throat, and politely asks her if she will join him at the Diner for breakfast.

It will be one of their last meals together and Tansy is quick to agree. She blinks rapidly as she passes me, hiding her tears.

It shocks me to realize that her tears are for me, not herself, when she touches my arm and says, "I'm glad you didn't have to say goodbye to Briar today. You don't deserve to lose anyone else. I'll come by later to heal your cheek."

She hurries away before I can respond. Her offer to heal me is unexpected. She knows I'm too proud to ask. The look in her eyes and the way she quickly assessed my stitches told me she will see me soon—whether I ask her or not.

Ridley is stern as he says, "You take her up on that offer, you hear me? I'm heading out to the Realm now. I'll be back to check on you."

I snag his arm. "Dad, it's not safe in the Realm."

Amalia proved she can breach Realms—a consequence of her power being used to create them. "Amalia could attack again at any time."

He gives me a quick hug. "That isn't going to stop me."

He strides away before I can argue, leaving me alone with Slade who asks, "Do you want to find Briar before we head out on our mission?"

I desperately do. I want to see her and hug that bony old woman until she doesn't have breath left in her body. But with every minute we delay, there's a higher chance Amalia will relocate her supplies from the warehouse we've identified.

On top of that, Briar is fiercely independent, a woman who flits between shadows. She could have come back to the Lane already, but she hasn't.

I shake my head. "Briar's more resilient than anyone I've ever met. If she hasn't shown up yet, it's for a reason. I won't find her if she doesn't want to be found."

Slade squares his shoulders, his jaw setting in a determined line. "Then we have a warehouse to destroy."

CHAPTER FIVE

We fly in hot and fast, soaring toward Amalia's warehouse located in Boston's south—a deserted stretch of broken buildings and graffiti-mottled alleyways.

We're both dressed in protective suits with multiple tranquilizer guns strapped to our chests. Slade carries the missile launcher in a harness on his back, his strength ensuring that its weight barely makes an impact on him.

Since we need to maintain visual contact at all times, we can only partially blur. The bright sunlight doesn't do us any favors, especially as it reflects off our wings.

We aren't under any illusions that we will be able to sneak in undetected.

Right now, speed is our friend.

Slade gives me a wolfish grin as the first chatter of machine gun fire tells us we've been spotted. "Meet me when you've taken them down."

My heart rate speeds up as he breaks off to the right, aiming for the shooters on the roof. I tilt left, pull out my tranquilizer gun, and zigzag through the air toward the shooters on the ground as a hail of bullets follows my descent.

I dive at the three men positioned at the door, fully blurring for a moment to disorient them before I take aim and fire three quick darts. I zigzag long enough for them to fall to the ground unconscious.

The first man's finger remains pressed against the trigger as he drops, spraying bullets at his comrades. Zooming in from the side, I grab the weapon just in time, aiming it high to avoid collateral damage.

Bending the barrels, I partially materialize again and fly around the corner.

My fist sends the man running toward me crashing into the side of the building. I shoot a dart into his chest as I race past, quickly blurring and firing into the oncoming group.

Five darts later, my gun is empty. I holster the empty weapon and pull the next, but the delay gives the final man time to leap over his tranquilized comrades, take a knee, and shoot wildly into the space where he last saw one of his comrades fall.

The bullets spray in a wild arc toward me.

I release my wings just in time, lifting myself above the danger. Ordinary bullets can't pierce my protective suit, but I don't want to take any chances he will get in a lucky shot across my eyes, which remain exposed.

I rise above him as he sprays bullets from side to side.

Taking aim, I pull the trigger and he kisses the ground.

Running around the perimeter of the building, I ascertain that I've taken care of the guards on the ground. I'll come back to drag them away from the explosion—and there are more shooters to contend with inside the building—but for now I soar upward, heading toward the roof, seeking Slade's location.

He spins in and out of invisibility across the rusty panels, appearing in one place and then the next, crashing through the guards before they have the chance to fire back. They at least have the sense not to fire at each other.

He is less agile with the weight of the missile launcher on his back, but he uses flight to give him greater impact as he slams his fist down on the last man. A tranquilizer dart meets his target's neck and the guy falls in a heap.

"Getting inside the building will be harder," I say, swapping out my empty guns for two fresh ones, testing their weight in my hands. "We'll need to shoot fast."

"Watch out for the upper right hand side window. There's a loft inside this building from which they can shoot. Last time, the guards inside used armor-piercing bullets." He shrugs and taps his shoulder. "I found out the hard way."

I shiver. That was the life-threatening wound I had to heal with my feather. Armor-piercing bullets are bad news. "Let's aim for that window first then."

We back up to the edge of the roof, facing inward, spread our wings, and drop, taking aim as we freefall.

A bullet whips past my ribs, nearly hitting my wings before I tilt in the other direction, locating the shooter and firing a tranquilizer into his shoulder. He recoils and drops, but two more men take his place.

Slade takes a more direct approach, tucking his wings and spearing through the window, guns outstretched. Glass sprays in all directions and the men don't stand a chance.

I follow him into a pit of hell filled with an upward rain of bullets.

"We have to blur!" Slade ducks and rolls across the loft,

shouting, "Go right. Don't come left without showing yourself. I can't guarantee that I'll sense you."

He disappears from sight and I follow his lead, blurring myself completely when I drop from the loft, kicking the nearest man and tranquilizing him before I land, one-knee bent, on the grimy floor.

The warehouse is filled with wooden crates. A large metal vault sits at the other end of it.

Before I can stand, a bullet bites my shoulder and passes straight through me. It was a lucky shot for the shooter while I'm invisible but very unlucky for me.

Pain explodes across my torso, the impact knocking me off balance.

I can't afford that. One bullet wound will take days to heal.

The pain makes me angry. My power surges to the surface, but as much as I'd love to fly around these assholes spreading death at a single touch, I can't kill any of them. This mission is off the books, unsanctioned.

I sprint toward the nearest stack of wooden crates, counting on the guards to be smart enough not to fire at the explosives. Darting behind it, I check my wound, grimacing at the flowing blood before I take a deep breath.

Focus, Hunter.

I'm still invisible, but the moment I start firing, they will know where I am. Shots from the other side of the room tell me that Slade is on the move and the men are struggling to keep up.

Arms outstretched, I rise up on one knee, take aim at the oncoming men and fire rapid shots. One, two, three, four…

I only have eight darts in each gun and I quickly empty all of them into the oncoming horde, pulling the trigger in quick repetition. Slade's end of the warehouse falls silent—he's got them all—but I'm out of tranquilizers and there are still four men coming at me.

I launch myself out from behind the crate. Just as I plan a reckless path into the spray of bullets coming my way, an invisible force rams through the men from behind, scattering them before four quick darts appear in each of their chests.

Slade materializes mid-spin. "You okay, Hunter?"

I adjust the harness I'm wearing so that it covers my bullet wound. If Slade sees it, he'll pull me out of here right away and we still have the vault to deal with. My black suit will hide the blood for now.

Satisfied that he won't see it, I let out my breath, managing a truthful answer. "I'm a little banged up."

He runs his eyes over me, closing the gap to check me over. I pull away before he gets too close. "We need to keep moving."

He gives me a growl that says he doesn't like my evasion, but he holsters his empty tranquilizer gun and hands me his spare. "Just in case."

I angle the weapon at the vault. "We need to know what's inside that vault."

We stride toward it before coming to a standstill. It's about nine feet high and just as wide—a big, gleaming metal box. The panel at the side tells me it's password controlled.

"Or not," I say, since it appears impenetrable.

Slade arcs an eyebrow at me. "Let me try."

I watch carefully as he closes his eyes. He has used his power to control doors before but unlocking a vault seems like a stretch.

To my surprise, he doesn't make a move. Instead, our surroundings change.

A long corridor appears, plain white walls rising up beside us. When I turn, it stretches in either direction as far as my eye can see.

"A Realm?" I ask, wondering how that will help us.

Slade says, "Take five steps forward."

I do as he asks, stopping when he places his hand on my arm. The Realm fades, replaced by darkness.

I blink into the dark. "Did we just step inside the vault?"

Slade's assassin's ring glows, filling the space around us with dim, silver light.

He smiles. "We did."

I turn in a circle, staring at the piles of cash and neatly-laid-out-jewelry that lines the shelves. It's all blood money.

"These walls are cast iron. We won't be able to destroy the vault from the outside. Do you have a match? We can light all this on fire and then get out of here."

His eyes gleam, silver light bleeding into them. "I think I can do one better."

He places both hands against the inside of the door and braces against it. I take a step back when the metal creaks and groans.

Slowly, he pulls his hands apart and the door splits in two, a small rip that grows wider the further he separates his hands. Sunlight gleams through the expanding crack. Screaming metal fills my ears and I flinch as the top of the vault rips apart, each side folding down toward the ground. The money rustles in the fresh breeze.

Slade turns back to me, the silver clearing from his eyes.

I stare at him in surprise. "How did you do that?"

He has used his assassin's magic to control the movement of objects and people before but not to this extent.

"The iron," he says. "It's like putty in my hands. Same with doors—it's not the wood but the hinges and the handles that I focus on."

I reflect on my power and Amalia's. Slade derives his power to make Realms from her. He got his wings from me. But he was already incredibly strong and that is because he is a ringmaker…

I shake off the direction of my thoughts and state the obvious with a smile. "Now an explosion will destroy it all."

Slade smiles. "Let's get the men out of here."

Ten minutes later, we've dragged or flown Amalia's guards well away from the warehouse, ensuring that they will be safe.

After asking me to stay at that distance and to be ready to fly, Slade wastes no time loading the missile launcher and firing into the empty building.

The explosion washes across me, wood and glass exploding in a satisfying plume of fire and smoke.

He heads toward the burning building and hoists the launcher off his shoulder. His muscles bunch before he throws it into the inferno. It spins through the air and disappears into the wreckage. Then he pulls out his burner phone complete with a voice distorter and reports the fire to the authorities. Not that the explosion wouldn't have attracted attention already.

The phone follows the same arc as the launcher.

He turns back to me. "We need to mo—" His eyes widen and his voice takes on a worried tone. "Hunter, you're hurt."

A brief glance at my shoulder tells me that all of the moving around has shifted my harness and revealed my bullet wound.

Slade immediately bends to one of the unconscious men and rips off his shirt, using it to bind my shoulder and staunch the blood flow. I'm reminded of Annabeth's mother. Now I'm the one with my enemy's shirt keeping me from passing out.

As soon as he's finished, Slade gathers me into his arms. "I'm taking you to Tansy right away."

I don't object. A week ago, I would have, but the blood loss has left me light-headed and I'm done pretending that I'm fine.

Slade holds me tight as he blurs and takes to the sky, speeding high above the rooftops. His warmth and energy are so strong that they tingle through me, making me feel less like death warmed up.

"Thank you," I whisper into his chest, even though I'm not sure if he can hear me.

He coasts for a moment, taking his eyes off the sky to drop a kiss on my forehead. "From now on, please tell me when you're hurt, okay?"

"Oka—"

Oomph!

A hard object smacks me right out of his arms, spinning us both off course.

My wings burst out of me as I fall. I spiral, quickly forcing my wings closer to my body to turn my wild tumble into a focused dive.

I dip and rise again, following Slade's path.

That's when I sense a presence in the sky higher above us.

Roses.

CHAPTER SIX

malia appears on my left, higher up and close to the cloud cover, her wings curving as she aims to fly back at me.

The last time I saw her, she threatened to take Slade's soul.

Panic spears through me and I shout to Slade. "You can't let her near you. I'll hold her off. Go!"

His fists clench, his wings beat, and he stays put. "You're hurt. I'm not leaving you."

I dive at him, pushing him away. "She can kill you, Slade. Go! Now!"

With a shout of frustration, he twists and plunges away through the air, casting backward glances my way until he disappears into the cloud cover.

Just in time. Amalia has almost reached me.

I fly at her, intercepting her downward path. She pushes backward with her wings, maintaining a safe gap between us. With a brief glance at Slade, she lets him go.

The sky rapidly darkens around us. Lightning flickers in

the distance. The air buzzes and the hairs on my arms stand on end. The storm grows far too quickly to be a natural phenomenon. Below me, the Earth is replaced by a sea of boiling clouds.

Amalia has trapped me in another Realm of her creation, this time an electrified storm. Relief fills me that Slade escaped just in time.

Her wings don't work as well as mine because of the Keres feathers she wears. I can beat her in the sky, so she is compensating by making me fight the environment as well.

I scream into the growing wind. "Coward!"

A bolt of lightning strikes close by, electricity sizzling the air.

Amalia's silhouette lights up in the bright bursts and her voice carries to me over the sound of the storm, amplified by her power. "Oh, Hunter. You don't look so great."

Damn the bullet wound.

"That wound won't heal without a lot of help," she says. "It would be so much simpler if you joined me. You could take a Keres feather and live like me."

I fly toward the edge of the storm, testing the limits of the Realm around me, sensing the boundary before I hit it. Then I fly the other way, testing its width. It is not as wide as I had hoped, not as much room to maneuver.

She has boxed me in.

I whirl back to her. "What the hell do you want?"

Her wings curve, creaking closed. Just like she did during the sandstorm she created last night, she conjures a platform beneath her feet that supports her in the air. "You destroyed my warehouse, Hunter. I'm a little upset about that."

"Good. That was the point."

She's wearing another dress, its length flowing around

her as the platform carries her to my position. I ascertained during our fight that her legs are her weakness, although I'm not entirely sure what's wrong with them, because she keeps them covered at all times.

Her radiant hazel eyes and glossy brown hair defy the fact that she is dying, too. She halts a few feet away from me. Every beat of my wings gusts across her, but she seems to delight in the sensation.

"I used to fly like you," she says. "My wings were young and strong."

"You didn't trap me here for a walk down memory lane, Amalia."

"Queen!" she snaps. "I am not Amalia to you. I am your queen."

No. I refuse to acknowledge her claim of power over me. "The warehouse, your money, and your weapons are gone. There's nothing more to talk about."

"But there is. There's the—" Her eyes suddenly narrow. She sucks in a sharp breath. "Oh… you don't know."

I demand, "Know what?"

She laughs, a delighted sound. "Poor Hunter is in the dark again."

I glare back at her as she floats closer. *What the hell is she talking about?*

She licks her lips. "Tell me, Hunter… Where is the Horde's Realm?"

It's such a sudden change of subject that I stare at her. "Why are you asking me that?"

She revealed last night that she has difficulty lying to me. It's why she stayed away from me for so long, but so far today, she has done a splendid job of resisting her impulses.

Not this question, it seems.

She blurts, "Because Cain has something I want and I intend to get it back. You will tell me where the Horde's Realm is hidden—"

"No."

She takes a threatening step toward me, teetering on the edge of her platform, floating higher than me so that she looms over me.

I rise to meet her, swallowing my anger. "I don't know where it is. I've never been there."

She snarls, "Damn. You aren't lying. I can tell when you lie to me." She tilts her head back and shouts into the wind, "Useless girl!"

I shake my head at her. I'm done listening to her riddles. I beat my wings, pushing away from her, prepared to beat down the walls of this Realm if I have to, but she lurches forward, barely remaining on her platform, to grab my arm with fingers that feel like claws.

She gives me a sly smile. "Tell me, Hunter, who do you think would win in a fight between Cain and Slade?"

Slade's name rises to my lips. He is the strongest assassin, with the most powerful assassin's magic. In addition, he is a Valkyrie. Cain is strong, but in a fight between them, there is no doubt in my mind who would win. "Stop playing games with me, Amalia."

"Queen!" She grinds her teeth but pulls back, her head held high. "Would it influence your answer if I told you that Cain wears a Keres ring?"

"What?" The exclamation leaves my lips before I can stop it.

The first-known Keres ring is a training ring that Slade used to wear. He assured me that when he became Master, he took it out of circulation.

The second known ring sits hidden in a drawer in my room.

Now Amalia is telling me that Cain wears the third. I'm not sure how that's possible. Cain touched me plenty of times. Surely the Keres ring would have burned me—

Except that he wasn't allowed to wear it in Boston. He only wore it in the Realm and I had no direct physical contact with him on those occasions.

Amalia floats closer to me again. "You'd better stop them fighting each other, Hunter."

"Why would they—?"

"Or the outcome will be devastating."

Why is she saying that Slade will fight Cain? They're friends. There's no reason for them to fight...

She's messing with me, that's all. She enjoyed telling me last night that I'm dying. She is enjoying the mind games she's playing with me now. Her sick revenge for her lost warehouse.

"Let me out of here!" I follow up my demand with a fist that she quickly blocks with her forearm. She uses the contact to push off from me, the platform whisking her away.

She shouts across the distance, "You will find out the location of the Horde's Realm for me or—"

I'm done taking orders from her. I soar toward her, reaching deep for my killing power as I sweep my wings and knock her off her platform.

As we drop through the air, my hand closes over her forearm, my power sizzles through my fingertips, and the nearest Keres feather bursts into flame.

The ashes rise like flower petals as we plummet, illuminated in the lightning that crackles around us.

Amalia's eyes shoot wide with fear. A scream dies in her throat.

Her wings snap open with a painful *crack* and she tears away from me, taking flight into the storm before I can get a tighter hold on her.

I follow her through the lightning. If she's going to box me in, then I sure as hell am going to make her pay for it.

Her flight is jagged and uneven, uncontrolled, but she has the advantage that she controls our surroundings. I zip and weave through the glittering lightning bolts she sends my way, barely escaping the path of the last electric strike before I catch up with her.

My hand closes over the top of her wing, yanking her backward.

I will make her regret coming near me. I will make her think twice about trying it again.

Her face lights up as the storm crashes around us. Off balance, she attempts to steady herself by grabbing my wing, but I angle out of her grasp.

I don't let her regain her balance, my furious fists striking her shoulder, cheek, and jaw. Her head snaps back before she can propel herself out of my reach. She manages to evade my next hit and the one after that, wobbling like a butterfly in the wind.

I increase the speed of my punches, forcing her to twist and spin to avoid me.

"I told you I will bring the Keres woman to you," I shout. "Stay the hell away from me until I do."

She launches herself backward with a scream. "You're lying! You won't do it!"

I break into a smile, easing up for long enough to allow

her to get her hands up to protect her face. "You have no power over me, *Amalia*."

Her chest heaves and for some strange reason, her focus darts down toward the ground, a slow smile growing on her face. "You think you can beat me because you've gathered the support of the Master Assassins. But I'm building my own army of assassins, Hunter. An army made of supernaturals who have been rejected and shunned by everyone around them. They will soon be ready to fight and then they will crush everyone you love."

With a snarl, she pushes away from me, flying into the storm. Despite her claim to power, her wing beats are painfully slow as she disappears.

I watch her go, my anger replaced with confusion and renewed fear.

Her threat that she's building some sort of army has sent a chill down my spine, but my more immediate confusion is caused by her threats about Slade and Cain.

None of what Amalia said makes sense to me. *What could make Slade and Cain fight? And why does she want to know where the Horde's Realm is located?*

I need answers but first I have to get out of this place. I also need help for my wound.

I soar toward the edge of the storm while the wind billows around me, strong enough to throw me off course.

The clouds break and rain pours down, fat droplets beating against my wings and forcing me toward the clouds below, until I adjust the angle of my flight to accommodate the extra pressure falling from above.

I wrench myself upward and to the side, banging against the Realm's boundary, anger churning inside me again.

Amalia left the Realm intact. *Damn her.* Could she leave

me here for days? Weeks? Longer? She probably thinks she can subdue me here.

I've faced assassin's magic before. I remind myself that her magic is my magic too—Valkyrie power. I never learned how to create a Realm. I don't know if it's possible for me, whether it's only something Amalia can do, but even if I can't make a Realm…

I'm going to learn how to *un*-make one. Right now.

The edge of the Realm is an optical illusion. It looks like sky and clouds stretch far into the distance, lightning reflecting inside them, but when I plant my hands against it, it is flat and solid.

I close my eyes and reach deep for my power.

I'm good at destroying things. This should be no different.

Power surges through my fingertips, a bright force that sparks through the barrier, threads of silver fire cutting across its surface.

Crack.

The barrier shatters like glass, jagged shards spiraling inward, cutting the air as they fly toward my face and body.

I fling my wings around myself and turn my back to the onslaught. Blades slice across my feathers, but my wings are strong, indestructible. Even in my weakened state, they protect me.

I huddle inside them, drawing my knees to my chest, curled up inside the cocoon I created.

Thunder cracks around me and then… silence.

The shards beating against me turn into cool rain drops, a final gentle shower of them falling across me.

I take the chance to open my wings, water dripping off me to the Earth far below.

An ordinary sky greets me, a weak sun peeking through the clouds.

The Realm is gone.

I quickly harness my blur to keep me obscured. My energy wanes, my vision swims, and my flight is unstable.

I can't pass out here. It's not safe.

I focus on my wing beats, praying I don't fall from the sky.

CHAPTER SEVEN

I stumble onto Saber Lane, making it no further than the entrance before I lose my invisibility.

Teetering beside the lamp post, I grab hold of it, but I can't stop myself sliding to the ground, my knees clunking against the cobbled stones.

"Hunter!" Slade catches me before my head flops to the ground, drawing me safely against his chest.

My ear rests against his heart and I exhale with relief, unclenching the hold on the fear that was building inside me. It's possible I might be going into shock. Not something I've experienced before but I've heard people talk about it.

"I don't want it," I murmur, trying to see where Slade is taking me. He veers quickly left and Tansy's face appears in my field of view. Vlad stands in the corridor behind her.

"Quickly," Tansy says. "Bring Hunter to the parlor and lie her down on the floor. Vlad, bring me my spellbook."

As soon as Slade sets me down on the carpet, the book appears above me for a moment before Tansy closes it, places it on the floor, and leans over me.

She presses her hand against my shoulder, closes her eyes, and murmurs beneath her breath, "Pictures not words."

Warmth from her power spreads across my arm and torso, radiating from the point of contact in all directions.

My body sinks into the floor, relaxing for the first time in days. Her healing power travels through my neck up to my cheek, and the sting from my stitches fades. A gentle tugging in that location tells me that Tansy is removing them with her power.

Heat continues to blossom across my shoulder, increasing until it is nearly too hot, before it recedes again.

I slip in and out of consciousness as she continues to heal me.

Regaining my senses, I catch glimpses of Slade pacing at the side of the room, stopping only to drop his head into his hands before he gets up and paces again. Vlad stands watch from the door, his expression closed off and masked.

Finally, Tansy, her eyes gentler than I've ever seen them when she looks at me, tells me she is finished.

She whispers, "Why aren't you healing like normal, Hunter?"

I test my arm. The pain is gone and the wound is mended, but I'm too exhausted to get up. I tip my head back against the carpet, my hair spreading out beneath me, pulled out of the braid I put it in this morning.

Unable to move, I'm at the mercy of Tansy's questioning eyes and the worry behind them. Both she and Slade know about me, but Vlad doesn't. The fact that she's willing to ask me questions in front of him tells me the extent to which she trusts him.

My heart tears a little for her. Vlad has to leave today and the chances of him coming back are slim. I know what it feels like to be torn apart from the person I love, and circumstances are not in their favor.

Slade kneels beside me, sliding his big arms behind my back to support my torso and help me sit up.

His cheek presses to mine, but when he speaks, he's angry, his words cutting across me. "Hunter, never tell me to run from a fight again. You can't use the bond against me like that. I nearly lost my mind when you made me leave."

I gasp. I *made* him go? Did I compel him against his will? If it wasn't for the bond, would he have stayed and fought Amalia?

I try to see his eyes, but he's holding me too tightly to tip my head back.

Kneeling beside him, Tansy exchanges some silent communication with him. When she and Slade first met, they were in danger of tearing each other's throats out, their reactions fueled by fear and misunderstanding, but now something has shifted between them.

Tansy's ferocious glare intensifies. "A Realm, please, Slade. So that we can speak in private. Vlad, step inside."

The giant assassin does as she asks, quietly pulling up a chair. I can't read his expression but that's not unusual for Vlad. Discerning his inner emotions is like trying to see through an opaque shield.

Once Vlad is seated, Slade shifts slightly and the air shimmers around us. The room doesn't change into another place, but silence descends, blocking out the sounds from the outside world. A gauzy veil appears across the windows, giving us privacy.

We are contained in a safe bubble where I can speak freely, but fear rakes through me.

I've been holding on to my secrets for so long, only

sharing them when they are torn out of me. Telling Vlad what I am and what's really going on is a leap of faith for which I am not prepared. Telling Tansy that I'm dying is a truth I'm not ready to speak. Telling Slade that I will never force him to run to safety is a promise I can't make, because if it comes to a choice between him or me, I already made that choice when I gave him my feather.

I've been alone for years, moving only by the power of my own two feet, living only by my own determination.

"No." I pull out of Slade's arms, wobble to my feet, and pretend that I'm not an unsteady mess right now. "I won't put any of you in danger."

Slade folds his hands across his chest as he stands, silver light bleeding into his eyes, an immovable force. "You have to tell them what's going on. Tansy and Vlad care about you. If they can help—"

"They're not allowed to care! Nobody is allowed to care. William cared and now he's dead." My shout shocks me, echoing back at me in the protected space. "This is my war, Slade, not anyone else's. At some point, I will have to break the Code. We both know it. When that time comes, I don't want anyone else tangled up in it."

Slade draws himself up to his full height, a growled response on his lips. "Hunter, you're very good at pushing people away, but I'm telling you right now, I won't be pushed. I'm staying right here."

My heart is brittle and bitter. "You're bonded to me. You don't have a choice."

He crosses the distance rapidly, but he doesn't touch me. "Choice? I chose you, Hunter. Bond or not. I don't believe for one second that happened against my will."

"But my Mom…"

His gaze softens. "No matter what happened between your Mom and Gareth, there must have been a time when they felt something for each other."

I whisper, "I'll never know. But I can't take any chances." I point out the window in the direction of the Lane, this place that is filled with humans and magical beings who all sought safety and freedom from their past—a safety that I could destroy. "I have to protect them... all of them... from Amalia."

"We will," he says. "All of us. Together."

He still doesn't touch me, but the air sizzles in a way that tells me he is about to access his power. The depth of trust and emotion in his eyes is too much for me.

"I know how hard it is for you to trust people," he says. "I spent most of my life in a fog of rage, making anger my shield, the mechanism I used to keep anyone from getting close to me. So... I'm going to take a leap of faith first."

Tansy has located herself next to Vlad. It's impossible to miss the way she has reached for his hand.

Slade says to them, "I trust you both with this secret."

His wings form at his sides, glowing and silver, the electrical currents of Valkyrie power streaking through them.

Tansy's eyes widen, but Vlad hardly reacts, a wry smile spreading across his lips.

Tansy asks, "How?"

Slade doesn't exactly answer her when he says, "I'm not a born Valkyrie. I became one."

Vlad's smile turns into a wolfish grin. "Now I feel a lot better about the fact that you beat me."

Slade turns back to me without putting away his wings,

tucking them close to his body. "This is my war, too. I'm fighting it with you, Hunter."

I have struggled for a long time to let Slade care for me. It's taken me a long time to let him into my heart. To really trust him.

When he reaches for me, his touch is impossibly calming, gentle, as if he's absorbing all my anger with every stroke of his hands across my arms and back.

"I want to be part of the battle, part of your life," he says. "Loving you is not about taking the good, it's about sharing the hard, about walking this path with you." He runs his hand across my healed cheek. "Your choice is whether you let me."

Cain and I once had a difficult conversation about accepting help. He said that if I was his woman, I wouldn't think of it as "help" because loving someone is not about obligation. Slade doesn't want to be seen as "help." He isn't treating me as if I'm not strong enough. He wants to fight with me.

"Will you let me?" he asks.

He has taken a massive leap of faith by revealing his wings in front of Tansy and Vlad, the kind I never would have taken.

I nod once, then stronger. "Yes."

Tansy's expression softens as she rises from her seat and reaches for my hand. "Please, Hunter. I lost William. I can't lose you, too. Something's wrong with your healing power and I need to know what it is."

I clear my throat, my eyes burning, struggling to speak through my emotions. "Since Vlad hasn't freaked out yet…"

"It will take a lot more than wings to freak me out, woman," Vlad grumbles at me. He rises from his seat and crosses the distance, a tower of muscle dressed deceptively in casual jeans and a gray t-shirt.

"I tell you what, Hunter," he says. "You and I seem to do well when we make deals with each other. So let's make a deal. You tell me one of your secrets, and I'll tell you one of mine."

I narrow my eyes at him as he challenges me with an arched eyebrow and a smile that I can't quite decipher.

"Deal," I say.

I spread my wings, not slowly like Slade did, but with power, stopping them scant inches from crashing through the furniture on either side of the room.

The sound of them spreading snaps through the silence.

They glimmer, every feather shining and radiant, the source of my power and my life.

Vlad takes a step back, eyes wide now. "Okay. Those aren't fairy wings." He side-eyes Slade, speaking in his blunt way. "No offense, but... uh... I figured yours were the result of some sort of magic spell, something connected with your assimilation with your assassin's ring whereas Hunter's..."

"It's not a spell," Slade says. "Hunter used a feather to save my life but as a consequence—"

He stops speaking. It's up to me whether I tell them the consequences.

He was right: I can't keep the truth from the people around me anymore.

I point to the gap in my feathers and say, "I'm dying."

CHAPTER EIGHT

I tell Tansy and Vlad everything.

I start at the beginning—my mother's bond with Gareth, her protection of the Keres baby and the baby's birth feather, and now my search for the Keres woman with the violet eyes.

I tell them who Amalia really is—my supposed queen—and how she survived all this time. I tell them the frustrating truth: only a Keres and Valkyrie together can end her. Then I tell them that my only hope is a hidden Realm that is fabled to contain the original birth feathers of the first Valkyrie and Keres.

Tansy is ashen when I finish. She smothers a cry with her hand. "It's my fault. I didn't heal Slade that night. You never would have given him a feather if I had helped you. You're dying because of me."

I take her hand, pulling it away from her mouth, holding it in mine the same way she took my hand after William died. "I gave Slade a feather because he was riddled with bullets from guns you didn't fire, Tansy. He was riddled with bullets because he chose to go on an impossible mission. He chose to take the mission because I asked him to become Master of the Legion. We are all responsible at one time or another."

She wipes her eyes. "I promise you, Hunter. The next time you ask me to do something, I will do it. No questions asked."

Vlad folds his arms across his chest. "The woman my former Master chased across the country and assassinated because of Amalia… She was Keres? And her child is the key to opening the hidden Realm?"

I nod. "That's correct."

He is thoughtful, his eyes narrowing, sifting through information in his logical way. "My Master chased her from the forests near Portland. It stands to reason that the Realm is located in the west."

Tansy gasps, her eyes flying wide. "West!" She grabs hold of my arm. "William said something about that yesterday. He wanted to write it down but there wasn't time before the attack happened. We had to protect the books."

Slade casts a hopeful glance at her. "I'm trying to decipher the books to know for sure."

"I can help you," Tansy says. "I was helping William."

"I would appreciate that," Slade says.

Vlad asks, "What can I do?"

"Find out everything your Master knew about that woman and her child," Slade replies. "Any clue might help."

"Consider it done. But I have to warn you, if the Realm is located in the forests, your path to it won't be easy." Vlad takes my hands in an unusual gesture. "We had a deal, Hunter. You told me your secrets, now I'm going to tell you one of mine."

He casts a gentle glance at Tansy when he says, "My mother was a witch."

Tansy's eyes widen again and I twitch with surprise.

"But you're human," I say. "You have no aura."

"Exactly." He sighs. "When I was born without any magical ability, my mother was cast out of her coven. It broke her. She took me to my father and then she disappeared. I searched for her my whole life and never found her.

"But her coven was not satisfied even then. They sealed off their territory in the forest so none of them could meet and fall in love with a human again. If the Realm is located there, you will have to get past Mother Serena first."

"We'll need your help," Slade says.

"You have it," Vlad promises.

I give Vlad a cautious smile. "That explains how you know so much about witch's magic."

He grins at my wings. "This explains how you took a death blow for me."

He levels his blunt gaze with mine as if he has read my mind. "We will end Amalia one way or another. But we will find a way to do it within the letter of the Code."

He knows me too well. Vlad is a bear of an assassin who speaks his mind, kills without regret, but treats Tansy as if she's priceless.

I know in my heart that the next time I face Amalia, it won't be as an assassin. It will be as a Valkyrie.

A distant *thud* makes me jolt.

Slade gives us a warning glance. "Someone's here." His wings disappear and my own snap shut, folding away while Slade removes the magic around us. As soon as the Realm disappears, Tansy strides to the door.

It bursts open the moment she turns the handle. I glimpse a green beanie and an old coat before Briar hurtles down the corridor toward me.

Briar shouts, "I went to the bookshop, but you weren't there."

My heart leaps to see her. I pull her inside the room and throw my arms around her bony shoulders, hugging her tightly. She thrums within my grasp, as if she's going to leap out of her skin.

"What's wrong?" I ask.

She pulls back, agitated, "Where is she?"

"Who?"

Briar jumps out of my hold, her wild eyes searching the room before she grabs my arm. "Where is Archer Ryan?"

I startle and glance at Slade and Tansy who wear equally perplexed expressions. Only Vlad is expressionless, a slight narrowing of his eyes conveying his bewilderment.

Archer Ryan fought Lutz this morning and saved Briar from assassination.

"Not here, Briar," I say. "Why would he come here?"

"Not he. *She*. I told her to come here where she would be safe!"

Briar rounds on Slade, her ferocious glare causing him to take a startled step back. She advances on him with a snarl, "This is Hunter's territory. You have no power here."

The determination on Briar's face and in her aggressive stance remind me that she was once a Horde assassin.

If she were holding a weapon, I would fear her right now. In fact, like Lutz Logan, she probably doesn't need a weapon to kill.

"Stop." I squeeze my eyes closed and take a deep breath,

stepping between her and Slade to demand Briar's attention. "You said: *she*."

Briar clearly struggles with my response, rounding on me. "I did."

"But Archer is Patrick Ryan's *son*."

"No."

"No?" My head spins. "A daughter?"

"It was a surprise to me, too. The first day I saw her was the day you entered the Legion to become a Novice. She uses an alias—calls herself "Grace"—but she told Lutz that her real name is Archer Ryan. I believe her. The way she fought him proves it. She even saw through his blur!"

"Wait, what? That's not possible—"

Briar rushes on. "She told Lutz to get off her turf or she would kill him."

That's exactly what Lutz reported.

But I shake my head again. "Archer Ryan can't be a woman. Archer Ryan is a cold-blooded killer. He was raised in the underground. He is Patrick Ryan's son. *Patrick Ryan.* The man Mom protected. And his *son*." I can't seem to stop repeating myself, as if the more I say it, the more real it will be. Not a lie like Briar is trying to make me believe.

"No!" She takes hold of my arms and shakes me hard. "Archer Ryan is a woman. A kind-hearted, caring, thoughtful young woman who hides her scars and knows how to fight dirty to beat assassins like Lutz Logan."

My stomach is sinking. I whisper, "Lutz said she threw a coffee cup at him…"

Briar's shoulders sag. "She was bringing me breakfast. Instead, she saved my life—"

"Why, Briar? Why would someone like Archer Ryan help you?"

Briar growls, "I'm trying to tell you! She gave me food. Every damn day for the last few months. She always carries a book in her pocket. She wears her father's ugly old coat. She lives in a rundown apartment and chews her nails when she's nervous. She is a good person. Now she's going to die because she helped me."

"No." I shake my head. "This can't be true…"

Briar's voice rises. "Don't you see? *Archer needs you!*"

The room suddenly spins.

Those words… Ridley said the same thing to me…

I sway on the spot, reaching out to plant my hand against the wall. *"An archer needs an arrow."*

Slade reaches my side, shooting Briar wary looks. "What is it, Hunter?"

"Dad gave me a message. The last time Mom saw him, she asked him to tell me: An archer needs an arrow. She gave me the name 'Glass Arrow.' She even designed my tattoo in the shape of an 'A.'"

Shock burns through me. Clarity is a sharp blade cutting through my thoughts. "I am the arrow and Archer needs me."

Slade's expression clears. "Your mother wasn't protecting Patrick. She was protecting baby Archer. Archer is the child your Mom saved."

I nod. "She hid the baby in plain sight with the fiercest protector she could find. Patrick Ryan wasn't Archer's real father." I spin and seize Briar's shoulders. "What color are Archer's eyes?"

She startles. "You think she's the girl you asked me to find?"

"Briar! Her eyes!"

"Blue, but she wears colored contact lenses. I know

because she dropped a case of them out of her shoulder bag one day."

I try to breathe. "Of course. She grew up in the underground. She would hide such a distinctive trait."

Briar shivers in my grasp. "She broke the fifth rule, Hunter. She's in danger. You have to stop the Guardian from sanctioning her death."

My heart rate speeds up. "It's already done. Archer has been given a death sentence."

Briar's face falls. "Already? I tried to come back sooner but Lady Tirelli's thugs were following her. I had to stop them. I told Archer to come here—that she would find help on Saber Lane."

I don't blame Archer for not following Briar's instructions. Someone like Archer who has survived the underground, lived in it her whole life and then run from it when her father was killed, will never trust anyone but herself.

There is no such thing as safe in a life like hers.

Briar eyes light up with ferocity. "She fought like you, Hunter. With precision. Finding her enemy's weaknesses. She is a force to be reckoned with."

Of course she is. She is Keres. A born warrior. As strong as me.

"You said she saw through Lutz's blur." I flick a glance at Slade. "He didn't tell us that."

"I don't think he believed it happened," Briar says. "But Cain's people were watching. They followed Lutz to report back on the outcome of my assassination. Archer bumped into Cain right after. She didn't look well and he helped her."

The mention of Cain rings alarm bells for me.

Amalia said something about Cain when I fought her. She

asked me where the Horde's Realm is and who would win in a fight between Cain and Slade.

Slade is a wall of stone. "I can't protect her, Hunter. I'm bound by the rules. If it comes to a fight between me and her…"

Briar doesn't know that I'm Valkyrie so Slade has to speak carefully, but his meaning is clear. If Archer is the Keres woman, then she can only be killed by a Valkyrie—or if she chooses to die. Slade is the first male Valkyrie. I made him so.

He could end her.

She could end him.

There is no good outcome to that fight.

In fact, any assassin with a ring powered by a Valkyrie feather could hurt Archer. Since most are, she is far more threatened by assassin's magic than I am.

"What about Lutz" I ask.

Slade says, "I told him I wouldn't kill Archer until he completes his surveillance. He may have approached Cain already." Slade's gaze drills into me. "You have to get her out of this mess. I can't go with you. The moment I see her, I'm bound to end her. You have to bring her back to your territory where I don't have jurisdiction. Then we'll find a way to save her. We have to."

Archer Ryan is the Keres woman who can open the maze and help us find the feathers.

She has the power to save me or let me die.

I can't waste another moment. I spin to Briar with my heart pounding. "Tell me where to find Cain."

CHAPTER NINE

I ignore my numb fingertips as I soar across Boston, my body blurred as I speed toward Cain's house.

Leaving Slade is like leaving the sun behind. I grow colder with every moment.

By the time I reach Weston where Cain's house is located, I can't feel my feet.

I sail past mansions and perfectly manicured gardens until I reach a massive white home surrounded by a wrought-iron fence that is laden with security. Cain once told me that he uses infra-red security cameras, so I land further down the street, well before I trigger the security system.

I walk the remainder of the distance on foot, fully visible, stamping the feeling back into my toes.

I stop at the gate and stare up at the security camera, waiting to see if I triggered anything. A moment later, I press the buzzer, braced and ready for anything.

A male voice that is not Cain's says, "Hunter Cassidy, we were expecting you. Please step inside."

The gate clicks open and slides wide enough to allow me through. In the distance, a man strides toward me. He looks vaguely familiar, definitely ex-military, and completely human.

I stop several paces away from him.

"I'm Ross, the head of Cain's security detail," he says. "We met a few weeks ago, if you recall?"

I nod. "Your people watched over Saber Lane for a while." That was after my first failure to heal properly. "I'm here to see Cain."

"I'm afraid you missed him. He left with his sister an hour ago. They're already on a plane to Austin."

"Only with his sister?"

Ross gives me a small smile, but doesn't answer my question. "This is for you."

He hands me a white envelope with my name written on it. I rip it open on the spot.

Hunter,

I'm taking Archer with me. She isn't what we thought she was. In fact, she is a lot of things we never suspected.

Tell Slade that if he wants to end her, he will have to go through me first.

All I ask is that he waits a week until I have been appointed as Master of the Horde. The Guardian can arrange the fight.

I won't give Archer up. Don't try to contact me. I won't respond.

Take care of yourself, Hunter.
Yours,
Cain.

"Damn." I rub my hand across my forehead, my stomach sinking so fast that I think I'm going to throw up. Cain is trying to protect Archer, but he's breaking the Code by interfering and for a Master to do that...

Slade is duty bound to challenge and kill him.

Amalia's laughing voice repeats on me. *Who will win in a fight between Slade and Cain?*

Damn! This whole situation just got a lot worse. I could have found a way to protect Archer, but now Cain has challenged Slade. Cain, who wears a Keres ring...

They could kill each other.

I scrunch the envelope in my fist, wanting to set it on fire. My timing is terrible. I should have been here an hour ago.

Ross asks, "Can I have someone take you back to Saber Lane?"

I'm already backing away. "No, thank you. I'll catch a cab."

I race along the pathway, the gate opening just in time to let me through before I pelt down the street. I run until I'm sure nobody is watching. Then I blur and take to the sky, welcoming the numbing cold this time.

I can't let them fight.

I land on Tansy's doorstep, put away my wings, and race inside.

Slade is the first to jump to his feet.

Briar hovers anxiously behind him. "Where is she?"

I press Cain's letter against Slade's broad chest. "I was too late. She's gone. Cain took her. He has challenged you, Slade."

Slade stares at the letter without touching it. "Cain has decided to interfere? *Damn.* Does the letter say why?"

"Read it."

Slade slips the letter out of my grip, but he keeps me in the circle of his arms. He curses softly as he reads. When he finishes, he hands the letter to Briar who passes it to Tansy and Vlad.

Slade rubs his fist across his forehead in frustration. "This situation just got a lot worse."

My heart is beating far too rapidly. "Amalia will do everything she can to find Cain and get to Archer. She told me she doesn't know where the Horde's Realm is so that's the only safe place for them. We need to get a message to Cain somehow—tell him to take Archer to the Realm. If I try to contact him, he will see it a threat."

Briar pipes up, declaring, "He will talk to me. I used to be a Horde assassin. I was second in command. He can't refuse my call." She pulls her coat from the back of the nearest chair. "I will get a burner phone from Ridley and make sure Cain takes Archer to the Realm."

"Thank you, Briar."

She touches my arm as she passes. "Is there anything else I should tell him?"

I look to Slade, who is resigned as he says, "Tell Cain I accept his terms. The Guardian will set it up."

As soon as Briar is gone, I take Slade's hand. "You can't fight him. His assassin's ring is powered by a Keres feather. You'll kill each other."

A sharp tingle of uncontrolled power rushes from Slade into me as he reacts instinctively to the news.

His eyes flood with silver but he inhales, quickly calming himself. When he drops his forehead to mine, closing his eyes, I sense that he is harnessing his good memories to stop his power from spiraling out of control.

Vlad shakes his head. "That is unfortunate. Keres rings are very rare. My understanding is that there are only three: one made from the feather of the Keres Queen and two from her young daughter. Both women were imprisoned before the ringmakers raided the Valkyrie home. It was always unclear how the Keres women escaped."

"The Keres Queen sold out the Valkyrie to save her daughter. I'm not sure if they died soon after anyway because they each lost a feather like Amalia did." I squeeze my eyes closed. If there are only three Keres rings—and we have the other two—then at least I can rest easy that no other assassin can kill me.

Only Cain.

I shiver. My hand shakes against Slade's chest. Cain will treat me like an enemy now, not a friend. Worse, his ring is powered by royalty like Slade's is. A fight between them will be devastating.

"Cain has given us a week," Slade says. "We can count on him to keep Archer safe for now. In fact, if he is determined enough to challenge me, then Amalia will have a fight on her hands."

He ticks off tasks as if none of it could mean the death of us. "In the meantime, Tansy and I will work on locating the hidden Realm. Vlad will find out everything he can about Archer's mother. Ridley can act as my second in command to take care of Legion missions. I will send Lutz to the South to keep an eye on Archer and make sure she's safe. If possible, he can bring her back safely. He won't hurt her."

I run my hand across Slade's cheek. "What if he can't bring her back? You can't fight Cain."

His lips set in a determined line. "In a week, I'll travel to Austin. You should come with me, and while I keep Cain busy, you can steal Archer away."

A laugh tears out of me. "It won't be that simple."

He presses a fierce kiss to my lips. "My only mission now is you. I won't let you die, Hunter."

The flicker of silver in his eyes sends sharp fear thrumming through me. His power is controlled by his memory of me. He controls it willingly.

But he is bonded to me.

If I die, he will break. Nothing will control him. He won't care about the Code. His humanity won't have a chance against his rage.

He was born with the strength of a ringmaker. Now he

has the power of a Valkyrie. He has wings and a ring powered by the Valkyrie Queen herself.

He will be unstoppable.

I'm not afraid of dying. I'm afraid of taking the world to hell with me when I go.

CHAPTER TEN

That afternoon, Vlad's giant form shadows the bookshop door, but he doesn't come inside.

Hoisting his backpack over his shoulder, he says, "I have to return to the Dominion. I'll do everything I can to help you. When the time comes, you have permission to enter my territory."

"Will you go to Cain's ceremony?" I ask.

"It's my obligation as a Master. In the circumstances, Slade said he will send Lutz instead."

"Okay." I swallow my sudden sadness. Saying goodbye to Vlad is hard. He fought beside me, brought me back to Boston, made me face my fears. I wish I could reach into his heart and steal a little of his unwavering objectivity and his dispassionate view of the world.

He lays a big hand on my shoulder. "I know we will meet again, Hunter Cassidy."

I grin at him. "In this life or the next, Alexei Mason. Besides, you owe me a favor."

He laughs, a deep rumble in his big chest. "I was hoping you'd forgotten about that."

I snag his arm before he can step away. In the distance, Tansy waits at the corner beside Vlad's beast of a motorcycle. She is subdued, her coat pulled tight around her slender shoulders, one hand resting on the handlebars.

If I can't find a way to beat my death sentence, this might be the last conversation I have with Vlad.

I clear my throat, knowing I'm overstepping boundaries but, *hell*, I'm dying. It's now or never. "Don't forget about Tansy. She may have shut herself off from the world for a long time, but that doesn't mean she doesn't have a heart."

His gaze softens as he turns in her direction. "There is no forgetting Tansy." His expression turns blank, the first true mask I've seen him wear, as if, for the first time, he has something to hide.

"Tansy is safe here," he continues. "Other covens crave her power. Her aunt was only the first. Once your mother stepped in, nobody dared try again. You may not realize it, but *you* keep her safe. Tansy would be hunted if it weren't for you. In fact, if a witch like Mother Serena was determined enough, she might even find a way to break the protective spell on this street."

Worry strikes through me. I might not be around much longer to protect Tansy. "What if I don't make it? Will you keep Tansy safe?"

His gaze quickly narrows, giving me an unwavering stare. "You're going to live, Hunter."

I clench my teeth. "Promise me you will come back for her."

Concern grows behind his eyes. "Promise me you won't step between Cain and Slade if they fight."

He stares even harder at me when I don't answer. He growls a warning, "Hunter…"

I demand, "Will you come for her or not?"

"Of course, I will."

I shake out the tension in my shoulders and unclench my jaw. "Thank you."

Vlad's shoulders hunch. "Tansy's home is here. As long as she is safe, I will never ask her to leave the place she loves."

He strides away from me. As he passes each of the shops, the residents of Saber Lane come out to say goodbye to Vlad. Christopher James shakes his hand outside the grocery store. The couple in the bakery give him a brown paper bag that is no doubt filled with cupcakes. Dean claps him on the back and Willow hurries after him, handing him a belt full of tranquilizer darts, saying, "Just in case Lady Tirelli's people try anything on the way."

We are all safe on Saber Lane, but the minute we step out of its protection, we have to be prepared.

I can't watch him ride away—another friend gone—so I hurry inside and lean against the bookshop counter until the motorcycle's growl fades into the distance.

The rest of the week is the longest of my life.

Slade is unbelievably focused. Every morning he joins me in the dojo, training with me, but after that he shuts himself in the bookshop with Tansy, pouring over the Keres Coda and the Valkyrie Vade. The rings around his eyes darken. Like me, he barely sleeps. He never shows his frustration, channeling his emotions into the task, but I know he's feeling it.

Halfway through the week, I come upon them staring at a page. They aren't writing or speaking and the silence in the kitchen is heavy.

Slade says, "We've deciphered more of the image, but it's not the location and it's not good news."

"I can handle it," I say.

He holds my gaze. "It says: *Only the reckless or the desperate will enter the maze. The path to the feathers is paved with death.*"

I chew my lip, clear my throat, and declare, "Well, call me reckless and desperate."

He breaks into a smile. "Okay then."

A little while later, Tansy stands up from the table and holds out her hand for me, "It's time, Hunter."

I grip the table. Entering a maze of death is far less daunting than the subject she and I keep avoiding.

I haven't touched William's things.

I can't.

I was shocked when Tansy told me that everything is mine now. Before he died, William changed his will. The legal process will take time, but he left the Tomb to me. He should have left it to Tansy and I told her so.

She takes my hand. "I will help you."

Three hours later, we have sorted through William's room, bagging up everything we can give to charity. The only item I keep is the t-shirt with a cartoon picture of a dragon on it that he loaned me the first time I stayed here.

I hug it to my chest as the sight of the empty bedroom saps my energy. I turn my thoughts to anger instead.

A daily stream of clients comes to the bookshop to write in my ledger and every night I head out into the dark, the grime, the parts of Boston that decent people never see.

My power is as merciless as my heart. I don't take a dagger or a gun with me now. I am unseen, invisible. My targets don't have time to plead for their lives before I take hold of their hands, their arms, whatever body part I can touch and I smoke their lives like the vulture woman that I am.

Twice, Amalia nearly catches me, but I evade her, making myself as insubstantial as the shadows that I live in now. I swore to tear down the underground and that's what I'm going to do.

By the night of Cain's ceremony, I have annihilated Amalia's prime support network and started in on the minor players.

Then Briar brings news that Amalia has disappeared.

Briar stands at the kitchen table where Slade and Tansy's notes have grown into piles of scribbled-out attempts to locate the hidden Realm. "Amalia has gone south."

"That's bad news." I pace the floor. "She must have found the location of the Horde's Realm. We have to warn Cain."

Slade leans across his notes and looks to Briar. "Is there any way you can contact him?"

She appears uncertain. "The ceremony has already started. Amalia was clever this time and covered her tracks. I didn't know she was gone until now."

I practically jump out of my skin. "Please, Briar. You have to try."

She doesn't waste any more time. She spins on the spot and hurries away.

I lean on the table, palms down, icing the panic that threatens to swamp me. "Archer's safety is down to Cain."

"He won't let anything happen to her, Hunter."

My forehead creases at the certainty in Slade's voice. "Why is Cain protecting her?"

Slade gives me a crooked smile. "The same reason I will protect you with my life."

My jaw drops. "He loves her?"

"According to Lutz's latest report, Cain will do anything to keep Archer safe. And apparently, Archer would do the same for Cain."

I run my hand across my forehead and sink into a chair. "What am I doing, Slade? If Archer and Cain have a chance to be happy, how can I ask either of them to risk that?"

"Asking Archer to help you isn't going to hurt them, Hunter."

"I don't know… The path to the feathers is paved with death, remember?"

Briar's heavy footsteps sound on the stairs. She appears in the entrance carrying a burner phone. She hands it to Slade. "The Guardian wants to speak with you."

Slade appears cautious as he takes the phone from Briar and quickly puts it to his ear. "Guardian?"

As he listens, the color drains from his face.

He leans forward, bracing his free hand on the table and closing his eyes. "I understand."

He puts down the phone and says to Briar, "Thank you, Briar. I need to speak with Hunter now."

"Of course." She hurries away while my heart hammers.

Slade clutches the burner phone so tightly that it's in danger of busting apart. Shadows cast across his face when he turns away from the light. "Lutz is bringing Archer here."

"Here to me or here to you? You can't kill her, Slade."

"The Guardian has agreed that if Archer trains as an assassin, she can't be a target anymore. The first rule will apply to protect her."

I breathe out my relief. "Really? That's a clever solution but who will train her?"

"You will. That is the Guardian's condition. Cain can't have anything to do with it."

I can't believe it. Archer is coming here. Brought to me with the Guardian's blessing, no less.

It almost seems too easy. It definitely doesn't match the fear in Slade's eyes. "What about Cain?"

"Cain has agreed to let her go." Slade stops speaking. His shoulders hunch. The dark expression on his face scares me.

It *is* too easy. My stomach churns with anxiety. "Slade, what happened? What aren't you telling me?"

"Amalia attacked the Horde tonight," he says. "All of the Novices were killed. During the fight, Archer tried to protect Cain and she got hurt. Very badly. She might not make it."

He reaches out to steady me, his hand firm on my shoulder. "If Tansy can't heal her, Archer is going to die. If she dies, so do you."

CHAPTER ELEVEN

My mortal enemy lies on a medical stretcher at my front door.

The moon sits high in the sky above us as Tansy and Slade stand with me.

Cain walks on one side of the stretcher while the Guardian walks on the other side with Lutz beside her. They are pale and tense in the moonlight.

I take a step toward the woman on the stretcher. *Archer Ryan.* The woman I've been looking for. The one Mom protected.

Archer's blond hair spreads across the mattress, matted with blood. Her eyes are closed and her breathing is shallow.

She's wearing an evening gown that might once have been baby blue with an embroidered corset and long fitted skirt but is now rich red, torn, and soaked through with blood.

Her body is broken in so many places that I can't identify any single point of impact.

My lips part with shock. "What did this to her?"

Cain is a tower of stone, his jaw set, his expression shadowed.

His assassin's magic flares, a copper glow that stops me in my tracks. The Keres power is sharp and stinging even from a distance.

Like all assassin's rings, Cain's is in a constant state of active power. Touching it will burn me, and if he chooses to lash out, he could kill me.

Cain's focus is on Slade who followed me down the stairs.

Slade pulls to a sharp stop, spreading his arms wide to show Cain that he isn't carrying any weapons and won't attack. "Archer has nothing to fear from me, Cain. In fact, I will protect her from anyone who tries to harm her."

Cain's anger turns to confusion, his forehead creasing. I don't blame him for not understanding. A week ago, Slade was duty-bound to kill Archer, and Cain knows that Slade always follows the rules.

He has no idea how important Archer is to us.

Cain's power fades. I can't help but notice the way his fingertips brush Archer's, never straying far from her for too long. Or the fact that he isn't wearing his assassin's ring on his forefinger like the rest of us do. Rather, it's on his ring finger, where a wedding ring would be.

I asked him what did this to her and he finally answers me. "Archer did this to herself. She was trying to save me."

Now that Cain has suppressed his power, Tansy launches into action. "I need to get to work immediately. Slade, please use your power to transport Archer upstairs—without jostling her around. She is in a very fragile state right now. I would do it myself but I want to conserve my energy."

Tansy spins to Cain, her golden hair flying around her face. I woke her an hour ago. All I had to do was ask and she hurried to help, preparing William's room and readying her spellbook.

She says to Cain, "I'm sorry to see you in these circumstances, Cain. You will come with me, please, so you can answer my questions about what happened."

The Guardian steps into his path, shaking her head. "I allowed Cain to travel with us to make sure Archer remained calm during the journey. He must return to his territory now—"

A sharp flicker of light bursts around Tansy as she faces the Guardian. "Do not tell me what Cain will do. If you want this woman healed, then he will come with me. He can go when I say so."

The Guardian lifts an eyebrow at Tansy, her lips parted in apparent surprise, but she doesn't argue. "Very well. I will be at the Diner. Lutz Logan, you will come with me."

Lutz gives Slade a firm nod before he spins on his heels and leaves with the Guardian.

As soon as they're gone, Slade lifts his arms to raise Archer off the stretcher into the air. I hold the door open so he can float her inside and up the stairs, Tansy hurrying ahead of her and Cain staying close behind me.

Now that the Guardian and Lutz are gone, Tansy's true concern shows through. "Onto William's bed, please," she says to Slade. "Quickly. She doesn't have long."

As soon as Slade rests Archer on the bed, he gives my hand a quick squeeze and leaves the room. He won't be far away but it's better if he gives Cain space.

We already set up Tansy's spellbook in the corner of the room and she located the healing spells she might need. For the last hour she has been repeating them to herself, trying to remember them so she can heal Archer as quickly as possible.

"Pictures, not words," she murmurs beneath her breath before she turns to Cain: "Tell me what has been done to help Archer already."

He kneels beside the bed, holding Archer's hand. "My medical unit used every power they had to stabilize her for the flight. But they couldn't do more than that. I used the power in my assassin's ring to keep her calm and help her sleep."

Tansy asks, "Your ring is powered by a Keres feather, is it not?"

As if on instinct, his free hand covers the ring. "It is." Cain's gaze drills into Tansy. His voice breaks. "Please, tell me you can heal her."

Tansy's fingertips float over Archer. Tansy is very pale as if the more she assesses Archer's wounds, the greater her despair. "She is completely broken. Her back is split apart. Her ribs, her internal organs, her heart, they're all shattered beyond anything I've ever seen. She shouldn't be breathing right now. I will do everything I can, but I won't lie to you, Cain. This will take everything I've got."

Every muscle in his body appears tense. "I can't lose her."

Tansy bends to him and places her hand over his heart, trying to calm him. "I understand. Now, step away please."

When he does as she asks, pacing like a caged beast beside the bed, she rests against it, one knee planted on its edge as she starts with Archer's chest, focusing on the location of her heart, her palms hovering above it.

Tansy closes her eyes, her body relaxes, and tranquil light builds around her like warm sunlight. *Healing light.* It's warm and soothing, just like the power she used to heal my wounds. It reaches out to me, drawing me closer, my own need to be healed taking me forward.

The moment I take a step, Cain stops pacing, his hands forming into fists as he swivels into a protective position between Archer and me.

I pull up sharp, wary of the way he's looking at me as if I could tear down his world.

His breathing is rapid. He is barely holding on. His voice is a dangerous rasp. "Do you know what Archer is?"

I take a quick breath. He said "what" not "who."

Damn. He knows. I stare at him in shock. But how much? Does he know about me too?

I shoot back. "Do you?"

He advances on me, copper light from his ring building around him.

I stand my ground even though his power stings like hell. Vlad said that the Keres rings were made from feathers belonging to the Keres Queen and her daughter. I have no doubt now that Cain wears the Queen's ring just like Slade wears my Queen's.

My queen. I shake off the thought. Amalia is no queen of mine.

I harness my own anger, my own power to protect myself. The pain in Cain's eyes is like a fire burning brighter and brighter. He doesn't really see me right now. He only sees another threat to Archer when she's already broken and vulnerable.

"Archer is Keres," I say. "The last of her kind."

His voice is like sharp wire striking across my skin, fierce and accusing. "Then you know there are only two ways she can die. One of those is by your hand."

My shoulders sag. *He knows what I am.*

A week ago, he stood beside me when I faced Amalia Avery. Before that, he brought me meals and made sure my wounds were stitched. He cared for me like a true friend. A week ago, he was my ally.

Now, the distrust in his eyes tears my heart apart.

He knows that I can kill her.

He must be terrified that I will.

I've lied a lot in my life. Always out of necessity, but I'm good at it. Only honesty will save me now.

I slowly draw off my jacket—the jacket I wear to stay warm because I can't keep myself warm anymore.

I harness my power carefully, cautiously, sensing my back shift.

Silver feathers unfold gently from my shoulders, spreading out at my sides. My wings give me the strength that I need right now. I allow them to spread to their full length, so large, so powerful that they touch the walls on either side of me.

Cain's green eyes widen like a growing storm. He must have imagined what my wings would look like but actually seeing them must be far more confronting.

His muscles flex as the copper power around him increases, glittering light swirling around his arms and legs.

He may not be Keres in the same way that Slade is Valkyrie, but the way his power grows tells me he has learned how to harness the Keres power to its fullest extent.

Speaking the truth, I say, "Archer can die in the same two ways that I can die."

CHAPTER TWELVE

ain's knuckles turn white. "You could kill her."

I tip my chin up. "She could kill me."

He inhales a sharp breath, but his power remains strong and biting, a crackling force around him. "Who are you, Hunter?"

I drop my gaze. *Who am I?*

"Sometimes, I don't even know." My shoulders rise and fall with my indrawn breath as I meet his eyes. "I am a killer. I am angry. I am…" My gaze falls on Tansy. Her eyes are still closed. She is completely absorbed in her task and her instinctive magic has clearly taken over now, a powerful force surrounding her and Archer within a protective dome. She used to access the full power of her instinctive magic only by accident, but the more she uses it, the more she seems able to draw it out and control it.

My gaze softens. "I am a friend. I was a daughter. But I will never be a mother."

A cautious expression settles on Cain's face. Despite his pain and his fear for Archer, he is listening.

He is willing to hear me.

"I am imperfect." I step forward, bracing against his power, flinching against the pain that strikes through me. I force myself to take it, deal with it, and put it aside. "How did you find out about her power?"

"Patrick Ryan told Archer a fairy story about the day she was born. He said that she was flown to him by a silver stork that turned into a wily fox. That was your mother. She was the Glass Fox and she was a Valkyrie with silver wings."

"Mom died to protect Archer," I say. "I, too, will protect her. I promise I won't hurt her."

"You're her enemy." His brow furrows at the way I've willingly stepped into the circle of his power. "Tell me why I should believe you."

I could tell him that I need her. That she's the key to reaching the feather that can heal me. That unless she and I work together, Amalia will be unstoppable.

But none of those reasons are good enough. The way he looks at her… It's the same way Slade looks at me.

Somehow, in the short space of a week, he has given her his heart.

"I know what it's like to watch the person you love dying and to know that you would willingly take their place." I point at his assassin's ring where it rests, like a wedding band on the ring finger of his left hand. "You love her."

He stands his ground, but his deep inhale answers my question.

"Do you remember the night Slade went on the mission that earned him the title of Master?" I ask.

Cain gives me a cautious nod. "I do."

"What you don't know is that he nearly died that night. He came to me riddled with bullets. I brought him here and I healed him in a way that—" I take a deep breath and force myself to speak the truth. "I healed him in a way that means I have chosen to die."

Cain's eyes widen. His power fades, disappearing from around his body. "Hunter—"

I hurry on. "Not today. Not tomorrow. But soon. I don't have long now."

I tuck my wings away, my shoulders settling as my wings disappear. I dare to step closer to Archer, to contemplate the terrible damage to her body.

Something tore her apart.

Tansy's healing power is like sunlight near my body, but I don't dare soak it in. Archer needs every bit of it.

Cain is pale when I look up.

"You love Slade that much," he says.

"I do." I allow myself to smile. "And he loves me. We have traveled a rocky path to get to this point, but it was worth it."

I dare to reach out, touching Cain's arm, grateful when he doesn't pull away. "Slade will never hurt Archer, and neither will I."

His big hand closes over mine. The tension leaves his shoulders and face. "I'm sorry, Hunter."

I bite my lip. "You said Archer did this to herself trying to save you."

He sighs. "For some reason, her wings are trapped inside her. She didn't even know she had them. It took us all week to figure it out. Every time she gets in a fight, she triggers her power. Her wings try to release, her back burns, and it's too much for her body. She collapses. That's what happened after she fought Lutz. She literally fell into my arms."

He shifts his balance but keeps my hand against his arm, maintaining the contact between us like a truce. "But this time, during the fight with Amalia, I died. Amalia did something to me. I don't know what exactly. Archer used her power to bring me back."

I nod. "The Keres have the power to take souls like the Valkyrie do, but they can also give them back. But Cain... Archer could only do that if she released her wings."

"She forced her power out," he says. "She ripped herself apart from the inside."

"Dear saints." My heart sinks as I sense my own wings, imagining what it would be like to try to release them forcefully from my body. They would shred me from the inside. "You never saw her wings?"

"Only as a copper glow across her shoulder blades as if they were sitting right beneath the surface."

"Not even during...?" I blush. How do I finish *that* sentence? To begin with, I shouldn't assume that they slept together, let alone that she would have bonded with him.

He tips his head to the side. "During what?"

I clear my throat. "We have to release our wings to use our power, but the other time is when we bond."

He gives me a blank look.

Oh boy. This is not a conversation I wanted to have with Cain. Or ever thought I would need to have.

Tansy shocks me when she sings out from beside me. "Keres women bond during sex, Cain. You might need to know that."

My face burns, but Cain is quiet. "I never saw her wings."

I swallow. Take a deep breath. "I recently found out that Mom put a spell on my wings to stop me from bonding. Then she burned my birth feather to make sure the spell could never be reversed. It's entirely possible that she also had a spell cast over Archer's wings, but it must be much stronger than the spell cast over me. To keep Archer's true identity a secret, she wouldn't have wanted Archer's wings to reveal themselves at all until Archer was safe from Amalia."

He nods. "I guess that would explain it."

I twist my hands. "There's more, Cain. Do you remember the Keres feather that Gareth showed us on the night you visited the Legion?"

Cain jolts a little. "That was Archer's?"

I nod. "I stole it. It's how I found out about Archer. It's how I found out that Mom was protecting her. But I didn't know Archer's name, only the color of her eyes."

"They're violet," he says.

It's the final confirmation that Archer is the Keres woman I'm looking for. "After I stole her birth feather, I burned it." My shoulders sag with the guilty admission. "By burning it, I would have locked in the spell. If her symptoms are getting worse, that would be why."

He is quiet and thoughtful. "There's no way to reverse it?"

I look hopefully at Tansy. She is more powerful than any other witch. If anyone can undo the spell, she can. I'm startled to see that she is floating off the floor now, the glow between her and Archer growing brighter by the second. Power streams between them, a kaleidoscope of colors.

Despite the intensity of her concentration, the way she interjected into our conversation before tells me that she's listening.

"Tansy? Can you help?"

Tansy's voice is silky soft. "I'm sorry. I can't unlock the spell that binds her wings right now. It would tear her apart even more. But I promise I will try when she's healed—if she wants me to. In the meantime..." She smiles. "Archer's wounds are healing now. She will be fine."

The brightness around the two women increases, a soothing calm that makes me ache.

The color returns to Archer's face, her lips relax, parting a little as her breathing deepens. The fissures in her chest and arms begin to close and her torso settles onto the bed as the bones in her back smooth into position.

Tansy exhales a sigh as her feet return to the floor. She gives Cain a small smile. "Archer has scars beneath her wounds. But her mind is clear. She won't forget you, Cain."

On the bed, Archer's eyes suddenly fly open, but she's unfocused, staring upward. She struggles to get up. She cries out, "Cain!"

Cain jolts as if she reached out and touched him, shuddering toward her.

Tansy steps between them, pushing him away. "She isn't awake. Not really. Please don't touch her or you'll interrupt her healing."

Cain backs away from the bed until he hits the wall, his chest rising and falling rapidly.

For a second, I think he's going to change his mind and go to her, but he says, "I can't be here when she wakes up or I won't be able to leave."

Tansy quickly brushes her hand over Archer's face, closing her eyes again.

Archer relaxes, sagging back to the bed.

Tansy, too, sinks to a sitting position on the bed to take Archer's wrist in her hand, checking her pulse. "She needs a change of clothes, but that can wait for now."

I reach out to Cain. "I promise I will look after her."

His movements are slow and heavy when he turns to the door. "You once told me that I could do better. Well, she is my better."

He glances back at the room with a suddenly wry smile. "Don't expect her to wake up meekly. She will hit first and ask questions later. Be warned, she can make a weapon out of anything. She's Archer Ryan. I suggest you strip this bedroom down to basics before she revives."

I give him a small smile. "I'll be prepared."

I follow him out to the little kitchen.

Slade stands up from his relentless study of the Coda. There's no doubt in my mind that he heard our entire conversation, including the part where I admitted that I can't fully bond.

He reaches for my hand, drawing me into his side, his gesture telling me it doesn't matter. He says to Cain. "You have my word that Archer will be safe."

Cain exhales carefully. "You and I were never enemies, Slade." He reaches into his boot and pulls out a dagger, turning it handle-first to give to Slade. It is etched with the initials "SL."

"Archer took this from Lutz when she fought him," Cain explains. "I'm officially returning it to the Legion."

Then he reaches inside his jacket and retrieves a hardcover book, which he places on the table. It has a slit in the middle as if it was cut through with a sharp object.

"This is Archer's," Cain says. "She loves to read. Make sure she gets it back. I'll have all her belongings sent here tomorrow, including the rest of her books."

He bows to me, but he lowers his eyes to the floor, a gesture of peace before he strides down the stairs.

The bell on the door rings and then he is gone.

ain's departure leaves us in silence.

Slade takes a deep breath. "I can't be here on Saber Lane when Archer wakes up."

I pull back to see his face. "Wait, what? You can't leave. You're safe here."

"Archer knows all about the Code and the fifth rule. She knows I was duty bound to kill her. She will treat my presence as a threat."

When I begin to argue, he strokes my arms, gentle but firm. "If I'm here, you'll lose her trust and never get it back. She'll run and never stop running. We know she's good at hiding."

Archer's history proves that she knows how to move undetected in the shadows. I press my cheek to Slade's. He told me that I was his mission. Now he's willing to go back to the Realm, away from the protection of Saber Lane, because he doesn't want to scare Archer.

"Amalia fled the Horde after Archer fought her tonight," he says. "She hasn't returned to Boston yet. What's more,

Gareth left the city this morning. I'm running surveillance and so far all indications are that they're heading west. I'll warn Vlad that they could be coming his way and then I'll leave Saber Lane at first light—"

"No." I place my finger against his lips, my voice stern. "Slade, you told me that you want to walk this path with me. Well, this is the part where you stay with me. Archer will react badly to your presence whether you're here when she wakes up or she meets you in a month. We both know I don't have that long. Besides, I have a feeling she's not that easily spooked."

He laughs, but it's a worried sound. "That's what I'm afraid of. A fight between me and Cain is one thing. But between me and Archer? Or worse, *you* and Archer. I never want to see that, Hunter."

"I won't lie to her about you. I'm done hiding, Slade. Cain and Vlad know about me now. If I've only got a few months to live, then I'm going to live my final days with honesty and truth."

Taking hold of his hand and asking him to come with me, I pick up Archer's damaged book to carry it to William's room—the room that I will need to start thinking of as Archer's. Assuming she will agree to train with me.

Tansy sits in a chair by Archer's bed, watching over her. She sits up when we enter. "I will stay with Archer tonight. You both should get some rest."

"Thank you, Tansy." I place Archer's book on the bedside table. The book is obviously important to her or Cain wouldn't have returned it like he did. If she values books, then I hope she might like living here. "How long before she wakes up?"

"She's a fighter. She's healing more rapidly than I

expected. I would say she could be awake in as little as two days."

"We need to prepare this room before then. Cain said she'll wake up swinging. I want to make sure she doesn't have any weapons at her disposal."

Tansy inclines her head at the bedside table. "What about the book?"

"Leave it there. It will be a leap of faith."

Two days later, I lean against the wall in Archer's room, waiting for her to open her eyes.

The Guardian left Saber Lane as soon as she was satisfied that Archer was healing.

Slade and Tansy have relocated themselves to Tansy's place for the day. Even though he agreed to stay, Slade drew the line at being present when Archer wakes up.

I had to agree that was wise.

Archer slept the entire time while Tansy visited regularly, keeping her nourished with magic, making sure her wounds mended completely. Tansy told me—with some annoyance—that Cain deposited a sizeable amount of money into her bank account. She grumbled, "I didn't do this for payment."

I took her hand and told her, "It's Cain's way."

Now, I'm alone with Archer.

Her hair is a paler blond than Tansy's, her lips crimson, and her eyes... *Well, we'll see.* Tansy removed Archer's contact lenses while she slept so I'm preparing myself for the moment I see her violet eyes for the first time.

She wakes much more calmly than I expected. In fact,

she's so quiet about it, it makes me wonder if she has been awake for a while.

Her gaze travels around the room, quickly sizing up the emptiness.

I took Cain's advice seriously. There is nothing in Archer's room now but the bed, a bare mattress, closet, and bedside table. Archer is dressed in my old sweatshirt and pants, soft and comfortable, but not the height of fashion.

Her focus settles on me—on my tattoo in particular—and there's no doubt in my mind that she has already determined the threat level I pose, deciding whether she can take me on.

The relaxed set of her lips and her even breathing tell me she's confident she can fight me—and win.

I hide a smile. I like her already.

"I'm sorry about your surroundings," I say. "I couldn't take the chance that you'd react before you let me speak."

Without moving, her electric eyes swivel to the book I left on the bedside table—the one with the slit in it. The growing tension around her mouth disappears, telling me she appreciates the gesture.

"I could probably throw my book at you." Her voice is soft, confident, but it carries an edge of threat that tells me she's prepared for anything.

I remain very still aside from allowing myself to smile. "Cain said you were resourceful."

She flinches as soon as I say his name. She can't hide her pain fast enough or disguise the hurt that creeps into her voice. "Where is he?"

I lift myself off the wall, my heart hurting for them. They don't deserve to be torn apart. The only blessing is that she didn't fully bond with him. "Where you left him. But not where he wants to be."

She sits up, sliding her legs over the edge of the bed, every movement careful and controlled. "Who are you?"

"I'm Hunter Cassidy. Perhaps you've heard of me."

She nods. "I'm told nobody messes with you."

Cain must have told her that. I guess that means he didn't see me as his enemy the whole time that Archer was with him.

I reply with certainty, "Which is why nobody will mess with you now."

She gestures at the room with careful movements. "What is this place?"

"I live above a bookstore. I believe that might appeal to you."

A small smile touches her lips before she hides it. Cain sent her clothes and a box full of books this morning. The size of the box tells me that Archer values reading well above her appearance.

There's only one more thing I need to ask her before I let her out of this room. "Are you willing to train with me and become an assassin, Archer Ryan?"

She considers me for a moment. She's still sizing me up. She slips off the bed, rising to her full height. Eye-height with me. She's curvy, tall, and moves with a grace I don't think she's aware of.

"Yes," she says.

I give her a firm nod. "Good. Then let's get started."

She looks surprised. "Right now?"

I fold my arms across my chest. "You need to become a fully-trained assassin. You already know how to fight. You wouldn't have survived a battle with Lutz Logan otherwise. As soon as I determine your strengths and weaknesses, I can send you on a mission. Then you can earn your status as a Superior Assassin."

Her expression shuts down so rapidly I nearly do a double-take. Her voice takes on a deadly edge. "I don't have any."

I blink. "Any what?"

"Weaknesses."

I stare at her. *Oh, wow. She's serious.*

In fact, she spoke with anger, a clenched jaw, and tense shoulders, not pride. I shouldn't be surprised. Her reputation is earned, not fabricated.

"My father beat any weakness out of me. Literally." She taps her finger against her thigh in a sign of irritation. "You can send me on a mission. I'll show you what I can do. Or ask Cain what I did with the shifters we fought in Texas. I'm sure that will convince you."

I make a mental note to ask Cain about that. "We'll see." Before she can argue, I turn away from her. "Cain sent your clothes and books—"

"My books!" She lurches forward but halts herself, quickly disguising her enthusiasm. She clears her throat. Reforms her expression into one of aloof indifference. "Thank you."

I press my lips together, finding it hard not to warm to the true personality she reveals in small glimpses when she's not maintaining her tough act.

Briar told me that Archer used the alias "Grace Kennedy" when she came back to Boston several months ago. She was a waitress, blended in, completely undetectable. Even Briar didn't figure out who she was until Archer revealed herself.

Archer is going to make a perfect assassin. But then, death is in her blood, the same as it is in mine.

Killing is what she does best.

"Your things are in the corridor," I say. "This is your room now. I'll get it set up with linen and make sure you have what you need. Get yourself dressed, put your contact lenses in, and meet me downstairs. We'll spend the afternoon training in the dojo at the end of the street."

"My eyes!" Her hand shoots to her face. I guess she didn't realize she wasn't wearing her contact lenses.

The questioning look she gives me tells me she's surprised I haven't reacted to her eye color. It's true that her violet eyes make her appear less than human, and very otherworldly, but that's undoubtedly the way I look when my wings are spread.

I smile. "They're gorgeous. I'm sorry you have to cover them up."

She gives me a guarded smile in return. I take it as a sign of trust when she leaves the book—her only possible weapon —on the bedside table before she follows me out of the room.

I continue, "Then we'll see if you have any weaknesses."

CHAPTER FOURTEEN

*A*rcher's fist is like a hammer.

Smack!

I allow her to land the blow to my shoulder so I can gauge her strength but I dodge her follow-up kick to my chest, ducking and whipping my arm against her knee to knock her off balance. Or so I expected.

She adjusts her balance and spins on the spot instead of falling, her fist shooting back toward my face.

She may as well be flying as she follows me around the dojo, attempting to get in another solid hit.

I asked Drake to give us space and he agreed after giving me a cautious look. Archer's reputation has made all of the inhabitants of Saber Lane wary.

When we arrived at the dojo, she took the suspicious look he gave her in stride, her head held high while she made only small, non-threatening movements.

It will be hard to convince them that she's not here to destroy the safe haven they have created. Tansy's decision to heal her helped a lot. Over time, I hope the others will come around.

If there's any blessing in her inability to spread her wings, it's that she can't inadvertently use her full power against me.

I'm safe, but that doesn't mean she couldn't shorten my remaining time on this Earth.

My biggest problem is how to tell Archer that I'm Valkyrie. According to Cain, she knows that our two species are enemies.

For now, that's a problem for future Hunter. Right now, I'm busy trying to avoid her fists.

I duck and dodge every attempt she makes to hit me, flowing with the punches, my back burning. Her presence triggers my inner power and the need to release my wings grows stronger with every attack.

I'm impressed to discover that she doesn't fight defensively, only on the offensive. She attacks with strength and purpose but she reacts like liquid to my responses, shifting out of the way instead of taking the hits.

I finally step in close when she isn't expecting it and sweep her feet out from under her.

She flips to the side before she lands on her back, her leg shooting out, nearly colliding with my calf: a hit that would have knocked me over if I didn't dance away from her in the nick of time.

I smile as she regains her feet. "Enough for now."

"You let me land that first hit, didn't you?" she asks.

My smile broadens into a grin. "I need to know how strong you are. In fact, I need to know everything you can and can't do. As your Master, it's my job to keep you alive."

She narrows her eyes at me. "I didn't think there were any female Masters."

I'm surprised. "Cain didn't tell you?"

She shakes her head.

"I'm a Rogue Master, like my mother was," I say. "That means I control my own territory but I don't have a team like other Factions do. It's just me."

A smile curves her lips. "Until now. Does that make us a fully female Faction?"

Sudden warmth fills my heart. "Actually, it does."

She plants her hands on her hips, appearing barely out of breath. She may be curvy but she moves like an elite athlete.

"You should know that I can kill anything with a single bullet," she says. "I can also break a man's neck with a single twist. Cain told me that I—"

She stops and exhales. Saying his name clearly hurts her.

A trickle of apprehension enters my mind. She may not have fully bonded with Cain, but I'm starting to suspect that her bond is like mine: partial and built on love, which actually makes it stronger. That sort of emotion doesn't disappear no matter how far apart they are.

I ask her as gently as I can, "What, Archer?"

"Cain said I fight with impact. That includes willingly taking a hit if it means getting closer to my opponent. I tend to approach a fight expecting to get hurt. He taught me how to shift out of the way and react with greater force."

"Wise advice."

Archer gives me a look I have trouble deciphering: challenge or doubt, I'm not sure which. "Lutz Logan implied that you and Cain were together," she says.

I choke on air. "Wow. Really? No. Cain is a kind and generous friend but nothing more. Lutz should have known better."

Especially because Slade is his Master.

I make a mental note to smack Lutz around the head the next time I see him. That's if I don't hug him instead. The rumor is that he not only protected Archer on multiple occasions while she was in the South, but he also looked after Cain's sister during Amalia's attack on the Horde.

Archer gives me another cautious smile. "I've hit a nerve."

I want to ask her if she has been taking "blunt" lessons from Vlad. My voice becomes wry when I say, "Lutz knows I'm with someone else."

She sighs. "It's hard to imagine having a normal relationship in this assassin's world. Not that I ever expected to have a normal relationship. It's impossible when you can't tell anyone the truth about your past, let alone your real name. Cain was the first man I couldn't lie to."

Hmm. Unable to lie. Another symptom of bonding.

When I separated from Slade, I was in a lot of pain. Archer is hiding hers well, but it's there, lurking in the crease in her forehead, the tension in her shoulders, and the way she visibly braces every time she says his name.

To hell with the Guardian's ruling. I have to find a way around the distance between them.

Archer inclines her head at the wall of weapons behind us and changes the subject. "I can throw knives just as effectively. I can use swords, too." She crosses to the end of the room where my katana rests on a stand.

"Do you like it?" I ask. "We can get one for you."

Her eyebrows rise. "It's beautiful. I would like that."

I consider her carefully. Cain said she collapses after a fight but so far she isn't showing any signs of physical distress. "Forgive me for asking, but how do you feel right now? Cain said that triggering your power has consequences—"

She jolts away from me, immediately on the defensive. "He told you what I am?"

I don't react to the fighting stance her body settles into, even if it does worry me a little. We are in a room surrounded by weapons and she has proven that she's strong enough to fight Amalia and win.

I have no illusions that I've seen all of her strengths yet.

I take a deep breath and say, "I know you're Keres."

She considers me with alarm and sudden distrust. "But you agreed to train me. Aren't you afraid of what I am?"

I calmly sweep my hand in the direction of the Lane. The dojo doors are wide open, the entire street visible to us. "You're not the only magical being on this street. In fact, this place is a safe haven for those who have escaped violent pasts. See the brownstone on the far corner? That's Tansy's home. She is known as the Saber Lane Witch and she's like a sister to me."

Saying those words brings home how true they are now. Like sisters, Tansy and I have fought, disagreed, even hated each other, but at the end of the day, we've come through for each other.

I continue, "That place over there is Dean's Diner. He's an empath."

"I've never met an empath. All magical beings have an aura, don't they?"

She peers at me as she speaks. *Hmm. She's checking me for an aura.* I wonder if Cain told her that Keres and Valkyrie don't have one.

"That's correct," I say. "It's better if you don't meet Dean until Tansy can protect him from your emotions. I hurt him badly the first time I set foot here. Something tells me you'll knock him out."

"I carry a lot of baggage." Her gaze is astute, intelligent. "The Keres are killers but… You really aren't afraid of me." She searches my eyes as she asks, "Why not?"

Slade said I should take things slowly.

I probably should, but every word I say to Archer counts. She is too perceptive to accept a lie.

I prepare myself for the moment of truth, the challenge of needing her to accept what I am.

CHAPTER FIFTEEN

I step back from the doorway so I can release my wings.

My heart is in my throat as I say, "I'm not afraid of you because I'm—"

"Hunter!" A shout from outside the dojo makes me jolt.

I hurry to the door to see Briar racing up the street, her beanie held in her hands, her wispy hair flying.

She speeds up the stairs. "We have another one!"

She skids to a halt when she sees Archer, pausing long enough to say, "Archer Ryan, you're healed! You gave us a big fright."

Archer returns Briar's smile with a genuine one of her own. For a second, I think she's going to hug Briar, but it looks like physical affection is not something she's comfortable with. "I'm sorry I didn't do what you asked and come right here that day."

"You trusted your instincts. That's never a bad thing." Briar spins to me, her sense of urgency returning. "Two mages are holding a boy for ransom. The mother is at the bookshop."

Deep anger spears through me. "When will these assholes learn?"

I pause only long enough to seize two daggers from the wall of weapons behind me, pocketing them so they're out of sight and I won't scare the client. "Come with me, Archer. You're going to get your wish today."

I hurry from the dojo, pleased when Archer keeps pace with me. Like Slade, she walks beside me, not behind.

The familiar bell rings when we enter the shop. The agitated woman pacing at the counter heads straight for me. She's dressed in a designer coat and clutches an expensive bag, pearls dangling from her ears. The rest of her is a trembling mess.

She nearly drops her bag when she grabs my hands. "Please, they said you can save my son."

I curl my hand into hers as gently as I can. She's shaking so hard she rattles and I'm worried she won't be able to write in my ledger.

I make no promises as I draw her to the counter, open my book to a fresh page, and press the pen into her hand.

"You need to write the details here. Then we will wait for the mission to be sanctioned. If it is, the men who are holding your son won't live to see another day."

The pen shakes, she tries to steady herself, but her tears keep flowing and the ink streaks across the paper. "Oh, help," she says, gulping, dropping her bag so she can grip the pen and book.

I want to help her and steady her but writing in my ledger has to be done of her own free will. I can't assist her to do it.

Archer suddenly swings around me and takes the woman by the shoulder, urging her to look up. "Your son is going to be okay. Trust us. We won't let anything happen to him. We will get him back."

Archer is standing with her back to me but I can see the woman's reaction—she swallows, takes a deep breath, shuts her eyes for a moment… And then a deep peace fills her expression. She stops shaking, the crease across her forehead disappears, and her tears stop.

At the same time, Archer's back glows. Gentle golden light shines through the thickness of the sweater she's wearing, spreading across her shoulders and down her spine.

I take a quick step back, the force around Archer's body biting my exposed face and hands like the lash of a whip, but the glow fades as quickly as it appeared.

Cain told me that he used the power in his assassin's ring to keep Archer calm. I didn't think much of it but what if Keres power can calm people's emotions?

Tansy always said that the Keres were the gentle ones.

Unlike me. My power only instils fear.

Luckily, Briar is standing on the other side of the woman, so she didn't see any of it.

The woman focuses on my ledger and begins to write. I recognize the men's names, both minor players in Amalia's game, both lesser mages, but I've been eager to make their acquaintance.

She places the pen in the middle fold and stands back. Within seconds, the Guardian's sanction appears across the page.

"Normally, we would be done at this point," I say. "But there's one more thing I need to do."

I take the woman's place in front of my ledger, carefully

considering the two men and what I know of them. Kurt is a fire mage, but not a powerful one; he can only wield a flame that is already lit. But he's also a straight shot with a gun. The other is Scott, an earth mage who prefers to play with his prey. He is an expert in close contact knife fights.

I circle Kurt's name and draw a line from it to the space beneath, where I write:

Archer Ryan will take this target. If successful, I will request her status be updated from Novice to Superior.

Archer murmurs at my shoulder, "Thank you."

"For what?"

"Assigning one of them to me. For giving me the chance to prove my worth."

I struggle not to react.

With great difficulty, I keep my breathing steady. "You can read what I wrote?"

She shouldn't be able to. Nobody but the client and I should be able to read it.

Archer gives me a guilty look. "I read Cain's ledger, too."

Another Keres power, then. I definitely need to ask Cain about those shifters they fought in Texas. Come to think of it, there was a rumor that a bunch of jaguars and wolves went down in a gang war outside Austin. Perhaps they didn't kill each other after all.

I hold my breath waiting for the Guardian's decision. It's early for me to put Archer to the test, but I hope her history will force the Guardian to agree.

The Guardian's golden writing gleams across the page.

Sanctioned. Don't get her killed or Cain will hunt you down and end you.

I smile and write:

Noted.

Briar quickly ushers the woman out of the shop, but before she leaves I ask her to verify the sanctioning with the Guardian over the phone.

Amalia may have disappeared for now, but I'm not taking any chances that she could have interfered with my ledger. Kurt and Scott aren't exactly her most loyal followers.

Then I swing to Archer. I have two challenges now: the first is figuring out where these assholes are keeping the boy. The second is getting Archer a protective suit. My suit has a bullet hole in it and I don't have a new one, let alone a spare for Archer.

Technically she doesn't need it but it's reckless not to suit her up—the kind of reckless that will make Cain beat down my door.

Just when I'm about to offer her my suit, she drags her focus away from the page and says, "We need to go right away. I know where these guys hide, but they're unpredictable. They work for Lady Tirelli. They've given the mother until midnight to pay the ransom but they're just as likely to kill her son for kicks."

She holds out her hand for one of the daggers I took from the dojo, saying, "I don't know how to blur but I don't mind hanging on to you so we can move around undetected when we get there."

Okay, then. She already knows the drill.

"You should wear a protective suit or Cain will kill me," I say. "I have one you can borrow—"

"No need. There are two suits in the box of clothes he sent."

She flips the dagger around in her hand in a way that tells me she's getting a feel for its weight. "I'll get dressed and meet you back here in a minute. We need to hurry."

She takes the stairs two at a time. She wasn't joking about hurrying.

I lean against the counter, mentally preparing myself for the task ahead.

Killing is so much easier when I can use my power but I won't be able to do that in front of Archer.

Relying solely on my weapons is dangerous for me now that my healing power is nearly gone—there's more room for injury and the consequences are far worse. I tell myself that if I have to, I can blur and use my power that way.

Except that Archer can see through blurs. *Damn.*

But can she see through *mine*?

It's a risk I can't take.

Weapons it is.

I hurry upstairs to get dressed, attaching weapons holsters around my body before I check the hole in my suit. It's small and shouldn't pose too much danger. My attacker would need excellent aim to shoot through it.

Archer appears in my doorway and quickly freezes, fixated on the picture of Mom on top of the dressing table. "I thought you looked familiar."

I'm surprised. "Did you meet my mother?"

"Not officially. I only knew her by name. In fact, I deliberately avoided meeting the Glass Fox." She slips into my room and picks up the photo. "I used to think that assassins were myths. But this woman... I did see her a couple of times. Only from a distance."

I want to tell Archer that Mom died to protect her, but how can I lay that on her?

Her fingertips linger across the image where little me smiles at the camera. Archer gives me a crooked grin. "You were a cute kid."

I laugh. "Don't let anyone hear you say that. You'll ruin my reputation."

She smiles. "Something tells me your reputation is more secure than that."

She hands me the photo and I press my finger beside my mother's image. Gareth killed Mom, but Amalia was the cause of it.

Somehow, no matter how much damage I do to Amalia's empire, it's never enough.

CHAPTER SIXTEEN

I check that Archer's harnesses are secure before I hand her a tranquilizer gun, as well as a gun loaded with bullets. "Do you know the rules of the Assassin's Code?"

She seems unbelievably calm. Even calmer now that she's carrying firepower. "Kills must be sanctioned. Collateral damage is forbidden."

"Good. The tranquilizers are for anyone who isn't your target. Collateral damage includes any injury that results from your actions so you need to be careful."

"So if my target shoots at me but kills the person behind me, that's on me?"

"Yes. For that reason, we should approach our targets in a secluded location."

She purses her lips. "That will be tricky, but not impossible."

"If we blur while we run, do you think you can keep pace with me without losing contact?"

Her answer is to clamp a hand on my arm. "Easier than a three-legged race."

I grin at her and mentally lose myself into my surroundings, drawing on my power to blur myself. It rises to the surface, a force that is like a deep current, flowing through me and calming me.

Too late, I realize my mistake.

The place on my forearm where Archer grips me flares, a spark shooting between us.

She cries out, wrenching her hand away, a lightning-fast reflex that carries her several feet from me in an instant. A safe distance.

She hugs her hand to her chest, taking glances at her palm. "What the hell?"

Oh... no...

I bury my power, switching it off cold, and take her hand, checking her over. Her palm is red, but luckily she didn't lose any skin. There are no deep burns.

I check her face and her eyes to make sure she doesn't have any delayed concussion. "Are you okay?"

"That was like electricity. Your assassin's magic is—" She forces a laugh. "*Damn*, Hunter. No wonder nobody messes with you."

She thinks it's my assassin's ring. I don't feel guilt very often—it's not in my nature—but right now I'm swimming in buckets of remorse.

I could have seriously injured her. This means that I can't harness my power at all while she's touching me.

"I'm really sorry. I didn't know that would happen."

She shakes off her surprise and pain faster than I expected, proving to me just how tough she is. "Okay, what do we do now? We can't run through the streets dressed like this."

I exhale slowly.

Slade would be seriously worried if he knew what I was about to do.

"Now we get changed into civilian clothing," I say. "We conceal our weapons on our bodies. I need you to watch my back. I might have a reputation but I can get hurt, whereas you…"

"I've got your back." She gives me a determined nod before she races to the bathroom to change.

Two minutes later, we leave the shop, dressed in jeans, t-shirts, cropped leather jackets, and boots. We each carry a tranquilizer gun and a regular handgun tucked into our jeans. Archer's clothing looks brand new. She mumbles something about how Cain "refreshed" her wardrobe. I hide a smile that quickly fades when we pass Tansy's place.

I half expect Slade to burst out of the house and ask me why I'm not wearing a protective suit. The honest answer will get me into trouble since it will involve mentioning in front of Archer that I'm Valkyrie.

A moment later, we turn the corner.

Without alarming Archer, I cast my gaze back toward the street, worrying at my lip, but all is quiet behind us.

When we arrive at the high-end casino, I'm sure we're in the wrong place. "This is it?"

I definitely pictured a dingy warehouse for these guys. Instead, we're surrounded by opulence: plush amethyst carpet, leather seats at the games tables, a chandelier for every ten square feet of ceiling, and sweeping drapes hanging beside marble columns.

"Trust me. They're brutes, but they like to live it up. They'll keep the boy bound up in their room while they enjoy themselves at the tables. They like to gamble."

I growl at that. "With people's lives. How do you know all this?"

She swallows. "Because my father once used me as bait."

She moves to step forward but I snag her arm and pull her into a side corridor.

"What?"

She sighs. "It was when I was a kid, maybe ten years old. They locked me in their room while they gambled and when they got back, well, I did a lot of damage to them and they agreed to do whatever Dad wanted. Kurt still has the scar I gave him."

I have trouble processing what she told me. For starters, she was only ten years old and also... "What sort of father uses his own child as bait?"

"But I'm not his child," she says. "I never knew my real parents."

She appears completely unaffected, but she can't fool me for a second. Pain is buried deep inside her, the same way Slade buries his rage and I bury my truths.

I exhale, deciding not to push it. "Okay, well, remember that they're both mages. They don't have strong magical abilities but they could use their powers against us. Now... they're at the far-left table. Name the plan."

"The boy is our priority," Archer says. "As much as I'd love to end these guys, his safety is all that matters. Give me a minute and I'll be back with their room number. Then we can get the boy out of here before we go after the mages."

I'm not sure how she's going to get their room number, but I let her go while I casually lean against the marble column, crossing one booted foot over the other in a nonchalant pose.

She keeps to the edges, gliding effortlessly through the crowd, drawing no attention whatsoever.

I quietly observe the way she casually assesses the crowd, the way she takes in the exit routes, the clusters of people, and the pathways between them. Her observations are quick, careful, and deliberate.

She moves behind a group of players standing near a table and then… I lose her.

My forehead creases as I search the crowd and all the possible places she could have gone, swiveling from the bar to the table where our targets are playing blackjack.

There's no sign of her until…

Well, what do you know?

She said she didn't know how to blur, but right now she's giving off a gentle glow that only I can see, her silhouette like glass, shimmering like a female-shaped waterfall as she creeps up behind our targets, bends to her shoe right next to Scott's chair, then carefully straightens and backs away. She glides toward me, stepping behind the same group of people before she becomes visible again.

Nobody else saw a thing and our targets are oblivious.

I wonder if she knows what she was doing. She lived her life in the shadows so blending into her surroundings would have been a necessary skill and second nature to her.

When she reaches me, she doesn't stop, pushing a cold object into my hand as she pulls me with her. "Room key. Let's go."

Taking the elevator to the fifth floor, we keep our

movements quick but calm, ensuring we don't draw attention as we stride to the room and unlock the door.

"Closet," Archer says, heading straight for it.

It has two doors, the handles chained together in the middle. She wraps her fingers around the chain and pulls it, snapping the metal with her bare hands. "Normally, I wouldn't do that in front of anyone, but you already know about me."

The boy is huddled in the bottom of the closet, knees drawn to his chest, his eyes closed. He's barely more than five years old, his forehead clammy, his hair plastered to his face. It's far too hot inside the small space.

"Those animals." Archer quickly takes his pulse. "Drugged. We need to get him to a hospital. I wish I could fly him there."

She brushes the hair from his face and picks him up, drawing him gently to her chest.

She is so careful with him, I'm reminded of Briar's description of her as a good person. It makes me wonder what kind of person she would have been if she grew up with her real parents.

I don't want to leave her, but at some point I will have to take another leap of faith and let her out of my sight. "Actually, if you give him to me, I can get him to the hospital and be back within five minutes."

She stares at me. "How?"

"If I blur, I can move really fast."

Her eyes narrow slightly. She's perceptive, but the boy's safety must be more important to her than answers, because she carefully transfers him into my arms. "Make sure he's safe. I'll stay here and wait for our friends."

I give her a hard look. "Stay out of sight until I return. Do not engage them. Remember you're only sanctioned to kill Kurt. Also, mind their powers."

She gives me a half-smile. "I guess I'll get myself a drink at the bar then."

"I'll meet you there in five minutes."

I race from the room, blur, and harness my power to give me speed, opting for the fire stairs rather than the elevator.

Once outside, I take off from the front steps, ruffling the nearby passersby with the sudden wind from my wings. Heading for the hospital where I took Annabeth's Mom, I arrive in two minutes flat, materializing at the side of the building before racing the boy inside.

The same nurse from that night runs toward me, quickly calling for help before he takes the boy from me.

"Kidnapped and drugged," I say to him.

I give him the boy's mother's name, but before I can turn away, the nurse says, "I know who you are."

I freeze, swivel my gaze in his direction, and assess his earnest brown eyes, before I check my surroundings, looking for threats. The exit is wide open behind me and I'm not opposed to blurring right in front of him. Nobody would believe him anyway.

"Many injured people used to come through these doors," he says. "Our streets are safer now. Keep doing what you're doing."

With that, he turns away, speaking urgently to the orderlies who hurry up to him with a medical stretcher for the boy.

I race back into the air, a strange warmth filtering through to my heart.

By the time I reach the casino, I've been gone for four and a half minutes. Long enough for anything to have happened.

Archer isn't at the bar. The men aren't at their table.

I hover, half-concealed behind an opulent drape as I scan the room for them, trying not to panic.

I need Archer for so many reasons, but I won't deny that she's finding her way into my heart. I don't want anything to happen to her. She doesn't deserve more heartache in her life.

That's when a hand lands on my shoulder—a big, sweaty man's hand.

CHAPTER SEVENTEEN

I grab the hand that landed on my shoulder and then I twist and push.

Kurt snarls and tries to wrench out of my grip, his brown eyes glaring at me as I propel him straight across the corridor and into an empty gaming room where we're out of sight and a fight won't draw attention.

The door clicks shut as soon as we pass through it.

I push him off me and whirl to find Scott leaning against the door with a big smile on his face.

I guess that explains why Kurt didn't fight back just now.

Archer is slumped in a chair on the opposite side of the large, round gaming table, her head and shoulders resting on it, her hair spread across its surface. Her hands are bound behind her back and her eyes are closed.

It's difficult to see if she's breathing, but the color in her cheeks is a good sign. The back of her shirt is flipped up high enough for me to see that her guns are missing.

Hmm. I watched this woman break a steel chain with her

bare hands. I'm not sure zip-ties are going to pose a challenge for her once she wakes.

In fact, I'm not convinced that she's unconscious.

"We thought it might be our turn one day," Kurt says. "So, we kept an eye out for you, Glass Arrow."

Scott joins his friend as they prowl toward me.

I back away, slowly rounding the table so I can move closer to Archer.

As the men follow me, their movements are so coordinated that I'm surprised they aren't brothers. Telepathy maybe. I'll have to watch out for that.

Right now, Scott poses the greater threat since there is a lot of wood inside this room. Kurt, on the other hand, carries an abundance of guns, which he isn't afraid to show me, pulling out a shotgun complete with a silencer.

He reveals that he now carries Archer's weapon tucked into the holster around his waist, along with her tranquilizer gun and three other weapons.

I assume that Scott has a similar arsenal under his shirt, but his would consist of knives rather than guns.

Kurt appears a little perplexed. "We thought you'd put up more of a fight."

I reach Archer's side, noting the flicker of her eyelashes.

"Oh, honey," I say to Kurt. "You thought we had a fight already?"

Archer opens her eyes, her arms straining for a second before she snaps her bindings and pushes back her chair.

The two mages freeze in their tracks. It never fails to surprise me how arrogance can cloud a person's judgment.

Archer rises to her full height. "Well, look where we are. An empty room. No collateral damage."

I give her a smile. *Nicely done, Archer.*

"The only damage will be to your face," Kurt snarls.

She smiles sweetly. "Yours first. Oh, wait. I already did that."

Kurt fires his weapon, aiming right at Archer's eyes, but she's already on the move, ducking and flipping the table.

At the same time, a plume of flame billows from Kurt's gun, spearing in my direction.

Damn! He can use the spark inside his gun to create flame. That would explain why they are his weapon of choice.

I back-flip out of the path of fire, checking Archer's position.

The table rises into the air, but it isn't Archer's doing. Scott lifts his arms, pushing his hands forward. The wooden table curves like putty in response to his magic, forming a three-sided cage that crashes into Archer.

She's ready for it, turning her shoulder to take the impact. In fact, she not only takes the impact, she launches herself at the table.

Crack! The table splinters against her body. My ears *pop* with the sound.

Scott recoils in shock as Archer plows through the explosion of wood and debris, deftly catching a spiraling wooden shard in each hand while she races toward him. He barely has time to get his arms up before she launches herself across the space between them. One spike is aimed for his eye, the other for his heart.

But he's not her target!

A shout dies in my throat.

At the last moment, she angles the wooden spikes away from his body, spearing them neatly through his clothing instead. The force propels him back against the wall and the spikes thud into it, pinning him.

In the next moment, Kurt is on me.

Like Archer, I'm facing the wrong guy. But unlike Archer, I have my tranquilizer gun.

It would be merciless to tranquilize Kurt and allow Archer to kill him in cold blood but I pull up the memory of the boy's flushed face and my conscience clears.

I race out of the path of Kurt's bullets, bouncing off a chair onto the wall, then leaping off it while spinning to avoid the spray.

He dashes left to narrowly avoid the tranquilizer darts I shoot at him, returning fire as he goes. A plume of flame bursts after me, singing the back of my shirt.

The next ball of fire comes right at me, forcing me to lower my firearm and duck beneath the flames. I take the heat as I opt for a more direct approach, barreling straight at him.

He knocks my tranquilizer gun wide and nearly gets off a shot at me at close range, but I come up under his gun arm and push it high.

His finger squeezes the trigger in reflex—his second-last bullet; I've been counting—and the weapon fires into the ceiling.

The bullet hits the ceiling, the plaster ripples, and the projectile disappears without making a mark.

Wait... what?

Only Realm magic can do that.

Is it Amalia? But I don't smell roses...

Kurt appears as surprised as I am, growling at me as he grapples to wrench himself free from my grip. "What game are you playing, assassin?"

"Only the one that gets you killed."

Behind him, Scott is pinned to the wall by a string of

wooden shards, along with daggers that Archer must have stolen from Scott's weapons belt.

He quickly frees himself, using his magic to remove the wooden shards and throw them at Archer's back as she zigzags toward me and Kurt, a dagger clenched in her hand.

Weapon raised, she launches herself at Kurt's back... her true target.

I grab one of the guns on Kurt's belt, wrenching the weapon free just in time. Archer is about to plow into him and I don't plan to be under him when she does. I let go of his weapon arm and slip to the side.

Kurt shouts as Archer hits his back, her dagger meeting his neck in one brutal plunge.

At the same time, I aim and fire three rapid shots into Scott as he launches himself off the wall. He crashes back against it, dropping instantly.

But Kurt's focus is still on me, the life fading from his eyes as he lowers his weapon arm, falling at the same time as he aims his gun squarely at my heart.

He pulls the trigger one last time.

CHAPTER EIGHTEEN

A warm object hits me from the side.

The floor rises up at me and I crash into it, a heavy weight descending across my torso. The air whooshes out of my lungs and blood splatters across my chest.

The bullet bites the floor beside me.

Everything spins.

I try to catch up with what happened...

Fall, floor, bullet. The bullet didn't hit me but there's blood... So much blood...

Slade materializes above me, his torso and one leg pressing down on me. He groans as he pushes himself up so I can see his face.

He clutches one arm across his chest. He's only wearing a shirt and jeans, not protective gear. He must have come straight here.

The bullet tore right through him at close range.

He groans. "I wasn't interfering..."

"I don't care about the Code," I say. "We need to stop the bleeding."

"I'll live," he says, attempting to lever himself off me, but his arm buckles and his eyes squeeze shut. He wheezes. "I might need a moment. I think it tore through my lung. If that bullet had hit you, Hunter…"

Across the way, Archer follows Kurt's body to the ground, landing with one knee across his back.

Her focus spins to me, her gaze landing on Slade. "Hunter! No!"

She launches to her feet, wrenching the dagger out of Kurt and leaping toward Slade. "Get off her!"

Oh, no…

Slade meets my eyes for a split second before silver light floods his own. He rolls out of the way just as Archer's dagger descends toward his spine.

She retracts her arm, flipping over me so that she doesn't hurt me, landing in a crouch beside me. Her hand descends to my chest, to the blood seeping across my clothing.

Her eyes are wide with shock and fear. She must think the blood is mine. "No. Hunter! I promised to watch your back…"

Her head snaps up to Slade.

She screams, "You hurt her!"

Slade steps backward, his power flooding his body in a silver haze, desperately attempting to heal his injury as fast as possible.

He lifts his free hand, palm out. He's trying to heal and speak at the same time but all his energy is being sapped by his body.

I recognize his open palm as a gesture of peace but Archer doesn't. The moment Slade moves, she pitches the dagger into the wall beside his face and leaps toward him.

"No, Archer!" I cry. "Don't touch him!"

If she touches him right now while his body is flooded with Valkyrie power, it will kill her.

Slade's eyes shoot wide as he realizes the danger. At the last possible moment, he shuts his power off.

Archer's fist connects with his face, knocking him backward. She follows it up with another, hitting him fast, furious. Brutal. Where before her actions were calculated and controlled, she is now a wash of emotions. She thinks she let me down. She thinks it's her fault.

I roll to my feet, launching myself forward.

Slade blocks her blows but it means releasing the pressure on his chest that is staunching the blood flow. Without his power, he isn't healing. He is barely conscious. She lands a hard blow to his shoulder, smacking him against the wall where his legs buckle and his chin drops to his chest.

Archer draws her fist back for a final hit.

I'm almost to her, reaching out to stop her, harnessing my power to speed my movements.

Just as I stretch toward her, copper light floods the space around her shoulders. A glimmer of power flickers through her arm toward her hand. A single spark to power her fist.

A deadly spark.

"Stop!"

My hand lands on her shoulder. I meet her power with a spark of my own.

Electricity ignites between us, a force that silences the space around us.

Then it explodes.

The impact throws Archer forward and me back. She hits the wall and I hit the floor, sliding across it into Kurt's body. I gasp for breath, the world spinning.

I try to stand, wobble, and then drop to the floor again.

My legs are numb, no feeling in them at all. *C'mon, Hunter. Get up!*

Archer lies on the floor, struggling to push up onto her hands, clutching her head with a groan of pain.

Slade slumps against the wall beside her, one shoulder lower than the other, his head dropped to his chest. Even from this distance I can see that he… isn't… moving.

Oh, please…

I can't spread my wings, can't find my power right now, so I drag myself across the floor, fear fueling my actions, giving me strength as I claw my way toward him, my useless legs trailing behind me.

I reach his feet and then his legs, grappling with the space between us, reaching his side and pulling myself up beside him, stretching for his face, his chest.

"Wake up! Slade, wake up!" I push and pull at him, shaking him, pressing my hands against his cheeks, lifting his head to see his face. His eyes are closed, his skin deathly pale, only the faintest breath of air passing his lips. "Use your power. *Damn you, Slade. Use your power!*"

He doesn't move, doesn't breathe.

Blood flows from his wound. He has already lost too much blood and he deliberately shut his power down so he wouldn't hurt Archer. He passed out with his power blocked and now…

He's almost gone.

"You are not leaving me. Don't make me give you another feather, Slade Baines." I clutch his face and scream at him. "*Slade!*"

Nearby, Archer pulls herself upright, pressed hard against the wall as if she wants to become part of it and disappear.

She glimmers at the edges, on the verge of blurring, her eyes wide, face pale with shock.

"Hunter?" Her gaze shoots between me and Slade. "Slade Baines… What the…? What is going on?"

I don't have time to explain.

I press my forehead to his, squeezing my eyes closed. The warmth is fading from his body, but he can't die… Not like this…

I couldn't save William but Slade's power is still there. Under the surface. Somewhere. It has to be.

I don't take my time.

My wings shoot out from my shoulders like silver daggers, spreading to their full width, my power sizzling around me, its fiery wrath roaring to the surface so fast that the air crackles.

Wasting no time, I take hold of a feather and prepare to rip it out.

CHAPTER NINETEEN

The sound of Slade's inhale is like a shriek in my ears. His hand shoots out and grabs mine, stopping me with a grip that is like a vise.

His command is powerful, ripping my heart into pieces. "No, Hunter. You will never do that again. Not for me. Not for anyone."

I drop my face to his, all my fear rushing over me in one massive wave. Tears run down my cheeks, leaking uncontrollably from my eyes.

His big arms rise around my back, drawing me close, pressing me into him, wings and all. "I'm okay. I'm not going anywhere."

I sob against his neck. "You scared me."

"I promise I won't do it again."

I raise my eyes to find a gentle smile on his lips. He wipes my eyes and presses a kiss to my lips that reminds me what I would have lost if he died.

His expression becomes very serious as he strokes the hair out of my eyes and turns his head toward Archer.

She huddles where she landed, close enough that I could touch her with my wings. I quickly tuck them back into my sides and bury my power again.

She has drawn her knees to her chest. She is very pale. Too pale.

I wait for her to speak, knowing there is too much for me to say. Not only has she seen my wings, but she knows I'm her enemy, and she knows I'm with Slade, the man who was meant to kill her.

When she speaks, her voice is a hoarse whisper aimed at Slade. "You weren't attacking Hunter, were you? It was your blood, not hers. You took the bullet that was meant for her because you love her. And then… I hurt you." Her breathing is rapid, sharp. "Like the killer that I am."

My lips part in shock. Of all the things she could have focused on, it wasn't my wings after all. Or the fact that I can kill her.

It was what she did, her own choices.

Her hands shake. She clasps them together, pressing them against her legs and forming them into fists as if she's determined to make the shaking stop but it's no use, they rattle against her knees.

"I'm a danger to you," she says. "I'm a danger to everyone—"

"No, Archer."

Her breathing is far too rapid. "You're Valkyrie."

Slade's arms tighten around me, but he remains silent.

I reply, "I am."

"We could kill each other," she says.

I nod. "We could."

"Did you know that when you agreed to train me? Did you know that I could kill you?"

"Yes."

"Then why did you help me?" Deep pain bleeds into her voice. "I'm Archer Ryan, killer, murderer, thief, criminal. You have no idea the things I've done to survive. You don't know how many people I've killed, how many times I've pulled the trigger."

She stares at her knees, her hair cascading across her shoulders. "You can't possibly trust me. Not after this."

I am in shock.

I expected her to retaliate. I thought she would fight me once she found out what I am. I anticipated violence, anger, even fear toward me, but not pain.

Briar told me that Archer was good and kind. She wears a tough face, a shell made of iron, but underneath it she is human, vulnerable, cruelly aware of the consequences of her actions.

"Archer." I can barely speak.

Slade's strong hand flexes across my back, his gaze urging me to speak the truth.

"I have, too," I say. "Killed. Hurt. Lied. But you protected Cain. You nearly died for him. He told us that you protected his sister, too. You saved Briar's life. For all of those things, I owe you... so much."

She doesn't look up. "I am a threat to you."

"No. You aren't." I drop a kiss to Slade's forehead and he gives me a gentle nod as I disentangle myself from his arms. He won't be able to stand yet, his healing power is still working its way through his wounds, but he will soon.

I approach Archer carefully, expanding my senses in case she is unconsciously harnessing her power, but if anything, the only sense I have is of emptiness, as if her power has been sucked out of her and drained dry.

I kneel, reaching for her hands. I'm shocked to discover that she is colder than me, her fingers like ice. I rub them between my hands, attempting to warm them.

Slade finally rises to his feet behind me, the color returning to his face, his wound visibly healed when he pulls up his shirt to check it. He keeps his distance though, giving us space.

"You were trying to protect me just now," I say to Archer. "You did a good job of it. If there's anyone I want watching my back, it's you."

She doesn't respond, a low moan sounding through her lips.

"Archer?" Alarm shoots through me. The sound she just made was physical pain, not emotional.

She groans. "I don't... I can't..."

Cain said she collapses after a fight. He thought it was because her power was triggered. Well, she definitely triggered it before, and now the sense I get from her is like an empty shell about to cave in on itself.

"Slade! She's shutting down. We need to get her back to Tansy right away."

"I'll carry her."

"No!" Archer shrinks against the wall away from Slade, fear seeming to make her lucid, but it's clear she is in no shape to defend herself. "You were going to kill me."

Any sensible person meeting Slade for the first time would run for cover.

He hasn't shaved today, the shadows across his jaw adding to the harshness of his features, his ferocious eyes a paler blue, the dark rims around them making his gaze even more piercing. The circles under his eyes—his lack of sleep—worry me.

Even kneeling down, he is one scary-looking man. My heart melts a little at the sight of him. He is *my* scary man.

He rests on his knees and very carefully takes her hand and mine into his, clasping them together.

He is warm, like a lifeline we both need. She gasps, her wide eyes shooting to his as our tangled fingers quickly thaw within his grasp.

He looks her straight in the eyes and says, "I promised Cain I would keep you safe. I won't do anything without your permission. Please, let me fly you back to Tansy so she can help you."

She chokes, "Fly me?"

Unlike me, he takes great care releasing his wings. For a moment, I'm terrified that releasing his wings will release his power into her and hurt her. He's taking a massive risk right now.

I hold my breath as the gorgeous electrical currents that form his wings unfold into the air around us, turning the air silver.

She doesn't flinch, isn't hurt, and I release my breath, grateful that the act of releasing our wings doesn't hurt her. I guess my wings and Slade's are extensions of our arms and legs. It's the same as taking her hand. We won't hurt her just by touching her, only if we are actively drawing on our power at the same time.

"My wings are a long story," he says. "We can answer all your questions once you're safe on Saber Lane."

She considers him for another moment, then gives him a quick nod.

He doesn't waste time. He scoops her into his arms, sweeping her hair away from her face. Fully visible now, her features are drawn and pale, her eyes squeezed shut.

Slade murmurs to her, "Hold on, Archer. We'll get you help."

He turns to me before he strides from the room. "I'll leave the Realm intact and send a clean-up crew. The casino-users won't know a thing. We need to blur."

I nod. I trust him with her. "I'll meet you back there."

CHAPTER TWENTY

I fly as fast as I can, beating Slade back by seconds.

I race up the steps to Tansy's place, but her door flies open before I even touch it.

"Hurry!" she cries. "Dean sensed you coming and alerted me. Bring Archer inside."

Tansy ushers Slade inside through the hallway and into the parlor on the right. He lays Archer down on the floor, the early evening glow from the fading sunset casting shadows across her face and body.

Her head nestles on the carpet. She is only half conscious.

Tansy kneels beside her. "Help me lean her on her side, please. I need to see her back."

Slade enfolds Archer in his arms, propping her on her side so she rests partially on his knees. Tansy runs her hands down Archer's spine with a gasp. "I can't sense her power at all."

I hover nearby, keeping out of the way. "Our powers collided."

She blows out an audible breath. "Okay, I'll see what I can do. Slade, if you will…?"

He gently places Archer back on the floor, lowering her head so it doesn't drop, stepping away to allow Tansy to get to work.

He joins me at the side of the room, taking a seat on one of the plush chairs. The seats are too narrow to share, so I hold his hand across the armrests instead.

I'm still shaken up by what happened. His torn and bloody shirt is a sharp reminder that I could have lost him today. In fact, none of us is looking great right now.

Even Tansy, dressed elegantly in a long, black dress, appears worn and tired. Like Slade, she has been spending hours trying to read the Coda and Vade each day.

Speaking of books… I glance at her spellbook. It sits closed on the pedestal in the middle of the room.

Interesting. She didn't open it. She just acted in the moment. I can't help the hope rising inside me that Tansy's power might finally be healing.

Her aura grows stronger as light glows around her, the same powerful healing light as when she helped Archer the first time. It wraps like ribbons around her body and Archer's, connecting them.

Despite what I've seen of Tansy's power so far—the way she spelled Cain's daggers and the force she used to create the protective spell over the Lane—it's her ability to heal that is truly remarkable.

The sun has set. Darkness creeps into the room before Tansy finishes. I don't dare turn on a lamp in case I disrupt her concentration. Her power is light enough.

She finally sits back, stretches her shoulders and neck,

and then leans forward once more to run her hand across Archer's cheek.

Archer's eyelids flicker open, her expression peaceful and calm, quietly taking in the room and everyone in it.

Tansy gives her a smile. "How do you feel?"

"Much better, thank you. Did you…" She falters. "Did you fix my wings?"

Tansy's face falls. "I'm sorry, Archer. I can't break the spell that locks your wings. It wasn't a particularly powerful spell, but when your birth feather was burned, it locked it in. Only a miracle will reverse it."

I grit my teeth, fighting the frustration that rises inside me. It was my fault. Now Archer is burdened with the consequences of my actions, the same way I will never be able to fully bond.

Archer draws slowly to her feet, saying, "Thank you for trying."

Tansy flicks on a lamp and Slade and I both stand in the silence.

"I think it's time to start over." I draw Archer's focus to Tansy first. "Archer, this is Tansy, the Saber Lane Witch."

Archer gives her a genuine smile. "You saved my life. Thank you."

Tansy isn't the hugging sort; she gives Archer a gentle nod. "No thanks are necessary. I'm glad to see you're looking much better now."

I indicate Slade who waits quietly beside me. "This is Slade Baines."

He extends his hand toward Archer, remaining at a distance. "Well met, Archer Ryan."

She considers Slade for a moment, sizing him up the

same way she assessed me the first time she saw me. "I'm surprised, Slade. Assassins never willingly shake hands."

"Well, we already got the fighting part out of the way." He gives her a cautious smile. "You should know that I'm not like other assassins."

She takes his hand, maintaining eye contact. She has a powerful presence, even if she seems unaware of it. "I have a lot of questions."

He glances at me before he says, "We have a story to tell you."

It's hardly a fairy tale. Tansy makes cups of apple and spice tea and Archer huddles over her cup, warming her fingers while we talk.

I start at the beginning: her mother's flight from the west with her as a baby, and my mother's part in saving her and hiding her with Patrick Ryan, including hiding her birth feather.

I don't leave anything out, including the truth about my mother's death, Gareth's hand in it, and the complexities of bonding.

I tell her about my quest to steal back the feather, how I didn't know what it would reveal, then my efforts to find her —the violet-eyed child. I tell her about the Keres and the Valkyrie, about the ringmakers and the betrayal that led to Amalia becoming the person she is today.

Slade speaks then, telling her that he is a ringmaker, that Amalia killed his brother, and that I gave him a feather to save his life.

I tell her that I'm dying.

Then we tell her about the Keres Coda, the Valkyrie Vade, and the hidden Realm.

Tansy fetches the books for her. "This is the Keres Coda. It's a history of your people."

Archer's jaw drops. She reaches for it before she stops herself. "May I?"

"Of course. It belongs to you." Tansy hands it to her, opening it to the picture of the woman with the two babies.

"This is beautiful." Archer lifts the pages to her nose and inhales, her eyes closing. "Oh, that scent. And these images."

"There's a code hidden in the illustrations," Tansy says. "And, as of two hours ago, we know what it says."

I nearly jump out of my seat. "You decoded it?"

"That's why I came looking for you," Slade says. "When you weren't at the Tomb, I asked Briar where you were. She told me where you went."

"Where is the Realm, Slade?"

"Where we thought: in the forests of Portland, Oregon, right in the middle of Mother Serena's territory."

I grimace. "That's bad news."

Slade holds out his hand for the Vade and the wad of handwritten notes folded inside it. "William was right. Nyx was the mother of the babies. Their birth feathers were so powerful that Nyx hid them in the secret Realm—a maze. She surrounded the feathers with monsters so nobody could get to them, and then she placed a Keres guard at the entrance. Only the Keres guard or one of her descendants can open the Realm."

He tips the book on its side to show us while he reads along the feathers that float on either side of the babies. "There's one more message in the feathers. William decoded the first part but we figured out the rest. It says: *Trust is shared. Only through trust can truth be revealed.*"

"I'm the descendant of the original guardian, aren't I?" Archer asks.

Slade nods. "That would be our guess."

"Do I need to release my wings to open the maze?"

I give her a curious look. "Possibly. Why?"

"When I fought Lady Tirelli—Amalia—at the Horde, she let me go because she said that without my wings I'm useless to her. I think that means I have to release my wings to open the maze, which means… I can't help you either."

She sinks back into her chair, running her hand across her forehead. "The irony is that the birth feather of the first Keres could be the miracle I need to unlock my wings. But I can't release my wings to get it."

She gives a harsh laugh. "And you know what's really ironic? If I can't release my wings, I can't use my power to kill Amalia. Even without those problems, if I don't find a solution, my wings are going to kill me. I can't release them, I can't control them, and I can't control what happens after I access my power. I can't keep ending up here with Tansy trying to heal me."

Tansy leans across to her. "We can't give up. I may not be able to reverse the spell, but maybe I can help you open your wings temporarily so we can access the maze."

I purse my lips for a moment. "Tansy, you said 'we.'"

"I'm coming with you."

All of Vlad's warnings rush back at me. He said that Tansy would be hunted if she left Saber Lane. Taking her to another witch's territory is the worst thing we could do. "It's too dangerous—"

Tansy ignores me, presenting me with her back when she swivels to Archer. "With your permission, I can look into spells that might achieve that."

Archer casts wide eyes between Tansy and me. The friction is hard to miss, but she shakes it off with a smile. "I would appreciate that, Tansy."

Slade touches my arm. "What about the Keres ring? The Valkyrie rings always had a negative effect on you, but what if the ring could help Archer regulate her power?"

I chew my lip. For now, I am forced to put aside my worry for Tansy. I'll deal with that when the time comes to leave. "It's a long shot, but it's worth a try."

To Archer, I ask, "Did you ever come into contact with Cain's ring?"

"Several times. His assassin's magic calmed my pain when I collapsed."

I smile. "That's good news. Even if it doesn't work, the Keres ring belongs to you. It's also the only one you might be able to wear as an assassin." I turn to Slade. "Would you mind getting the one from my room?"

He immediately nods. As soon as he's gone, Archer tucks her feet under her bottom and considers me over the top of her cup. "So… you and Slade."

I give her a grin, the first today. "You and Cain."

She smiles and there's a little less pain in her expression. "I didn't think I would ever meet anyone like him. I want to believe that one day…"

"You will," I say. "I don't plan on leaving this world before I kill Amalia *and* make sure you can be with Cain."

I also give Tansy a hard look but she chooses to ignore me. She won't speak with me about Vlad.

Archer's forehead is suddenly creased and her question is quiet. "You don't expect to survive, do you?"

I stare at the floor, then at Tansy, then at Archer's cup. "I have to plan for a scenario where I don't. You know… There

142

was a time when I was terrified of meeting a Keres. But a good friend taught me that enemies are made, not born. I want to make sure that when my time is up, I've done what I needed to do." I swallow the lump in my throat, suddenly scowling at Archer. "It's really hard to lie to you, do you know that?"

She shrugs. "I find it difficult to hide my thoughts around you."

"Well, at least it's fair."

"You… I never expected…"

I smile. "What? To meet someone who fights like you?"

She sighs. "You're cleaning up the underground."

I fold my hands in my lap. "Mom had a reason for protecting Patrick Ryan, but now that reason is gone. So, yeah, I'm chewing on its bones and spitting them out again."

Slade returns with the Keres ring safely tucked into Mom's glass case. The first time I saw this ring, it was an object of horror. I hope something good can come of it now.

Slade opens the case and offers it to Archer. "Hunter and I can't touch it without burning ourselves. Other than Cain's ring, there is only one other Keres ring, so you should avoid coming into contact with other assassin's rings altogether."

She asks, "Where is the other one?"

"In my bag," he replies.

I sit up with a start. "You brought the training ring with you?"

He shrugs. "I didn't want to leave it in the Realm in case Amalia broke in again."

Archer reaches for the ring in the case. "Cain's magic didn't hurt me. In fact, it helped me when my wings were burning. But this one…" Her hand hovers over it. "It feels different."

"Don't touch it if it hurts you. Mom couldn't go near assassin's rings. They made her feel ill. I wasn't as badly affected, and the impact was variable, but sometimes I couldn't wait to take mine off. That's why I wear a glass ring."

Archer plucks the ring from the case and slides it around the forefinger of her left hand.

The magic in it takes hold and the ring resizes itself to fit her finger. She purses her lips for a moment, waiting to see what will happen.

Then she smiles. "It feels calm. May I see the other one?"

Slade brings his bag to her, withdrawing the training ring contained safely in a small leather box.

She turns it around in her fingertips. "I could wear this one too, but I think it might be put to better use." Her features set in hard lines. "Amalia threatened to take your soul, didn't she?"

Slade stiffens but nods. "She has to be within eyesight to do it. She can't take my soul from far away. But she can do it."

Archer's expression is dark. "I've seen it happen. I held Cain's soul in my hand after Amalia ripped it from his body. I won't let that happen to you."

Archer places the training ring in the box and passes it back to Slade. "I want you to use that ring against her."

"But how?" he asks. "I can't touch it."

She smiles at him. "You're a ringmaker. The ringmakers turned feathers into rings. I don't know how they did it, but I'm giving you permission to turn this ring into a bullet."

Her eyes meet Slade's. "A bullet for Amalia's heart."

CHAPTER TWENTY-ONE

lade stares at the ring. "I wasn't trained as a ringmaker." He gives me a worried look. "I'll have to take the ring to my parents, but I haven't spoken to them in a long time."

I touch his arm. "I'll come with you. You'll need backup."

He gives me a nod. "It's time for them to answer my questions about my family's history."

"While you're gone, Archer and I can start packing," Tansy says. "From now on, I will go where Archer goes, in case she needs me."

Tansy gives me a hard stare. So that's her trump card. If Archer gets hurt, Tansy needs to be there. Which means I can't tell Tansy to stay behind.

As much as I want to protect Tansy, we're about to head into Vlad's territory.

Maybe her determination to help isn't her only motive for coming with us.

I test my theory, saying, "Vlad will be happy to see you."

Tansy flushes.

Bingo. Well, as far as I'm concerned, that's the best reason for her to come with us.

I'm on edge from the moment Slade and I leave Saber Lane. A lot has happened already today and I don't know what to expect from his parents.

Slade and I blur and take to the night sky, both wearing protective suits this time. The Keres training ring rests in the glass case in a satchel secured to my waist. Slade's blur is so complete that it's nearly impossible for me to detect his presence, but we decide that is best so we can remain safe.

I land at the back of his parents' home in the same back yard that I saw in Slade's memories: a large, well-kept lawn with a high wooden fence to keep out prying eyes. As soon as I materialize, light floods the yard. I must have triggered a sensor light, but I don't see anyone around. I hurry to wait in the shadows at the corner of the building.

Tucking away my wings, I lean around the corner to check whether Slade has landed…

I lean straight into a fist.

The woman at the end of it doesn't give me time to speak.

I jolt backward as she follows up with a kick to my side, her foot a blur. I don't have time to identify her and the backyard light doesn't extend around this part of the house.

All I can do is duck when she spins and tries to land another kick at my face. I rise before her foot finds the ground so I can deflect the blow and shove her off balance.

She wobbles backward onto the open lawn, fully into the light.

I recognize her from Slade's memory: dark brown hair and pale blue eyes, rimmed in black like his.

I immediately ease up, dancing out of her reach. I don't want to hurt his mom.

She snarls, "Valkyrie! What do you want?"

Surprise is a hot dagger through me. "How do you know what I am?"

"I knew as soon as I touched you. Tell me why you're here before I end you."

At the same time as she speaks, my shoulders tingle. It's an unfamiliar sensation, like fingernails scraping down my back. *Is she doing it?* I roll my shoulders, trying to shake it off and focus on the problem at hand: convincing this woman I'm not here to kill her.

I opt for the closest truth I can. "Relax. I'm not here to hurt you. Slade is with me."

Her eyebrows rise as she registers what I said, but she stands her ground while she glances around the yard. Again, my shoulders prickle, an itchy sensation that makes me twitch.

An indent on the grass tells me that Slade has landed. He materializes without his wings, a wise move since we could be seen. Fighting his mom out in the open is bad enough but at least she and I were mostly under the cover of shadows during the fighting part.

Slade is a tower of strength as he strides toward us, each step purposeful. Even though his focus is on his mother, the flicker of his gaze toward me tells me he sees the way I'm holding my fists.

His mom twists her head toward him—a deceptive move, because at the same time she lets fly another punch in an attempt to smack me on the chin.

I evade the blow, narrowing my eyes at her.

That extra hit was completely unnecessary. She's definitely making it hard for me to like her.

I remain on guard while she takes rapid steps away from me, glancing between Slade and me, her expression turning to dismay. I guess she thought I was lying.

"Slade, why is this creature with you?"

His jaw clenches. He comes to a standstill several paces from her. "I know I'm a ringmaker, Mom. I know why Foster died and who killed him."

The blood drains from her face. She stumbles away from him so fast that she bumps up against the side of the back porch, the impact juddering through her. She is suddenly beyond pale. "If you know that her kind killed him, why have you brought her to my home?"

Slade's assertion is heartfelt. "Hunter is not our enemy. We can't change the past, but we can change the future. Right now, we need your help."

His mother plants one palm against the building at her back to steady herself before she draws a deep, shuddering breath. "Then you should come inside."

She whirls and stumbles up the stairs, regaining her poise by the time she opens the back door to let us in.

Slade's steely-eyed expression hasn't softened for one second, not even when he spoke to her.

Despite my instinctive dislike of her, I catch his arm before he follows after her. "Don't forget, she's your mom."

His gaze softens when he looks at me but hardens just as quickly. "Her name is Melinda. She is cunning and tough—and always ends up getting what she wants. Don't let down your guard."

Inside, the house is exactly like Slade's memory, right

down to the floral dish towels and the drawings stuck to the front of the refrigerator. The scent of apple pie rushes into my head the moment I step inside. It's the perfect picture of a family kitchen, right down to the freshly prepared food.

Without speaking, Melinda stalks to the oven, pulls out the pie, and busies herself preparing plates and making coffee.

I position myself on the left of the dining table in a clear space so I can move if I need to. Slade remains close to me but also with enough space around himself to deal with anything that might come his way.

My heart bleeds that he feels he can't trust his mom.

Without turning, she says, "You're Master of the Legion now, Slade."

"That's correct."

Her voice is crisp. "You know I don't approve of that life."

Slade's tone remains matter of fact. "We've had this conversation, Mom. It's time for a new one. Tell me about Grandma Baines."

She stiffens, her hands resting out of sight inside the sink, supposedly washing a spoon. I study the way she holds her head and the tension in her shoulders. I should have asked Slade for more details about his relationship with his mom. Slade said his parents tried to make him normal, that they wouldn't answer his questions about Foster's death.

I always assumed they were trying to protect him like my mother tried to protect me. Now that I've seen Melinda in action, I'm not so sure.

"Or better yet," Slade says, "tell me about Josiah, the man who massacred the Valkyrie. And put down the knife while you're at it."

A clatter inside the sink tells me she dropped a utensil.

She turns to us, sweeping up a dish towel to dry her hands. "Josiah Baines wore the same ring that you wear now. A ring made from the feather of the Valkyrie Queen."

Her gaze flicks to me and again I sense the same disconcerting tingle in my shoulders.

"He created the three Realms and wrote the Assassin's Code. Until that time, assassins were mercenaries, without masters. In return for their loyalty, he gave them rings. He gave them strength and power."

"And the ringmakers?" Slade asks. "What about them?"

"Josiah Baines was the first ringmaker. He gathered a group of his most trusted followers to share his power, but only his descendants inherited his true power. Some of his descendants became assassins like Grandma Baines. Others hunted the remaining Valkyrie and Keres to extinction to create more rings—five hundred over time."

She squares her shoulders. "In case you're wondering, I am the ringmaker, not your father. I married him because he had nothing to do with that life. A baker. Although he knows all about it of course."

Slade curls his fingers around the top of the nearest wooden chair, choosing to remain standing. "Josiah was just a man. How did he have the power to imprison the Keres and Valkyrie?"

"He sold his soul to a sorceress in exchange for..." Her gaze flicks to me again. It's the thousandth time she's done that and it's starting to get a bit too intense for my liking.

She suddenly fixates on me. "I can smell your feathers."

I blink at her. "What?"

Slade quickly moves to stand between her and me, a position that forces his mother to focus on him again. "What did Josiah get in exchange for his soul, Mom?"

"Unnatural strength… and power over metal." She side-steps, sliding against the sink so that she can see me again. "All ringmakers are drawn to metal that carries magic."

She inclines her head back at the sink. "I can manipulate that knife into any shape I choose, make it do anything I like, but add magic into the mix and it's intoxicating."

Slade shifts to block me again and I have no problem letting him. His tone remains calm as he says, "That's why Foster died, isn't it? He couldn't stay away from that Valkyrie."

"I thought she was the last but it looks like I was wrong." Melinda shakes herself but her pupils dilate as she cranes her head to see me. "Not every descendant of Josiah is born a natural ringmaker. My sister wasn't. Your cousin Thomas wasn't. I, on the other hand, had two sons both born with the power and the… impossible pull…"

Her hands suddenly shake. She clenches them together, rubbing her fingers. "Slade, I don't know how you're resisting your impulses, but you really should take her away before I…"

A force plucks at my back like invisible fingers. What was only a tingle before is now an intense pull.

I gasp and jolt to the side, my back suddenly burning but not in the way I'm used to when I call my power. This burn is like my wings being grabbed from the inside and forcibly wrenched out.

My feathers grate against my ribs inside my back, forming far too fast.

I wince and fight it, clenching my jaw, bracing against the force. "Slade!"

He swivels from his mother to me. Then back again. "What are you doing?"

Melinda's pupils are dilated, the blue taken over by darkness in the same way that silver floods Slade's eyes. She remains focused on me, her body locked in a concentrated trance. "I want to see her wings. Her feathers call to me…"

I cry out as my feathers scrape me from the inside, a painful burst. They're going to rush out of me fully formed. If I fight it, they'll tear me up from the inside just like Archer's feathers did to her…

"Stop!" Slade leaps the table and slams into Melinda, his fist glancing off her jaw.

It's a blow that would have knocked anyone else out but she barely flinches. She hits back, making Slade dance out of her way.

A knife rises from the sink behind her, slicing through the air toward him. He steps aside, avoiding the dagger, but in the next moment the kitchen drawers fly open.

Knives, forks, and spoons rush out of them, a barrage of weapons flying straight at him.

He shouts, "Mom! Stop!"

With a flick of his hand, a transparent shield appears between Slade and the weapons—a partial Realm—filling the space from floor to ceiling.

Like hailstones against it on the other side, dents appear on its surface where the implements clang into it. They quickly clatter to the floor. He flicks his hand again and the shield disappears.

His momentary distraction was all Melinda needed.

Against my will, my wings spread, shooting out so fast that they rake across my skin. I let them release, knowing it's the only way they will form without tearing me apart.

The angle at which I'm standing means that one of my wings hits the kitchen table and the other crashes through the glass cabinet at the side of the room, breaking the pretty porcelain cups inside it.

My feathers shiver, my wings drawing forward while Melinda's outstretched fingers curl up like claws.

She's pulling them.

She is going to pull them out.

CHAPTER TWENTY-TWO

nger pulses through me.

I've already lost one feather. I won't lose more. Not to this woman.

I stop trying to pull away and stride forward instead, the force easing now that I'm moving in Melinda's direction. Rather than leap over the table like Slade did, I shove it with all my strength, ramming it against her stomach.

She screams, suddenly pinned between the table and the sink.

I scale the table, adding my weight to it as she tries to push it away. I crouch on top of it and grab her throat.

Despite the threat I pose, her gaze remains on my wings. She reaches for them, leaning, grappling with the table in her quest to touch them.

Intoxicating? Far too much, it seems.

She is two seconds away from yanking the nearest feather from my wing. I am seconds away from releasing my power.

Her neck smokes beneath my fingers.

My voice is dangerously low. "Stop or I will kill you."

Slade lands on the table's surface with a thud and a wash of silver light fills the air. His electric wings shoot across my vision, encircling me. I'm forced to let Melinda go as he swiftly pulls me away from his mom, dropping us to the floor.

The visual disturbance created by his wings acts like a shield between her and me.

She shakes her head, blinking rapidly. Her hands slowly lower. She stares in shock at Slade's wings, her mouth gaping wide. "Slade... how? Even Josiah couldn't give himself wings."

Slade's protective growl sounds close to my ears, his arms tight around me, his wings a cocoon through which the world around me shimmers. "I am Valkyrie now."

Her pupils constrict. "That's not possible."

"It happened." He pauses to demand one last answer. "Am I the last ringmaker?"

"Yes. The power will die with you." She reaches for him, the darkness invading her eyes again. She shoves at the table so hard that it slides all the way across the room and hits the wall, cracking the plaster.

Her breathing is rapid, but also panicked. "I am what I am. Get out before I hurt you both!"

Slade draws me away from her, picking me up in his hurry, keeping his wing between her and me. Her hand rises and the force she was using to try to take my wings plucks at me again, weaker through the protection of Slade's wings but still painful.

She shouts, "Don't come back, Slade. Never come back."

He races away with me, carrying me away from the kitchen that smells like cookies and cinnamon, away from his childhood drawings and his deadly mother.

His wings retract as soon as we shoot through the door. I force my own closed, swallowing a scream at the effort it takes. Damn her, she's still plucking at them.

Slade's urgent voice meets my ears. "Can you fly?"

"No! She'll pull me from the air."

"Then, let's run," he shouts. "Don't blur. I need to see where you are."

As soon as he puts me back on my feet, we jump the fence and pelt through the neighbor's yard, leaping over the next fence into the playground beside it.

Our feet fly on the pathway through the open area, darting around the play equipment. Normally, we would never wear protective suits without blurring, but luckily nobody is around at this time of night.

The pull on my wings finally releases. I speed up at his side. "I can fly now."

Slade says, "Back to Saber Lane."

No arguments here.

We dart into a group of trees and out of sight so we can blur and take to the sky.

The wind rushes past me and relief floods me.

As soon as we land on Saber Lane outside the bookshop, Slade pulls me close to check me over, running his hands over my back and shoulders. "Did she hurt you?"

Trying to ease his worry, I attempt a smile. "I'm okay. Really." My smile turns crooked. "Do I need to remind you that I can't lie to you?"

He blows out an exhale, his remaining worry still creasing his forehead as he draws me inside the bookshop.

I close and lock the door and we catch our breath, both of us leaning against the counter. We're more out of breath from shock than anything else.

I don't hear anyone upstairs so I assume that Archer is still at Tansy's. In fact, they are probably having dinner at the Diner by now. We won't travel west until tomorrow, so we have all night to prepare.

The revelations from his mother are still sinking in. "You have the ability to control metal... *and* change it."

From the beginning, Slade had questioned how the rings were really made and how they carried so much power.

"It explains how the ringmakers were able to take the feathers without being killed when they touched them," he says. "And then to manipulate the feathers into rings without damaging the power inside them."

"It also explains how you tore an iron vault apart." I run my palm across his cheek. "I'm sorry about your mom."

His shoulders hunch a little. For a second, the mask he wears to hide his pain slips over his features, but he shakes it off. "She couldn't control her impulses. I understand now why my brother didn't stay away from Amalia."

I tangle my fingertips in his hair. "But you did. You gave Amalia back her feather. You never tried to hurt me." I search his eyes. "How are you different?"

His expression becomes reflective. "I was drawn to Amalia's feather. Just like I was drawn to you, I won't deny that." He laughs suddenly. "Wanting you in my bed in the dorm wasn't just about needing you to watch my back."

I smile at him, warmth filling my stomach at the way he strokes my back. "But?"

His forehead crinkles. "Tell me something, Hunter. When was the first time you touched me?"

I think back. "Maybe in the men's showers after Fallon knocked you out."

"You did something to wake me up, didn't you?"

I nod. "I drew out your consciousness."

His arms slide all the way around me. "I think you left a little of yourself behind. Is it possible that you curbed my power? Or at least gave me the ability to control it on a subconscious level?"

I press a kiss to his lips before I tip my head back. "Not on purpose."

"Well, something happened."

"Maybe it was something I did, maybe it wasn't. You made different choices throughout your whole life. You held Amalia's feather in your hands and you chose to give it back. You chose to control whatever impulses you were born with, the same way I control my impulse to kill everything that breathes. We all make choices."

I withdraw my arm and pull the glass case from the satchel around my waist. "What will we do now? Your mom didn't help us."

He smiles. "Actually, I got everything I needed."

"You did?"

He reaches for the case. "May I?"

He places it on the counter and opens the lid. "Let's see what I can do."

Without touching the ring, he hovers his palm over it, a look of concentration falling over his features. I step back, the feeling of having my wings wrenched from my back still too raw in my memory to want to be near that power again.

When he lifts his hand higher, the ring rises too. He shifts a little on the spot, his focus becoming even more intense. The Keres ring lifts into the air between his two palms.

He twists his hands side to side in opposite directions and the ring twists around on itself, forming a shape like an infinity symbol. When Slade draws his hands apart in increments, it stretches the ring until the shape separates.

There are now two smaller rings floating in the air between his palms.

He closes his fists and the rings compress, each forming a solid ball, which rapidly elongate and round out at one end, flattening at the other.

With a satisfied smile, Slade allows them to lower back to the glass case, flat ends resting downward. His concentration lifts. He snaps the case shut and holds it out to me so I can see its contents.

I consider the two perfectly formed bullets made from Keres power. "You did it."

"Two bullets," he says, but he becomes very serious. "I want you to know that I will never use my ringmaker power on you."

"I know—"

He captures my gaze, compelling me to hear him. "But I also need you to know… that I won't use it on Archer."

My lips part. Of course. We need her to release her wings to open the maze. If we can't get inside the maze, then I won't survive.

Slade could force her to do it. He could rip her wings out of her back but it would tear her apart.

"I would do anything to save you," he says, "but I will not break her."

Tears form in my eyes. "Whatever time I have left, I want to live it to the best that I can. I won't give up, Slade. But I won't make compromises either. We will find another way."

He rubs my arms, kisses me with soft lips, and rests his forehead against mine. Then he smiles. "We need Cain's jet."

My senses light up. "Yes, we do."

Slade gives me a slow grin, confirming my thoughts when he says, "They have been apart for long enough."

A few days is a lifetime when you love someone the way Cain and Archer love each other. With a smile, I say, "Hand me your burner phone."

I lay the phone on the counter and put it on speaker.

Cain answers with his Master Assassin's voice, stern and uncompromising. "What's wrong?"

I reply, "I'm calling in the favor you owe me."

"Hunter?"

"It's me. Slade is here with me."

There's a pause. "And Archer?"

"She's safe, Cain. She completed her first mission today and I'll recommend she be promoted. She fights as well as you said she does."

There's another silence. I picture the phone held in his ever-tightening fist. "What's the favor?"

"I need your jet. There's a chance I can be healed. We need to go west to Vlad's territory—"

"It's yours. It will be waiting for you at the airport in the morning."

"Thanks, Cain." I smile at Slade. "But that's not the favor. When I returned your dagger to you and you said you'd help me… well… I'm not about to waste that on something you'd do for me anyway."

His response is cautious. "Then what do you want?"

I inject as much steel into my voice as possible. "You're coming with us."

CHAPTER TWENTY-THREE

We only take what we can carry on our backs: our protective suits, including one for Tansy and a new one for me, along with a few changes of clothes and our weapons—mostly tranquilizer darts since none of us is sanctioned to kill, although we each carry multiple daggers and handguns.

Tansy's spellbook takes up a lot of room in her bag so I carry some of her things in mine. I also take my katana, and as a last-minute thought, I place the verdan plant in my bag too. I don't know what we'll encounter in the maze and the sap is fabled to kill anything, assuming I can access it in a dark environment.

Before I leave Saber Lane, I say goodbye to Ridley. It's an emotional moment. He doesn't know all my secrets, but if I get through this, I'm going to tell him everything. If I don't get through it, then I don't want to die regretting my last words to him.

"Thank you, Dad, for being there these last few months."

His response is a gruff hug. "Whatever mission you're going on, just make sure you come back."

"I will, Dad."

He hugs me tight, clearing his throat, trying not to show his emotions. "Then give the fair lady hell, Hunter. For your mom."

"I'll do that." I press a kiss to his cheek and hug him once more before we leave.

An early spring frost sparkles on the tarmac as we approach the jet just after sunrise. I closed out yesterday's missions in my ledger last night, and then wrote a blunt message to the Guardian:

You said Cain couldn't see Archer again, but I'm afraid he owes me a favor that he is required to honor. We're traveling into Vlad's territory. No rules broken.

Her terse reply came back to me: *You're testing the boundaries of the Code and my patience, Hunter.*

To which I replied: *I'm Rogue, remember?*

There was a long pause in which I practically heard her sigh, and then she wrote: *Be safe.*

Now, Cain waits on the tarmac at the foot of the stairs.

He is a tower of muscle and strength but his black hair emphasizes the rings under his eyes, his features carefully set in a controlled expression. I guess nobody has been getting a lot of sleep.

The moment we step out of the SUV, his focus is on Archer.

She lags behind while Tansy strides ahead to greet Cain first. He gives her a polite nod. "Blessings on your power."

"Thank you, Cain. We need all the blessings we can get."

She glides up the stairs and inside the plane. Slade and

Cain bow to each other, never taking their eyes off each other in the customary way.

I, on the other hand, give Cain a hug, dropping my head to his shoulder for a moment. "Thank you for coming."

I walk slowly up the stairs, wanting to give Cain and Archer space, but I also don't want to leave her alone in case it's too much for her. She chewed her nails in the car all the way here, such a ferocious woman terrified of her own emotions and afraid to show them.

She is completely blank, controlled as she steps up to him. "Cain."

His expression softens, the light returns to his eyes, and he takes a careful step toward her.

He murmurs something in her ear. Not many men, let alone women, are as tall as Cain, but Archer barely has to tip her head back to meet his eyes.

Whatever he said, all of the tension leaves her shoulders. She turns her cheek into his for the briefest moment, pressing her face to his in a gesture of trust.

Before they move apart, he plants a gentle kiss on the corner of her lips.

She turns away from him and hurries after me, her eyes downcast, but her body is lighter, happier. "Let's go."

Cain takes the steps two at a time after us and tells us to settle in to the plush leather seats. There are eight, all single, situated on either side of the passenger cabin, grouped in twos that face each other.

Slade and I take the two at the front on the right, facing each other. I indicate the set on the left for Archer. Cain sits opposite her. Tansy mumbles something about being the "fifth wheel" as she takes a seat in the back, but she smiles as she says it.

"How long will it take to get there?" I ask, sinking into the immaculate seat.

"Four hours."

I'm surprised. "Only four?"

"This jet is the fastest on the market." Cain gives Archer a secret smile as he says, "I like to travel fast."

I arch an eyebrow at them. I'd love to know what went on between them when they were together, but what I already know about Archer is that she's an incredibly private person so I'm not about to ask.

Taking a seat, Cain doesn't waste time leaning across the aisle to Slade and me. "Tell me what I've missed."

By the time we land, he knows the whole story. He takes it in his stride, but his focus is frequently on Archer, his expression darkening when we tell him she needs to release her wings to open the maze.

Slade doesn't leave anything out, including his power to control metal and the fact that he could hurt both Archer and me.

The tension inside the passenger cabin rises ten thousand percent at that point.

Cain's power swirls around him, a bright threat that increases with every word Slade speaks, until Slade says, "I won't do it, Cain."

It's clear that Cain doesn't believe him, apparent in every line of his tense face and coiled muscles, menace hanging in the air between them. He was prepared to fight Slade to the death for Archer. Judging by his response now, his determination in that regard hasn't dimmed.

"Hunter will die if we don't get inside the maze," Cain says. "You would do anything for her—"

Slade leans in to the haze of power surrounding Cain,

flinching against the biting pain but holding Cain's eyes, his response barely more than an instinctive growl. "I will die when Hunter does. I want to believe that will be in a really long time from now. But when I go, I will go with a clean conscience."

I lean across the distance and reach for Slade's hands.

I don't know what will happen to him when I die. In fact, I don't know what will happen to me if *he* dies. Either way, we are living for these moments together, making the most of them, making them count.

"If we never open the maze, then Amalia will die too." I give Cain a deadly grin. "Silver linings."

Cain leans back in his chair, his power fading, his expression incredulous. "You really mean that?"

"I do. *We* do."

Cain says, "That's why you've annihilated her operations."

I give Cain a pleased smile. "She has nothing in Boston now but an empty brownstone with a rose bush out the front. If I wasn't worried about the people living next door to her house, I would have destroyed that, too."

Cain considers me carefully for a moment before he turns to Slade. "Who will succeed you if things don't go to plan?"

"Ridley is looking after the Legion for now. But I've given him the name of my successor."

Cain doesn't let it go. "Who?"

"Lutz Logan."

Cain taps his thigh before he leans forward on his knees, giving Slade a shake of his head. "No."

Slade glowers at him. "You don't have any say in it, Cain."

Oh boy, these two. I prepare to jump into the conversation when Archer speaks up, the tone of her voice allowing no argument. "Lutz Logan belongs with Parker."

We all stare at her in surprise.

"Cain's sister?" I ask.

She shrugs at Slade. "Lutz won't ask you for his freedom, Slade. That arrogant bastard doesn't think he deserves it. It's true: he doesn't. Nobody deserves Parker. But nobody will ever love her the way he does. If you saw him with her..." She shakes her head with a laugh. "It's like a monster protecting an angel. I've never seen a brute brought down by a single smile before."

Cain sighs. "Lutz protected Parker during Amalia's attack. My sister has been through a lot. She trusts Lutz and he is very good with her."

Cain takes a deep breath and speaks aloud what I believe we're all thinking. "Nobody on this plane is getting a happy ending." His focus remains on Archer. "I want one for Parker."

Slade gives them both a helpless look. "Assassins don't leave their Faction. That's like inviting death to your door. Lutz would have a target on his back for the rest of his life. It would put your sister in danger."

"Not if you make him an ambassador," Cain says.

"A what?"

Cain leans forward again. "It's about time we had better communication between Factions, isn't it? We should each have an ambassador in the other territories."

Slade barely hesitates. "Done. Think carefully about who you send to the Legion, Cain."

Cain smirks. "I'll give it some thought."

I laugh. "Don't even think about sending someone to my territory."

"Not even your father?" Slade asks, quieting me with a disarming smile.

I laugh. "Okay, I'll admit, I would welcome my father. But I can't reciprocate. There's only Archer and me and—"

Oh, Cain, you clever assassin.

Cain gives me a hopeful look, the most vulnerable look he's ever given me. But he doesn't say anything, doesn't ask for what he wants: for Archer to live with him.

Carefully, I say, "We have to convince the Guardian to sanction the whole thing."

Cain growls, "She won't be the Guardian much longer. She has a year to hand over her title now that I've ascended."

He gives me a look.

My eyebrows lift. *Me?*

I give him a small shake of my head. Of all the choices for the best person to hold up the Assassin's Code, it isn't me. *Won't happen.* And yet…

I look between Slade, Cain, Archer, and Tansy, who has remained quiet. The relationships between the people in this cabin are incredibly complicated and astonishingly simple at the same time.

We are bound up in rules that are wound so tightly around us that we can barely breathe. Cain and Archer want to be together. I want to be with Slade. Tansy… well… she won't admit it but the further we fly, the more often she looks out the window as if the time isn't passing quickly enough.

We all want to break free.

We all want a different way.

But we're all ignoring the fact that we're about to go into battle and we don't know who will be alive at the end of it.

CHAPTER TWENTY-FOUR

The jet touches down in a private airport outside of Portland.

True to Cain's prediction, we arrive mid-morning, which will give us plenty of time to travel to the forest during daylight. We change into our protective gear before we land but pull on everyday clothes over the top to appear more normal, ready to travel from the moment we arrive. I silently kick myself that I didn't think for Archer and I to do this when we went on the mission to fight the mages.

Vlad waits on the tarmac with one other person by his side, but his greeting is *not* customary.

Instead of the usual bow, he hugs me, his big bear-like arms wrapping around me and lifting me off the tarmac.

I freeze with shock.

He raises his eyebrows at me, still squishing me like crazy. "I have to hug you at least once, Hunter. I figured I'd need to take you by surprise for you to let me."

"Ah. Yes. That would be correct." I side-eye the female assassin waiting with him before I relax and hug Vlad back.

It's a bit like hugging a tree, difficult enough to get my arms all the way around his chest, let alone keep my feet on the ground. "You're going to ruin my reputation."

He grins. "Along with my own. Don't worry. You can trust Kirrily." He puts me back on my feet to introduce her. "Kirrily is my second in command and the best tracker in all of the Factions. She has been following Amalia's movements and I'm afraid to say, Amalia is closing in on the location of the maze. We don't have a lot of time. The cars are ready to take us to the forest. You can trust my drivers."

Slade and Cain both give Vlad customary bows but Cain's brow furrows. "You knew about all of this already?"

In his blunt way, Vlad says, "You were the last to know. We should get moving right away."

Contrary to what he said, Vlad stays put as we file around him toward the vehicles.

He greets Tansy with a rare smile and she lights up the space around herself in response. Her green eyes sparkle and her instinctive magic ignites soft rainbows that swirl around her face and body. She is also dressed in a protective suit, over the top of which she's wearing a soft sweater and long pants that hug her curves.

Vlad is transfixed as he says, "Blessings on your—"

"Alexei Vladimir Mason." She takes his hands, her small ones disappearing inside his big fists as she rises all the way up onto her tiptoes to plant a kiss on his cheek. "I missed you."

He freezes, his smile disappearing. An intense fire lights his eyes and he sweeps her off her feet. One enormous arm wraps around her slender waist and the other across her shoulders, pulling her close.

She gasps, her head tilted back to see his face, her focus dropping to his lips, then rising to his eyes.

But the smile on her face rapidly fades, seemingly replaced with confusion.

They're barely inches apart but he doesn't close the gap, frozen like that, his ferocious gaze burning into hers.

Her lips part as the moment stretches. The tiniest crease appears on her forehead, an expression of puzzlement more than anything else and then… a shot of despair.

Vlad's expression changes from fierce to gentle to oddly resigned. "I missed you too, Solnyshka."

He carefully places her back on her feet, clearing his throat as he waits for her to precede him. The rainbows that glistened in the air moments ago vanish into the background as she hurries away from him.

I catch her arm before Vlad joins us, his footsteps unusually slow and heavy behind her. "Tansy?"

She gives a shake of her head. "It's nothing. I'm fine."

She's definitely not fine. She brushes past me, hurrying toward the SUVs parked at the side of the building.

I've never been able to make Tansy tell me anything she doesn't want to, so there's no point in pushing her, but it worries me what passed between her and Vlad just now. I can't even put it down to Vlad's ability to offend people with his bluntness, because he barely said anything to her.

The others are waiting at the car for us but I grab Vlad's forearm and pin him with a hard stare. "What just happened?"

His shoulders are sunk so low that he is nearly eye height with me. "She figured it out."

"Figured out what, Vlad?"

"You'll find out soon enough." He lumbers past me. His answer isn't good enough but we don't have time to waste.

I slide into the first vehicle with Slade and Tansy, choosing the seat facing Slade, hoping Vlad will join us, but he takes the other vehicle with Cain, Archer, and Kirrily.

Tansy stares out of the window as the landscape passes us by.

What the hell happened? All they did was hug and now they're avoiding each other.

Slade shakes his head at me—a non-verbal "stay out of it" —but I can't abide it. *Damn it,* I'm running out of time to say what I think and the least I can do is make sure Tansy is happy when I leave this Earth.

I reach across to her. "What happened? You were so happy before and now…"

She continues to stare out of the window. "Vlad can't love me. I don't know why he pretended to care."

"What are you talking about?"

"Stop asking me questions, Hunter."

"But—"

She covers her eyes with her hand, turning as far away from me as she can so I can't see her face. "Let me close off this part of my heart in peace."

I persist. "No, you need to—"

"Stop!" She spins back to me and her power flares out from her hand like a whip across the gap between us, a dark lash made of light striking across my torso.

I jolt back in my seat as the lash disappears. Smoke rises from my t-shirt where the whip burned it apart.

Holy… Only the protective suit saved me. I gape from the damage to Tansy.

"Hunter!" She stares at me in shock, her eyes wide, tears leaking from them. "I'm sorry! I didn't mean that to happen."

I cough out the smoke that rises into my nose.

Slade twitches opposite me and I can tell that he is seriously restraining himself right now, the silver glow growing at his edges telling me she set off his protective instincts and he's fighting to restrain himself. It's lucky her magic stopped as suddenly as it started or we could have had a war inside this vehicle.

I take a deep, calming breath, keeping my response soft. "It was your instinctive magic. It's stronger now that you're away from Saber Lane."

She whispers, "It's stronger when I'm upset. I'm truly sorry, Hunter. I know you want to help me... I know you care... but nothing can fix this."

She hugs her arms to her chest and turns away again, curling up on the seat.

Slade's power fades and calms. He of all people understands rage, the deep burn at the center of your heart. He surprises me when he reaches across the seat to plant his hand on Tansy's back, rubbing it the same way William used to calm her.

"We're here for you if you need us," he says.

She hunches over, but doesn't shake him off, accepting his touch, her voice a quiet whisper. "Thank you for not killing me just now."

He smiles even though she can't see it. "Something tells me you would be hard to kill."

A sad smile ghosts around her mouth, visible from the side. "Probably."

We spend the rest of the trip in silence. The landscape

changes as we take the Wilson River Highway deep into Tillamook State Forest. Trees rise up around us, a thick canopy that obscures the view left and right, even thicker when we turn off the highway onto a dirt track, traveling only a few minutes along it before the vehicle comes to a stop.

We will have to walk from here.

I follow Slade out of the vehicle, retrieving our backpacks from the trunk and quickly pulling on a new shirt before anyone notices my torn one. Nobody needs to know what happened between Tansy and me.

I check on Cain and Archer, hoping they had a less momentous trip. They appear relaxed, at ease with each other. Cain helps her secure her backpack before she checks over their weapons.

He brought more weapons than we did and I'm not sorry to see Archer don an additional harness sporting multiple daggers and guns. She and Cain are like a well-oiled machine, working together without speaking, but every now and then Cain touches her hand or her shoulder, little touches that tell me he's worried about her. She's the only one who can give us access to the maze.

If Archer is feeling pressure about releasing her wings, she isn't showing it.

Right now, we're all ignoring the fact that we have no idea how she's going to do it.

Vlad plows forward, indicating the path at the side of the clearing. His weapons belt is also laden with daggers and guns of every sort. I guess I know where to go if I run out of ammunition.

"As soon as we step onto that path, we will be in Mother Serena's territory," he says. "The entrance to the maze is a two-mile hike from here. We'll be lucky to creep in unnoticed so stay on your guard."

Kirrily says, "Amalia was last seen in this location. You need to be alert for her as well. As you know, she and Gareth are skilled at blurring—"

"Wait... Gareth?"

Kirrily gives me a serious nod. "Your former Master is here, too. I will leave you now, but I hope to see you again soon—safe and sound."

The last is said to Vlad. She may be his second-in-command but it's clear that she cares about the outcome of this mission. For a second, I wonder if she is the reason Vlad can't love Tansy, but I dismiss that idea. I'm not sensing any romantic vibes between Vlad and Kirrily, only mutual respect.

When Kirrily leaves, I turn to the others. "Amalia and Gareth will follow us. They will wait for us to do the hard work finding the maze and opening it. That's what I would do. We need to keep an eye out behind us."

I scan the visually impenetrable tree line ahead, wondering if I will be able to sense Amalia when she's close. She will hold off coming anywhere near us until we clear the way for her. Especially getting through the coven.

I'm filled with sudden dread. I'm giving Amalia everything she wants. I will lead her to the maze she's been searching for. Archer will open the door. If we get inside, then she can too, and if she gets to the feathers before us... Will anything kill her then? Will she be invincible?

The feathers were hidden for a reason. Guarded by monsters for a reason...

I stop so suddenly in my tracks that Slade catches me before he bumps into me. "Hunter?"

"We should turn back. I can't be this selfish."

"What are you talking about?"

"We're leading Amalia right to what she wants."

He takes my hands in his. "I know what you're thinking. *Don't.* This is a chance worth taking. It's a fight worth fighting. I'm not walking away from this place without trying. Archer needs this as much as you do."

He taps the gun resting in a holster across his chest. It contains the Keres bullets. "We are as strong as we will ever be Between us, we have everything we need to end her."

I look him in the eye. "Ending her is more important than healing me. Agreed?"

"One goes hand in hand with the other, Hunter. We will get to the feathers first."

Hope is an awful, treacherous thing. It gives me no choice but to believe him. Despite the churn in my stomach, I nod and take my first steps down the path toward the maze.

CHAPTER TWENTY-FIVE

It's impossible to walk quietly.

Every footstep carries the crunch of leaves and debris, the ground changing from spongy moss to brittle twigs and back to moss depending on how close we are to a water source.

We follow one of the many creeks for a mile while the stillness of the forest around us grows heavier with every step. Only the sound of rushing water signals movement, becoming more distinct as we follow Vlad's directions to the location of the maze.

Eventually, he stops, his forehead creased and head tilted. "Do you hear that?"

The whooshing water is loud enough that it doesn't sound like the creek anymore.

"It has to be a waterfall," I say.

He presses his lips together in an uncertain line. "Yes, but there aren't any natural waterfalls around here."

"Do you think the coven made it?" I ask.

"Maybe. Or maybe it's the entrance. It won't be on any

map. We've been walking steadily uphill for the last mile. It's not impossible that there could be a waterfall around here."

Tansy has stayed away from Vlad for the entire trek, but she approaches us now, saying, "I sense magic here. It could be the witches or it could be that we're close to the maze."

"I feel it, too." When I glance at the others, both Cain and Slade are accessing their power, carefully maintaining a safe distance from each other so their powers don't collide. Luckily, Archer has remained calm and is staying close to Cain. The last thing she needs is to trigger her power unnecessarily.

We push ahead for another half a mile until the pathway suddenly ends.

Two steps ahead of me, Vlad jolts to a stop, teetering on the edge of a yawning cliff.

My hand shoots out. I grab his shirt and pull him back to safety. The others were further behind so there's no danger of them bumping us off the edge.

I signal to them to stop before I creep up to it, crouching low.

A ravine roars below us and the waterfall we could hear crashes about fifty feet to our right, the water flowing fast and furious hundreds of feet below us.

A bridge stretches from one side of the ravine to the other, positioned right in front of the waterfall, the spray making the gray stone appear glossy.

Vlad checks our coordinates on the map, tapping it to indicate our current location. "According to the map, this waterfall doesn't exist."

"It shouldn't," I say. "The terrain in this part of the forest doesn't allow for a waterfall."

I squint at the waterfall, attempting to estimate its height.

The environment is misty high up, difficult to see beyond, as is the rest of the ravine to our left, telling me strong magic is at play here.

Vlad says, "That bridge has to be the gate."

I can't help but snort. *A bridge that is a gate.* It seems exactly the kind of contradiction that would indicate the entrance to a maze.

As the others carefully crowd around the cliff's edge, I murmur, "There's no direct path to the bridge."

Further along the cliff, an enormous tree blocks either end of the bridge, beside which other trees soar high and thick. The entrance to the bridge on both sides is completely blocked.

Archer says, "It isn't accessible by foot. It looks like we have to fly over there."

"That's fine," I say. "Slade and I can fly each of you across—"

At the back of our group, Tansy suddenly whirls to face the path behind us. "Hunter! Look!"

A woman steps along the path, black hair flowing across her shoulders as she glides toward us. She wears a gentle smile, but her eyes are cold and dead. The back of her burgundy gown slithers across the mossy ground, her effortless ability to navigate the path without making a sound giving her an air of power.

She hasn't made any aggressive moves but my skin prickles with every step she takes toward us.

Vlad launches into action first, making it to Tansy's side in several strides. I catch Slade's eye before he joins me and we move quickly with Archer and Cain to form a protective semi-circle around Vlad and Tansy, staying well away from the edge of the cliff.

The woman says, "If you're here to cross the bridge, you will fail. Nobody has stood on it for…" Her gaze flickers to Archer. "Twenty years."

Vlad's expression is set like stone, harder and colder than I've ever seen it. "Mother Serena, you will leave us alone."

She smiles. "Hello, Alexei. Look how you've grown."

He narrows his eyes at her. "Look how you've aged." His blunt response tells me he intends the insult for once.

"Oh, Alexei. That isn't polite. After all I've done for you." She takes a step forward, but it's a sudden move, a single pace that carries her across the distance, her form rushing in a blur to stop right in front of him.

A wash of power flows with her, her magic rushing around us, making my skin crawl.

Her gown floats around her legs as she rises into the air until she is at eye-level with Vlad. She smiles. "How is that spell working out for you?"

Tansy's hand shoots out, her expression dark. The same inky light that Tansy struck me with forms around her silhouette, biting the air. "Get back, witch."

Serena's gaze swivels to her, a curious smile touching her lips. Despite the deadly vibes Tansy gives off, Serena floats right into Tansy's outwardly stretched palm, pressing against it as if she doesn't care. Her gaze follows the shadows that swirl around Tansy's chin, cheeks, and eyes.

"Little Tanzanina Gray," she says. "You left your safe cocoon at last."

She takes a deep breath, her cheeks flushing and her eyes brightening as she inhales the darkness around Tansy. The older woman runs her tongue across her lips as if she's tasting the power in the air.

"I see why your aunt tried to steal your power." Her

forehead creases. "But such repression... It isn't healthy, Tanzanina."

"My name is Tansy. Only my mother called me 'Tanzanina' and if you don't back off, you'll find out exactly what I'm repressing."

Serena floats away from her. "That would be unwise."

The nearest tree shimmers, its branches lowering all the way to the ground in an unnatural movement, its trunk shifting around on itself, as does the one next to it, and the others.

Our semi-circle closes in toward Vlad and Tansy so we can form a circle, our elbows touching as we carefully drop our bags and reach for our tranquilizer guns.

I scan the environment, uncertain what could be coming our way.

The trees continue to shift, their bark peeling back toward their lowered branches, the woody surface smoothing and transforming from rough to silken red material.

A woman unfurls from within each one, the tree branches morphing into arms and legs, the trunk into flowing hair and bodies swathed in diaphanous silk that doesn't leave much of their bodies to the imagination.

Twelve women rise up around us. Serena makes thirteen. The only advantage is that now the space around us is wider.

"Sisters!" Serena calls. "Today we will take the power that belongs to us. We will share it as it should be shared."

Archer murmurs beside me, "Can we kill these witches?"

"Not sanctioned."

She curses. "We can't let them get their hands on Tansy."

I angle toward Tansy and whisper, "Get back inside the circle. Go to Slade."

I meet Slade's eyes across the way. He knows exactly what we need to do.

Tansy steps backward as our circle closes around her. She slips toward Slade's position while the witches glide forward, all of them chanting in unison. At the same time, Slade darts inward and catches Tansy's arm.

They disappear.

Slade's absence is so complete that my heart wrenches. He has never stepped into a Realm of his creation without me. I didn't realize how completely he would be gone. I can't sense him at all. My heart squeezes, because it's almost like death.

Serena screams and whirls, searching the space before she snarls at us. "Blurring will not save that little witch from our spells."

I give her a smile. "She's not blurred. She's gone. Somewhere you can't touch her."

Serena's eyes shoot wide as she catches on. "A Realm? That's not possible. Only the Valkyrie Queen could create whole Realms. No assassin has ever accomplished it. Not even Josiah Baines."

I don't give her time to think too hard about it. "Well, then, it's a mystery you'll never solve."

Now that Tansy is safe, talking time is over.

Vlad wastes no time striding forward, headed straight for Serena, but three other witches fill the space in front of her, their pale hands outstretched.

From what we saw of their ability to conceal themselves in nature, I'm guessing their power will be connected to the forest around us. As will their weapons.

A storm of leaves and debris whirls up from the forest floor around us.

Before it can obscure our view completely, I duck to allow Archer to shoot three perfect shots in rapid succession over my head with her tranquilizer gun, surprising the witches immediately in front of me since their focus was on me.

I grin as they drop to the forest floor, but my smile fades.

The other nine won't be so easy.

CHAPTER TWENTY-SIX

Cain plows ahead of me through the ever-thickening storm of debris to barrel into the nearest witch, knocking her out with a blow to the head followed by a quick tranquilizer.

The next witch leaps on him, her fingertips stretched for his face. The moment she touches him, he freezes, half crouched, pain shooting across his face, caught in some kind of trance.

Coming to his defense, Archer leaps, gun aimed, and shoots the witch in the back of the neck.

"Look out!" I barely have time to shout before the nearest tree branch swings into Archer, knocking her backward, but not before the witch that had captured Cain drops unconscious to the forest floor.

Seven witches are left now. They link hands and lift their arms, chanting in unison.

The ground trembles as the nearest trees uproot themselves, their bark and branches shifting and transforming again, this time into creatures that shouldn't exist.

Disfigured giants with clubs for hands and upturned tree roots for hair tower over us, a configuration of magic, ten feet tall.

Cain lurches to his feet, his power streaming around him, arcing through the still-swirling leaves toward Archer.

She shouts, "Please tell me we can kill those."

I grit my teeth. "They are conjured, not real. We can kill them."

I'm not entirely sure how. There are four of them—I spin. But where is Vlad and Mother Serena?

Through the trees, I catch sight of a moving form and Serena's burgundy robe. Electricity lights up the space around them as Vlad ducks and rolls away from the spell she cast at him. He retaliates with a dagger that she doesn't deflect with her magic in time. It barely misses her face.

I narrow my eyes. For once it looks like Vlad intends to break the Code. "He's trying to kill her…"

I don't have time to think. A giant wooden club appears through the leaf storm, aimed squarely at my head.

I duck, harness my power and run straight toward the giant's torso, punching into it with all the force I can muster. It's like slamming into a brick wall, but the giant wobbles and leans on his back foot to keep his balance.

Hitting his chest, I use it as leverage, propelling myself back into the air and releasing my wings at the same time.

I access my killing power, my fingertips tingling, and fly straight back at him. Now that my power flows through my body, I can sense much more around me. The giants are like glowing pillars of magic, Cain is a copper silhouette, Vlad is a silver one, and Archer…

She is a bright spark of energy as she launches herself at the nearest giant, leaps from his knee to his shoulder, launches herself at his throat, and rams her dagger into the side of his neck.

She quickly rips it out, stretches upward, and thrusts it into his eye before she drops to the ground.

Damn, she's beautiful with a knife. Any weapon actually.

Despite the damage, the giant continues to function, swinging his fist at her, clipping her shoulder before she can get out of the way.

"Archer!" Cain shouts, and launches himself at the giant, leaping onto its back, shooting bullets into it as he goes. The giant topples and Archer rolls out of its path just in time.

Despite the bullets and the knife wound, the beast is still alive.

I fly back at my target. He swats at me, crashing back into the nearby trees. I avoid his fists, aiming for his heart.

My power sizzles through my fingertips as I brush them across his chest in a searing line. My power collides with the magic being used to power the giant, slicing neatly through it.

With a creak and a groan, the giant splits down the middle, its body returning to its original form and solidifying on the spot, now a misshapen tree cut down the middle.

I glare at the witches. It's a cruel abuse of nature.

I have no choice but to go after the other three giants.

The one that Cain shot rises to its feet.

"Cain! Use your magic!" I shout. "Only magic works against them."

Cain shouts an acknowledgement but Archer gives me a helpless look—she can't help us—before she ducks and zigzags to avoid the giant fist that sweeps low to the ground, the giant behind it trying to scoop her up. Using her power is the most dangerous thing she could do.

It's up to Cain and me.

He darts behind the recovering giant, a burst of copper light sparkling around him as he launches himself onto its back again, moving his own massive form with more grace than I expected, grabbing the creature around the neck and pressing his hand to its temple. Searing light splits the clearing and the creature drops to its knees, solidifying as it falls.

I fly at the final two, forcing them to give me their attention to lead them away from Archer. My power cuts through them in a single line from one to the next. Two misshapen trees creak and groan in the suddenly quiet clearing.

I drop to the ground in front of Archer. Even though we defeated the creatures, the witches remain.

And… boy… they aren't happy right now.

Snarls on their lips, they chant in unison once more, but this time their focus is on me.

My skin crawls, the air around me thickens, and suddenly… I can't breathe. My wings snap closed as I cough, and water spills from my lips.

Water… coming from inside my lungs…

They must be drawing it from the ravine. I try to release my wings again, but my body won't respond. In fact, my arms and legs won't move. *I can't… move.*

Cruel sneers light the witches' faces as they close in on me.

I try to draw a breath, coughing out more water, splashing water and blood onto the ground as I double over.

"Hunter!" Archer reaches my side, immediately ripping out her tranquilizer gun and firing it.

The witches are ready this time, using their power to deflect the darts. Cain's gun follows as they disarm him with their magic. His weapon hits the nearest tree and shatters.

Archer screams. "Let me kill them!" She runs toward the nearest one, hitting an invisible force and rebounding, held down by another force.

I double over, gasping and reaching for my inner power. I have to dispel this water. I have to get it out! I spit and cough but as fast as I spit, my lungs fill up again.

"Enough!" Tansy's voice rages over me. She appears beside me, her arms outstretched. "The assassins can't kill you, but I can. Stop or you will die."

The women laugh. One of them speaks with a soft voice, "You are powerful, Tanzanina, but you will not save your friend. You will all die slowly and painfully—"

Quick and brutal, a tree branch spears through the woman's torso. Shock pierces her expression before she flies back against another tree with a *crack*, and drops, lifeless, to the ground.

In an instant, all hell breaks loose and it's… *all* Tansy.

She barely makes a sound as Cain's fallen dagger thumps into the heart of another witch. At the same time, a metal shard from his broken gun strikes another witch through the neck.

The entire clearing swirls with deadly debris that flies over and past Cain, Archer, and me, spearing toward the witches. Most stand their ground but two try to run, their feet suddenly enslaved in vines, one falling on a sharp branch, another thrown backward against the tree she turned into a giant, her back broken.

Within seconds, the remaining six are dead.

Tansy isn't done. "Where is Mother Serena?"

Through the trees, Vlad's form is a flicker of silver light.

Tansy takes off running in that direction.

With a quick glance at the others, I race after her, darting through the trees, jumping bodies and branches.

Tansy screams into the small clearing where Mother Serena holds Vlad pinned and kneeling on the ground, her fingers pressed to his temple. Dark mist surrounds Vlad's face and his expression is vacant.

Mother Serena sneers at Tansy. "You can't control your power, Tansy. You can't defeat me—"

Tansy grits her teeth and says, "You really shouldn't upset me."

Tansy exhales and then she inhales a slow, deep, sucking breath, her fingertips spreading, her chest expanding with such force that I step away from her.

Mother Serena's eyes grow wide. Her fingertips tremble. Her whole body shudders. A wail builds on her lips as she stares at her hands.

The mist around Vlad's face clears and his stormy eyes become clear.

Vlad's big fist darts out and squeezes around Serena's throat.

She hisses and strikes out, thumping him, pressing her fist into his chest, but her eyes pop wider when her hand hits his shoulder without impact.

Her gaze darting to Tansy, she gasps, "What did you do?"

Tansy is unsmiling, hard as granite. "I took your power. It's mine now. You will never get it back."

"Or your life." Vlad is as cold as an ice serpent as his hand squeezes tighter.

Serena is deathly pale. Panic spreads across her face. She tries to free herself, her voice hissing beneath the pressure around her throat. "No… please…"

Vlad is unmoved. "The spell you cast over me worked out really well, Mother Serena. Your spell took away my emotions. Because of you, I have no feelings. I don't feel fear. I don't feel love. I see only truth and logic. And logic tells me you must die."

"Alexei…" Her voice diminishes the tighter he squeezes. She tries one last time. "Vlad…"

He shakes his head at her. "I feel your neck in my hands, but I feel no pity. No remorse."

Her neck snaps.

Despite how coldly he killed her, Vlad lays her down gently on the mossy earth, straightening her limbs, smoothing out her hair, and closing her eyes.

When he's done, he rises slowly, but he doesn't look up. "Mother Serena's name was written in my ledger six months ago. I was biding my time. I haven't broken the Code."

Vlad told me that we would work within the Code, that he wouldn't break it. He has proven that time and again, but this time feels harder, a victory that cost too much.

He continues, "Out of respect for my father, I didn't look for my mother while he was alive. After his passing, I sought Mother Serena's help to find her. She not only refused, she took away my pain. She said it was a gift."

He looks up, but his focus is on Tansy. "Because of the spell she cast, I see the world in black and white. I see strategy, logistics, moves, and countermoves. I don't… *feel*… anything."

Tansy told me that Vlad can't love her. I thought she

meant he wasn't free to love her or that she doubted he loved her, but she meant that he literally *can't.*

"That's why Dean can't sense your emotions," I say.

Vlad nods. "I am not troubled by them."

Vlad told me once that he sees the world with clarity, not clouded with feeling, but once again I narrow my gaze at him.

It can't be true.

Dean said that Tansy had broken through to Vlad's heart. I've seen the way he looks at her, the care with which he treats her...

Vlad's suddenly hard gaze locks on me. "Logic," he says, as if he reads my mind.

He swings away from me, striding toward Tansy, stopping inches away from her. "My mother was a witch so it's logical that I would be drawn to one. Logic also dictates that the woman I choose will be the most powerful witch, because what idiot isn't drawn to power and beauty. But none of it is love. It can't be..."

His furious gaze rakes across her. "Tanzanina Gray, you are nothing more to me than a chess piece and I don't—"

Smack!

Unlike the time I slapped him round the head, Vlad responds to Tansy's fist with a sharp movement out of her path, as if it hurt far more than any fist ever did before.

He gulps out the rest of what he was going to say, speaking to the ground while he rubs his jaw. "I don't want to treat you that way."

Some of her anger fades, but not all. "Stay out of my path, Alexei Mason."

She spins and stalks away from him, heading back toward

the cliff. Now that the witches are out of the way, our next problem is getting to the bridge.

With a brief comforting press of his hand on my shoulder, Slade says, "We'll go with her."

Cain and Archer follow, but I storm up to Vlad. I have to restrain myself before I slap the assassin's mask off his face. "That was the biggest lie I've ever heard from your lips."

"It was more truth than I've ever spoken, Hunter."

I shake my head. "You feel something for Tansy. I've seen it."

He doesn't reply. His expression, his gray eyes, are like storm clouds tightly controlled that will never break. "It's better for her this way."

"How? By breaking her heart?"

"She deserves more."

"She wants *you*!"

When he stares back at me, his expression unyielding, I fist his shirt and drop my forehead to his chest. "I might not come back from this, Vlad. I need you to be there for her."

"I will be."

I tip my head back and search his eyes. "How?"

"As her friend." He clears his throat. "Without emotion, I am a much better protector than I would be with it."

As he gently disentangles my fist and walks away from me, I shake off the fairy tale I had naively clung to.

Cain was right.

Nobody gets a happy ending.

CHAPTER TWENTY-SEVEN

When I reach the cliff, Tansy is calm and in control.

She and Archer are deep in conversation, pointing to the bridge, while Slade and Cain pick up the dropped weapons and take stock of what is broken.

Archer voices my thoughts when she says, "It can't be as easy as flying over there. Or at least… I think it would be dangerous for us to try without testing it carefully."

I nod. "There are bound to be security mechanisms."

I scan the horizon. Most of our daylight is used up. The sun is sinking and will hit the horizon in less than an hour. After that it will become bitterly cold and I don't want to try anything in the dark.

Archer touches my arm, drawing my attention back to her, her blue eyes bright. Outside of Saber Lane, she has resumed wearing her contact lenses. "It's weird, but I *want* to be here. I don't remember this place, not exactly, but it feels familiar."

"If your mother spent her life guarding this place, then she would have lived around here."

Archer inclines her head across the ravine. "On the other side maybe. There could be a cabin over there that we can't see."

"It's possible. She had wings so she could have easily flown over. Let me go and see."

I spread my wings, careful not to bump into Tansy or Archer, and rise off the ground, aiming for the cliff's edge. I glimpse the ravine below and then…

Thump.

I hit an invisible wall. My wings fly forward, splatting against the unexpected surface. I try to gain purchase, but slide down the shield, landing in an ungainly heap on the cliff.

"Are you okay?"

I squint up at Archer, rubbing my head since I banged into the shield head-first. "Ouch." Rubbing my neck, I say, "It's shielded."

She hides her smile as she reaches forward—*Yeah, that wasn't the most graceful thing I've ever done*—testing the air with her hands, leaning as far as she can out from the edge without endangering herself. She presses up against a solid boundary. "For me, too."

Tansy peers at the place where Archer presses her hand. "Just because it's shielded here doesn't mean it's shielded everywhere. We should follow the cliff's edge and see if there are any openings along the way." She grimaces at the trees blocking our path. "As best as we can, that is."

Slade hands me my backpack before he slides his onto his back. "That sounds like the only plan we have for now." He checks my scalp and presses a kiss to my smarting head. "No damage."

Cain also hands Archer her backpack but Tansy snatches hers up before Vlad can do anything with it. The tension between them isn't any worse than it was before, but it grates on me. Mostly because I can't do anything about it. I can't make people's choices for them.

Vlad stays at the back of the group while we step through the forest at the edge of the cliff, pressing our palms to the invisible shield as we go.

Every now and then, but only when there is a large enough break in the trees, I spread my wings and fly, testing the height of the boundary. Toward the top it curves over in an arch. Still no way in.

When I return to the ground, Archer surprises me when she asks, "What is it like to fly?"

I smile. "It feels like freedom, but you will know for yourself one day."

She gives me a doubtful look but it carries a spark of hope.

Finally, we reach the bridge. Or, at least, we reach the large tree blocking the bridge.

Archer plants her hands on it, standing in its shadow, studying its bark and curves.

The trunk is easily seven feet wide—as wide as the bridge —so enormous that the lowest branches hang high above us, leaving the air clear on either side. The closest tree to the left is another seven feet away, not as close as it previously appeared, although there is a closer one on the right hand side—the side with the waterfall.

Tansy hovers behind us. "This place has strong magic. I

can sense it in everything around us: the trees, the moss, the light…"

The sun hangs low in the sky now. When Archer moves out of the tree's shadow she squints into the light, turning to me with an expression of disappointment. The sound of rushing water here is so loud she has to shout. "I was hoping something would happen when I touched the tree."

The sunlight glints off her eyes as she turns into it, and for a brief moment I am completely blinded by the reflection.

My hand shoots out. "Stop."

She jolts and gives me an alarmed smile. "What is it?"

I study her face, her eyes, the way the setting sunlight gleams off her skin. I'm blocking half of her body, but the half that is doused in sunlight… gleams.

She side-eyes me when I say, "Do me a favor and take off your contact lenses?"

She arches her eyebrows at me.

Cain looms behind her. "What is it, Hunter?"

"I have a hunch. I don't know exactly but… humor me?"

Slade and Vlad stand further back. Slade leans against a nearby tree and Vlad is a quiet force on the other side of it, avoiding Tansy at all costs.

Archer dips her head, carefully removing each of her contact lenses, crouching to return them to the case in her bag before she rises into the sunlight again.

I inhale. Catch my breath. Release it. "Oh."

Without taking my eyes off her, I signal for Cain. "Look."

Archer's lips purse into an uncertain expression as Cain joins me. His sudden stillness tells me I'm not imagining it.

Sunlight glints off Archer's eyes, reflecting back so

strongly that the moment she pins me in her gaze, I have to shield my eyes.

Her gaze passes to the right and her pursed lips drop open.

I can't hear her gasp beneath the roar of rushing water but the quick movement of her chest tells me she's surprised by something behind me. Slade also jolts upright and Tansy steps forward, both focused on the tree.

Sunlight glints onto it, reflected from Archer's eyes. Where the sunlight hits the tree, the tree doesn't exist.

Within those small patches of light is clear blue sky.

CHAPTER TWENTY-EIGHT

rcher closes her eyes and the patches of sky disappear.

Without her body reflecting it, the sunlight would never reach this part of the tree. The thick canopy on its eastern side prevents morning sun from reaching it and its trunk blocks the afternoon light from touching this location. The mossy undergrowth tells me this side of the tree is forever in the shade.

But not with Archer reflecting the sunlight.

I inhale a breath of hope. "You have to release your wings. They're copper. They will be like a golden mirror…"

She keeps her eyes closed, squeezing them shut. "But I can't."

I say to Tansy, "Please tell me there's a way to help Archer release her wings without hurting her."

Tansy's response is grim. "The only way is if I continuously heal Archer while she accesses her power. I can keep her alive while she forces her wings to release."

I smother my frustration. "That's too dangerous. She will rip herself to shreds."

"I'll do it."

"No, Archer. It could kill you. Let's figure out another way—"

She levels her gaze with mine. "I need that feather as much as you do. Neither one of us has a choice here." She steps back from me. "It's not just my eyes, is it? It's my skin, too?"

I nod, fear settling into the pit of my stomach. "It is."

Tansy says, "It must be the magic here. Your body is reacting to it."

"Okay then. It's time to wear my birthday suit." Archer's serious lips lift into a smile when she looks at Cain.

She is trying to lighten the mood but he is having none of it. "I've always supported your right to make your own decisions but this time Hunter's right," he says. "You can't take this risk."

She presses her finger to his lips, grazing his bottom lip in a way that turns him into a statue. His arms rise as if he would wrap them around her but he stops himself.

She gives him another smile. "I'm doing this, Cain."

I swallow my fear. If Archer is going to strip naked as the day she was born, then Slade and Vlad need blindfolds. I stride to the back of the clearing and rummage around in Slade's bag for a moment before I drag out one of his shirts and hand it to him.

He takes it with a worried smile, pausing to catch my arm and lean in close. "Don't push her, Hunter."

I draw close so he can hear me without shouting. "I won't let her continue if it's too much for her. No matter how determined she is. Clear conscience, remember?"

He presses a kiss to my cheek and another on the corner of my lips, stopping the breath in my lungs. The way he tucks the hair behind my ears tells me he will always have my back.

Vlad has already retrieved a shirt and wrapped it around his own eyes, both men calculating the distance to the bridge before they cover their eyes and lean against a tree to keep their bearings. They fold their arms across their chests to wait.

Archer quickly pulls off her outer shirt and pants, and carefully peels off her protective suit. Cain focuses on the horizon, the tense edge of his jaw telling me he's beyond worried.

I figure it's up to Archer to ask him to put on a blindfold, so I leave him alone.

Sliding off the last of her clothing, Archer's skin sparkles and her hair shines, its pale blond color catching the light and reflecting it. She is dazzling and completely determined. Her hands form into fists, her fingernails pressing tight. "Tansy?"

"I'm ready." Tansy takes up a position at Archer's back. Her power glows, her own hair a golden flame in the light, as she directs it toward Archer's spine.

I locate myself on the other side of the clearing, my heart thudding.

This has to work.

Archer focuses on a spot in front of her. "Let's do this."

Her focus is pinpoint, but also far away, unseeing of the things around her. Within moments, it's as if she is in another place. Copper light spills from her shoulder blades, the light emanating from them making me gasp.

Her wings become visible, the delicate shape of her

feathers pushing outward but they are clamped beneath her skin, stretching against her rib cage. She hunches, a moan on her lips, audible enough to tell me she's already in pain. She bites her bottom lip hard enough that blood trickles from it. Her fists turn white and her face drains pale.

Her wings writhe against her spine.

I can see the damage they're doing inside her body.

Fear fills Tansy's face as she digs in her heels, her fingers spanning out, her power a growing force. She shouts, "I can't heal her fast enough!"

I immediately stride forward. "Archer, stop."

"No." Her eyes fly open and her hand shoots out to stop me. I leap backward from her power and its biting sting, unable to go near her.

Archer's shout turns into a scream. Her back splits up the middle in a single horrifying moment, but even then her wings remain locked, writhing beneath the surface. Tansy heals the wound but another crack appears in Archer's back and all I can do is shout, "Archer, enough!"

Cain flinches on her other side, backing away to thump his fist against the nearest tree, over and over again, until his fist is bloody, releasing his fear into it. "Archer! Listen to Hunter. You tried!"

Archer's outstretched hand swivels past Cain… to Slade.

"Slade," she screams. "You have to pull out my wings!"

Slade freezes, his hands turning slowly into fists, but he relaxes them and shakes his head, still blindfolded. "No."

He turns his head, indicating that he won't reconsider.

Sobs tear from Archer's throat. "Cain?"

Cain stops pacing, his gaze flashing from her outstretched hand to her face. He closes the gap between them, three powerful strides taking him to her.

He sweeps her up into his arms, both hands pressing her shoulder blades, trying to ease the pain in them. His head dips. He is seconds from pressing his lips to hers.

She melts into his arms, her whole body pressing forward, her head tipping back, the tension fading from her body for the first time. I shouldn't watch, but I can't tear my eyes away. I need to be ready in case she needs me. Tansy, too, maintains her focus, her power glowing, healing the cracks that appear in Archer's back.

Cain whispers something to Archer, and this time I read it on his lips.

He asks, "Remember?"

She gives him the smallest smile before she rises on tiptoes and presses her lips to his. "Always."

His hands flex against her back before his palms press along her spine, smoothing down her back. Under her skin, her copper wings respond to his touch, moving toward his palms, following his touch, and then...

Out.

Cain draws his hands away from Archer's back and her wings unfold, spreading slowly while she kisses him. Her copper feathers glisten like suns, her golden wings extending all the way across the clearing. She leans back under their weight, but Cain supports her, his arms folding securely around her.

Tansy steps away from them, cautious, but casts me a look of deep relief. Her power is still glowing, still healing. Archer isn't out of danger, but... Archer did it.

Cain opens his eyes a little, his mouth still pressed to Archer's, his lips curving into a smile. He murmurs against her mouth, drawing apart just an inch. She smiles up at him, her hands tangled in his hair.

"I won't leave you," he says.

Without removing his hands from her, he glides around her body, ducking under her wings, wrapping his arms around her from behind, dropping a kiss against her neck. Now that he isn't blocking her body, the sunlight hits it fully, the glow across her wings blinding.

I can no longer look at her. Ahead of us, the tree disappears in the light that Archer's body and wings reflect. Instead of the tree, a bridge stretches into a misty sky, but it is a different bridge, not the wet stone that exists in the ravine. There is no waterfall beside it, only mist that swirls around its white marble edges.

Tansy's urgent call compels me into action. "The sun is setting. Archer can't keep her wings open for long. We need to hurry."

I run to the back of the clearing. "Slade! Vlad! The gate is open."

I freeze, my hand inches from Slade's arm. His blindfolded face jolts in the same direction as mine.

He senses it, too.

Roses.

Putrid... damn... roses.

CHAPTER TWENTY-NINE

The time for blindfolds is over. I rip Slade's off his face, calling to Vlad at the same time.

Vlad's lip curls. "I smell her. Gareth will be with her." He fought Amalia briefly on Saber Lane, as well as on the night of her attack on the Horde because he was there for Cain's ceremony; he knows what her presence feels like.

He pulls off his blindfold, draws a dagger and gun from his arsenal of weapons, and scans the forest behind us, weapons ready. "Go! I'll hold them off."

Backing toward the open gate with Slade, I try to sense Amalia's location. She and Gareth must be blurred, not visible, but there's so much magic in this location and the power streaming around Archer is so intense that it's difficult to focus.

Amalia's presence was always a war of contradictions to me—forceful because of her power but reduced by her state of health.

A flicker to my right snatches my attention, already past

Vlad's position. He senses it at the same time as I do, turning and hurling his dagger.

I follow the knife's movement, sprinting in that direction. If the dagger disappears for even a second, it means it entered her blur…

The dagger spears through the air, disappearing before it reappears and thuds into a tree. It must have nicked her.

She is moving fast, must be running for the open gate, and judging by the dagger's arc, she is closer to it than I want her to be.

I chase after her, running along the only path she could travel around Cain and Archer. They stay where they are, but I catch the alarm on their faces.

Bullets and knives won't stop Amalia. I have to get to her.

The air shimmers ahead of me; her blur fails for a moment. She stumbles—she must be injured so she has to draw on her power to heal herself. It gives me the time I need to catch up before she blurs again.

Slade powers toward her location from the other side, leaping in front of the gate to block the path at the same time as I launch myself into the space where I pray she will be.

My fist closes around something solid. Material rips.

At the same time, Slade ducks his shoulder and barrels toward me, his arms closing around the solid shape I'm holding on to.

Amalia appears, squeezed within Slade's grasp, but just when I think we've succeeded, she releases her wings. Raking metal forces Slade's arms apart. He falls back as she rises into the air, her fist shooting out to catch him on the chin.

My hand brushes her wings… and her feathers slip through my fingers.

She sails through the gate into the mist.

"No!"

My frustrated shout is swallowed in the roaring water and the sound of Tansy's scream behind us.

Her voice washes over me in one terrified shout: "Vlad!"

A wash of power charges the air and Tansy's scream ripples through the clearing with so much force that it buffets me to the side. I collapse and crawl across the ground, making it beneath Archer's wings before I see what happened.

Archer and Cain turn toward the back of the clearing, their faces filled with shock. Tansy stands behind them, one hand palm out pointed at Archer's back, still healing her.

Tansy's other hand stretches toward Vlad...

He kneels on the ground at her feet. Blood bubbles up between his lips.

The front of his protective suit is full of holes that quickly fill with blood.

Gareth materializes behind him, dropping a rifle to the ground. It must have contained armor-piercing bullets. His gloating eyes are as cold as glittering gems.

Gareth jeers, "He wasn't my intended target, but he'll do."

Vlad's shoulders slump, he sags, but his gaze remains on Tansy, whose eyes are wide with fear and pain.

"No." A sob tears from her lips. She can't help him while she's healing Archer.

Vlad's lips part. He says to her, "It's okay."

That's when I realize he took the bullets intended for Tansy.

It must have been Gareth's job to kill Tansy and ensure that Archer would die, stopping us from following Amalia into the maze.

Rage spears through me, burning my heart and soul like ice, a burn that I can't put out, can't extinguish, because Vlad is my friend. My true friend. No matter what he says about logic and strategy, I know his heart. He has comforted and supported me. He has been there by my side every step of the way, steering me in the right direction.

Gareth darts to the side, using our moment of shock to run toward the gate, his arms pumping.

I move faster.

I launch myself over Archer's wings, spreading my own, sailing into the air. Just as Gareth reaches the gate, a smile growing on his face, I crash into him, tumbling across the leaf-strewn ground with him.

If he had chosen to blur like Amalia, my task would be harder. She knows her own weaknesses, but Gareth's arrogance is his downfall.

I smash into him, my power rising into my hands.

He falls to his stomach, kicking up leaves and twigs. He manages to scramble forward and twist onto his back before I drop my knee onto his chest, constricting his lungs, my weight bearing down on him.

I dodge the first fist he aims at my face but I don't bother avoiding the next.

The Valkyrie power in his assassin's ring has no impact on me as he tries to strengthen the blows he lands on my shoulders and ribs while I tower over him.

Every time he thumps me, he shouts, "You. Can't. Kill. Me."

I don't care about the Code.

I don't care about the consequences.

And I sure as hell will not let him live.

My voice rises up. "Gareth, former Master of the Legion,

you have killed another assassin and broken the first rule. Your punishment is death."

I have no feeling in this moment.

I am empty.

My mother's voice fades into the darkness of my heart. *Just because you're born into darkness...* There is no escaping the darkness for this man.

My killing power is a void that sucks life into it but is never filled.

It is an endless cold pit into which Gareth's soul will sink and never return.

I clutch his face in my hands, squeezing my fingers against his temples. He shouts and struggles, trying to get up, trying to dislodge me, desperation fueling his movements.

Leaning down close, I whisper, "This is for my mother."

I release my power and it springs from me so easily, coursing through my hands, a liquid fire that smokes against his cheeks and steals his breath.

I meet his eyes and take his life.

CHAPTER THIRTY

My power fades. I remain leaning over Gareth as my wings fold and disappear.

Tears drip down my cheeks, cold in the fading sun.

Cain shouts my name, appearing beside me, dragging me upright. "We have to go!"

"No! Vlad is hurt!"

Slade runs toward me, leaping over Gareth and scooping me up at the same time, throwing me over his shoulder and running toward the gate.

We punch through, and I sense the ripple of his power as he fights the urge to release his wings.

I gasp a breath. Inhale mist. "No—"

Cain charges along behind us, carrying three packs, but his left arm is outstretched, holding onto Archer's hand.

She runs behind him. The light from her wings is still blinding as I lift my head, trying to see back into the clearing.

I need to know what is happening to Tansy and Vlad.

Archer bursts through the gate, crashing into Cain's arms as he pulls her through. They drop together onto the bridge, arms and legs tangled, her wings curling around them both for a moment before they snap closed, finally disappearing.

She slumps in Cain's arms, leaning into him, her chest heaving.

Slade skids to a halt and hurries to put me down, racing to grab a bag from Cain from which he quickly pulls out a blanket, wrapping it around both Archer and Cain.

He says to Cain, "Keep Archer warm. She could go into shock."

Knowing Archer is safe, I race toward the gate, shouting, "What about Vlad?"

The gate is closing, fading, turning into mist. I can't see Tansy or Vlad!

Slade's pounding footsteps catch up to me and his strong arms wrap around me, pulling me away from the opening. "We can't help him."

"No, let me go back!" I fight him, struggling and hitting at his arms, trying to pry them open. *Damn him for being as strong as me.*

"Hunter! Listen to me. Tansy will heal him. She needed us gone so she could try. She couldn't heal Vlad while she was helping Archer. The longer we stayed, the less time he had."

Slade spins me around to see his face but I'm still fighting him, panic raging through me. "I need to go back! I need to go… back…"

He takes my face in his hands, his voice lowering. "You have to trust Tansy. She won't let him die."

"But what if… What if she can't save him? And now she's alone in that forest…?"

He levels his gaze with mine. "She's strong, Hunter. It was the only way. She told us to go." The barest smile ghosts his lips. "I wasn't going to argue with an angry witch. If she heals him—and I know she will—she might just kill him herself."

He's trying to make me feel better but it doesn't change the fact that I don't know if Vlad is alive or not. I don't know if Tansy is okay or not. They have both been a part of my life for long enough that I can't imagine my life without them.

I turn within the circle of Slade's arms, allowing him to hug me as I shiver, forcing myself to take a deep breath. Not knowing what is happening outside the gate is killing me, but what's waiting for us in the maze could be far worse.

The message in the Coda warned that this place is filled with monsters. We're about to walk a very dangerous path.

I force myself to relax. "You're right. Now that the coven is destroyed, she's safer out there. We don't know what's waiting for us in here."

"We need to get off this bridge as quickly as we can," Slade says. "I don't want to push Archer, but we don't have much light left."

The bridge we are standing on could be a walkway or it could literally be a stone slab floating in space.

It's difficult to place our location or judge the true nature of the stone beneath our feet given that thick mist surrounds us on all sides. The only similarity between the real world and this one is that the light is fading at the same rate as it was in the outside world.

We only have an hour of twilight left before night falls.

I drop my head against his neck for a moment. "Do you really believe that Vlad is okay?"

He nods. "I have to believe he is. I might have tried to kill him once but he and Cain are the closest I have to brothers."

I tip my head back to consider the seriousness of Slade's statement. He lost his older brother when he was young.

Vlad and Cain have fought beside him the same way they have fought beside me. Their interests haven't always aligned but they would fight to the death for each other.

I kiss his lips, accepting that I have no choice but to move forward. "Then let's get through the maze."

When we return to Archer, she has pulled on her protective suit again but she is still wrapped in the blanket, taking the possibility of shock seriously—especially since Tansy isn't here to help her now.

Archer laughs self-consciously. "I've never been butt-naked in front of a bunch of people before."

Slade gives her an honest smile. "For what it's worth, we couldn't see anything. Your wings were too bright."

"Thanks," she says, accepting his word for it.

I quickly check my bag before I hoist it onto my back again. Everything is where it should be, including the verdan and my katana. I'm grateful that Cain was able to grab my things before he ran through.

I ask Slade and Cain, "Can you use your assassin's magic here?"

Cain clenches his fist, a copper glow building around it, the light swirling in the air as he moves his hand. "It looks like it."

Slade, on the other hand, has a creased forehead. He turns his fist in different directions, taking a moment to answer, his gaze becoming unfocused before he returns his attention to me.

Silver light glows around his body but he says, "My assassin's magic feels normal, but I can't create Realms here. The magic in this place is probably protecting itself."

"I guess we'll discover what else is different as we go along," I say.

Cain nods and tucks the blanket closer around Archer's shoulders. "We're ready to move."

Cautiously approaching the end of the bridge, I try to see through the mire, but the fog obscures everything in every direction. Talk about a literal leap of faith.

"Okay," I say. "I'm going first. If it's a drop, I can release my wings."

I slide my foot out from the ledge. Finding nothing beneath it, I carefully lower my boot, and am relieved to find a solid object beneath it. The mist suddenly clears around the step I took. I take another and the fog clears again but only around my location. I still can't see beyond it.

"It's stairs," I shout. "I don't know where they're going, but it's all we've got…"

The others follow cautiously behind me.

Half an hour later, I take another step and the mist suddenly clears around us, revealing a clear night sky, a bright round moon filling the space with light.

I stare behind us at the mist that still lingers over the top of the staircase, obscuring them high up. I'm stunned to realize that we have literally walked out of the clouds.

The staircase spirals toward the ground hundreds of feet below. Beyond its base is the maze, a labyrinth of rock hundreds of feet wide and deep, consisting of twisting and turning pathways, all visible from this height. It looks like a puzzle: the kind with dead ends and deceptive entrances, a place where you could get lost and never find your way out. The pathways are also made of rock.

So far, there is no sign of any monsters. No sign of Amalia, either. No life at all.

In the far distance, at the end of the maze, an island floats in the air. A castle rises up from the middle of it that appears to be made out of something reflective—maybe glass—its surface glinting in the moonlight.

Archer edges up to me. "That's where we need to go."

"Are you sure?" I ask.

She nods. "I don't know why, but I can sense it."

Her eyes glow in the dark. This place might be still and quiet but Archer's body hasn't stopped coming alive ever since we arrived. Her eyes appeared otherworldly outside the Realm but here… they are breathtaking.

I ask, "What are the chances we could fly to it?"

"Given the protective mechanisms around the gate just now, I would say slim."

I grimace. "I don't see Amalia anywhere."

Archer squints. "The maze can't be what it appears… I'm not sure if my mother ever came here. Her job was to guard the gate, but I sense this place has layers, maybe even realms within realms. Amalia could have gone in already. Once you go in… who knows what really happens."

I shiver but Archer continues, "Do you think you and Slade could fly us down the stairway? We've already lost daylight."

I swallow a sudden grin. "I'm not sure if Cain will appreciate being carried."

Archer glances back at the two men, several paces behind us.

Cain arches an eyebrow at her, making her smile.

"You're right," she says. "It's better to go cautiously anyway. The steps it is, then."

By the time we reach the bottom, the moon is full and high in the sky and Archer has confidently removed her blanket. It's a blessing that we can see clearly in every direction but our surroundings are overlaid with an unsettling silver sheen.

The front of the maze stands fifty paces away. It has two openings, each situated ten feet apart.

As we draw nearer, they both appear identical: yawning gaps in the rock wall. Behind each, the path leads left or right, depending on which entry we choose. It's impossible to make out anything else.

Slade takes my elbow, saying, "I also sense multiple realms in this place. We could step into one without warning."

"We need to stay close and stick together," I say. "First things first… which entry do we choose?"

Slade checks the entrance on the right and I step left. I attempt to peer around the corner to get a sense of where it leads, then the rock shifts beneath my hand.

I leap back at the same time as Slade does, both of us jumping away from the entrances.

Chunks of stone lift off each side, big slabs of misshapen rock creaking and groaning as they rise and spin, pulling together to form two giant humanoid shapes, one standing in front of Slade and the other in front of me. At least ten feet tall, the rock giants take a step to block and stand guard at each entrance. Glowing silver eyes appear like moonlight through slits in their heads.

While the one in front of Slade remains silent and still, the one in front of me bends down, its eyes narrowed, a mouth forming between chunks of rock.

Its voice is a soft rumble, "Who are you?"

"My name…" Cain had asked me the same thing and I'd told him everything I was and could be, but this place… nothing is the same here.

So far the rock giant hasn't made any aggressive moves, but I'm wary of any sudden hostility.

I answer its question with a question. "What are you?"

It says, "I am rock."

"How do you have a voice?"

The rock giant's face contorts into an expression that might be a grin. "All creatures in this place have a voice. It is your decision whose voice you listen to. You must choose wisely."

"What is inside this maze?"

The giant's moonlit eyes swivel to the other giant. "She asks a lot of questions."

The other one rumbles, "She is Silver Wings. You must answer."

The first giant doesn't seem perturbed, its rocky features taking on a curious expression. It gives me a faint smile as it returns its attention to me. "Inside this maze are more worlds than you could ever imagine. Worlds above you. Worlds beneath your feet. Worlds within the air you breathe."

Its face contorts into a definite grin this time. "Be careful what you inhale."

I plant my feet. "How do we get through it?"

"You will face three gates and three challenges. If you survive each one, you will ascend to the castle. But what awaits you may not be what you seek."

Damn riddles.

Its face descends closer to mine. "Now. Who are you?"

CHAPTER THIRTY-ONE

I reply, simply, "I am me."

"So you are." The giant leans back. "This is the first gate. You must choose which entry to take. I am Conflict." He indicates the other giant. "My brother is Combat. Which do you choose?"

Conflict or Combat? I turn to the others. "Neither sounds good."

"We should choose Conflict," Archer says. "Conflict can be resolved. Combat only ends when one side wins or the other surrenders."

I smile inwardly. I would have chosen Combat because that's how I tend to resolve my conflicts but I have to trust Archer's instincts. When both Slade and Cain give their agreement, I say to the rock giant, "We choose Conflict."

The giant nods and angles sideways, opening the way for us. "Very well. You may pass."

As we stride past him, I pause. "Which door did the other Silver Wings choose?"

The rock giant raises its head. "She chose Combat."

That doesn't surprise me. Amalia and I are similar in many ways—and completely different in others. "Thank you."

It seems surprised. "I have never been thanked."

Before I can take another step, a rock hand lands on my shoulder, heavy enough to weigh me down. The giant leans in again, close enough that its eyes become enormous in my field of view. "I have also never seen anyone return from the maze alive. Remember what I said about voices."

"I'll remember," I whisper, finding myself thinking about worlds not voices, because when I peer closer into its eyes, the bright sparks contain a multitude of tiny shapes.

I gasp. *Is there a world within each of its eyes?*

It steps away from me, its pieces separating again, spreading out to neatly slide into each other and seal the way behind us. There is now a solid wall at our backs.

There's no way out. Only forward.

Or not.

Now that I'm inside, I discover that we are walled in on all sides. Only the sky above us is open. "What...?"

Just as quickly, the wall in front of us separates brick by brick, clunking as it opens to reveal a sunlit plain made of... "What is that? More clouds?"

"Mist," Slade says, wading ahead into it. "Step carefully."

The sudden sunlight is disorienting, overly bright, and glints across his weapons as he moves.

As soon as I take a step into the mist, the rock maze disappears completely. There are no longer any walls behind or around us. No sign of the maze at all—or the floating island that we need to get to.

The misty plain stretches out as far as I can see, obscured

just like the bridge was. At least on the bridge we could see what we were stepping on.

Slade wobbles ahead of us, quickly regaining his balance. "The ground beneath is solid, but it's uneven."

Cain and Archer venture ahead of me, their hands touching every now and then as they check each other's position.

Running my fingers through the mist is like touching water, little droplets clinging to my fingertips when I raise them, but the moisture rapidly evaporates in the sun.

The silence is oppressive and it's starting to get to me.

The rock giant said that there were worlds within worlds in this place. I can't see anything above us so maybe that means there's something below—

With a shout, Slade drops out of sight, disappearing completely through the mist. Closer to him, Archer races forward, taking two steps before she plunges out of sight with a scream that is cut short just like Slade's.

I freeze. Did something pull them? Did they fall? "Slade! Archer!"

Cain crouches close to the ground, sinking so low that the mist rises to his shoulders as he swivels in my direction. "There are holes in the ground! Hunter, you need to—"

He jolts backward, disappearing a second later. There might be holes in the ground, but something definitely pulled him down.

I take a deep breath. The rock giant said I should be careful what I inhale. I hold my breath as I lower myself into the mist. I fan my hands across the ground, tracing Slade's steps and searching for the place where he fell. For all I know they could have fallen into separate tunnels. The ground is rough, oddly woody like… tree bark?

Branches!

We've been walking on branches and we didn't know it. I quickly adjust my backpack and release my wings, beating them once so that the gust of wind carries the mist away.

The action reveals a branch that is so wide I barely catch sight of the edge of it before the mist closes in again. If this is the size of its topmost branch, this tree's trunk must be at least seventy paces wide, which would make it astronomically high.

Slade has wings, but Archer and Cain do not. Unless they managed to catch hold of a branch on the way down... I have to get to them.

A fork in the branches two steps ahead is where Slade fell. I tuck my wings to my sides and run for it, having memorized the path before the mist returned, and prepare to launch myself off it into the vapor below.

An enormous shadow passes across me seconds before a screech sounds in my ears and sharp talons pluck at my back.

I swivel just in time to catch sight of a giant eagle swooping at me, its wings spread far wider than mine ever could as its massive talons aim to snag me. They are as big as one of my arms.

I dodge its path, ducking and rolling, narrowly missing the fork in the branches. With a shriek that splits my ears, the bird circles back and flies at me again, plucking at me. Its wings are so black that they appear almost purple, its head covered in creamy feathers and its beak and talons as golden as Archer's wings.

I would think it was majestic—if it wasn't trying to kill me.

I'm not about to become its dinner.

Digging in my heels and spinning, I launch myself

upward, crashing into the bird as it speeds toward me. Knocking it off course, I grab hold of its neck, my arms only just reaching all the way around. I spread my wings and wrench down, plunging us both into the mist.

We hit a branch, catching the edge of it. Only the eagle's body stops me breaking my ribs against the wooden limb. The bird twists wildly as it falls, but I manage to hold on, beating my wings and directing us at full speed toward the next branch.

The bird shrieks as we plummet onto the wooden surface, its body beneath mine cushioning the impact. It is stunned for long enough for me to reach for my katana and raise it above my head, ready to end its life.

Lying on its side, one golden eye pins me.

It gasps, "Do you know what you plan to kill?"

My chest heaves. We tumbled through space so suddenly, but I was holding my breath the whole time, not wanting to inhale the mist. The eagle is much bigger and more powerful than me. I caught it unawares, but I will only have the upper hand for a moment longer.

With one fist firmly planted on its neck, I shout, "You speak!" Then I shake my head, preparing to drive my sword through its neck. "Of course you speak."

It says, "But are you listening?"

I halt. My hand shakes around my sword. The rock giant told me I should choose wisely which voices I listen to, and now this creature is asking me to listen.

"You were going to kill me," I say.

"Was I?"

My eyes narrow, my focus narrowing with them. The mist wafts in again. I don't know where Slade, Cain, or Archer are and sudden panic floods me.

The eagle asks, "Who are you?"

This time the answer comes quickly. "I'm an assassin. Killing is what I do best."

"How do you choose who dies?"

My forehead creases. "All of my kills are sanctioned."

"By a Guardian who makes choices for you. What if you were the Guardian? How would you choose?"

I swallow. The Guardian's choices were never my business. How she made her decisions wasn't something I had to worry about, but I always trusted her. She was harsh at times, a rule-follower when I hated the rules, but she was a constant, steady force. Reliable. Even formidable.

The eagle peers at me. "It is not so easy anymore, is it?"

This creature isn't trying to kill me. In fact, it might have been trying to help me. Whatever grabbed Cain might have been about to grab me, too. With a grimace, I release the eagle, stepping back but remaining ready in case it tries anything.

As it rises in slow movements, keeping its eyes on me, I ask, "Who are you?"

"I am Justice."

"And this place?"

The eagle ruffles its feathers and settles onto the branch. "This is Yggdrasil."

I can't hide my surprise. "The World Tree?"

That would explain why the tree is so enormous, but if the myths about the tree are even remotely true, then there are other beasts living in and beneath it—beasts I don't particularly want to meet, including Nidhogg, the serpent that dwells beneath its roots and gnaws on its foundations.

The eagle says, "Your friends are at the bottom of the tree. They are alive but in danger. I wanted to spare you from what lies beneath, but it seems conflict is in your nature."

I grit my teeth. "I don't see good where there could be evil."

The bird's eyes fill with sadness. "You distrust even those who love you."

I swallow again. I distrusted Slade, even Vlad and Cain, and definitely Tansy, but not anymore. "I'm learning… slowly."

The eagle says, "I only control the sky. I can't go with you to the ground beneath the tree. Beware of Ratatoskr on your way down. He is malicious and enjoys conflict. He grabbed one of your friends but I don't think Ratatoskr anticipated your friend's strength."

The bird must be talking about Cain. Slade and Archer fell, but Cain was pulled under. If any one of us had a chance against a malicious beast, it is Cain with his ability to see into the heart of things.

The eagle's eyes twinkle as it spreads its wings. "It is good to know that Malice was defeated for once. Fly now Silver Wings. Your friends need you."

It takes off, rising into the mist, its wings beating away the cloud cover for a second before it disappears.

I peer into the gloom below, unable to see beyond a few feet, preparing myself to dive once more into the unknown.

CHAPTER THIRTY-TWO

sail through the clearing mist, hundreds, maybe thousands of feet down, the air growing warmer the further I descend.

I fly as wide of the branches as I can, keeping my eye out for Ratatoskr, and catch sight of the creature as I pass.

The squirrel is hard to miss. Like the eagle, it is massive, its burnished orange fur standing out against the bright green leaves. Its black eyes dart to me, quickly narrowed and unwelcoming. It nurses its side, but it doesn't appear wounded. It chitters at me. *Maybe only its pride.*

The further I descend, the more worried I become.

I can't see Slade, Cain, or Archer. The land below is lush and green, a grassy meadow around the base of the tree. The roots twist across the earth, large thick cords that plunge beneath the surface.

Nihdogg hides under there. I will need to watch out for him.

I wheel around the trunk, finally spotting the others at

the base of the tree on the other side. They stand apart from each other, Archer beside Cain, both of them facing Slade.

As soon as I land and fold away my wings, Cain repositions himself in front of Archer, his posture taking on the appearance of a protective shield.

He urges Archer to back away from me through the rich grass, one hand raised up as if to ward me off, a dangerous warning in his voice. "Stay away from us, Hunter."

My lips part in surprise. "What? Why?"

I look to Slade whose expression is set in hard lines. A dagger gleams in his hand, raised in a defensive position as he holds his other hand out to me, beckoning urgently. "Hunter, come away from Cain."

"Why are you both...?" I take glances between them before I plant my hands on my hips, not moving. "What's going on here?"

Cain's glare is searing, focused on me with more vehemence than I've ever seen. I was just telling the eagle how far I've come with trusting people and now I've fallen right into the middle of a situation where Cain and Slade are giving off killing vibes. Killing *each other* vibes.

Cain's anger is like a whiplash. "Where were you, Hunter? Were you trying to get to the feathers on your own? Were you going to leave the rest of us to die?"

I flinch at the accusation in his voice. "Of course not! I ran into trouble up there. I want a feather for Archer too."

"You're a liar, Hunter. You lied about what you are. You lied about why you became an assassin. You're still lying. You never stop."

His accusation hits me hard. I stumble toward Slade, my heart squeezing tight in my chest. It's true that I have lied. Constantly. I justified my actions, believing them necessary, but ever since I fought Amalia at the ball I've made it my mission to speak the truth, even when it hurts or endangers me. Cain should know that. As an assassin, he should understand it.

Slade growls from behind me. "Cain only came with us because he wants the chance to kill you, Hunter."

"What?" I shake my head, vehemently. "That's not true. Cain would never hurt me."

I turn back to find Cain breaching the distance between us, his power glowing around him as he strides toward me. His assassin's ring gleams, its force sparking across the distance as he pulls a dagger from the belt around his chest.

I flinch, my guard flying up. When he first brought Archer to me, Cain was worried and angry, fearful that I would hurt her. I thought I convinced him that I never would, but now the look on his face tells me he has stopped believing she is safe.

But, why? What changed his mind?

Cain growls as he walks, "I will kill you before you kill Archer."

Slade leaps in front of me, his Valkyrie power washing through him so fast that it makes me gasp. It fills the space around us, forming an instant shield from the Keres power radiating from Cain.

Slade shouts, "I won't let you hurt Hunter."

Cain ignores him. "I won't let Archer die!"

The two men are like electrical currents about to ignite. When Archer's power and mine touched, we were blown across the room—and that was a small spark. Slade and Cain have released their power at a thousand percent.

My back is to the tree and I have nowhere to go.

Off to my right, Archer stumbles away from the fight, her

face pale, one palm pressed against her temple, the other pressed against her ear as if she is in pain.

Her gaze is unfocused, distant. She staggers but I don't have time to see what she does next because Cain charges.

"No! Stop!"

My scream is futile. The air explodes, the blast splitting the space around me, knocking me into the tree. My head thumps against it, my lungs compressed, and my spine bashed like a twig.

Pain explodes inside my skull and through my back, and the air is knocked from my lungs.

Slade and Cain are blasted apart from each other, tumbling through the grass on opposite sides of me, their daggers flying wide.

Ears ringing, I drop to the ground at the base of the tree, trying to breathe, wanting to scream.

Slade rolls to his feet, his forehead bleeding, and races back to me, shouting my name but Cain beats him to me.

I duck and roll just in time to avoid Cain's fist.

He hits the tree instead, splintering the bark where my face used to be. He isn't harnessing his power this time, so I guess he has decided to end me the old-fashioned way.

A voice in the back of my mind whispers: *He was always going to kill you. Trusting people only makes you vulnerable.*

In the next second, Slade crashes into him, the force of the collision driving Cain away from me. "Get away from Hunter!"

Cain responds with a powerful fist, crunching Slade's cheekbone. When he follows up with another fist, Slade grabs it, holding tight and pushing back, blood running down his face. The strength between the two men as their hands lock causes their arms to shake, muscles straining as they push against each other. With a final twist, Slade forces Cain's hand down but Cain retaliates with a boot to Slade's chest, sending him flying backward again.

With a snarl, Slade releases his wings, powerful currents filling the air as he flies back into the fight. The two men are brutal with each other, every fist, every hit smashing its target. Within seconds, they both spit blood, and they don't stop.

I clutch my chest, trying to find my voice, my stomach roiling. Amalia asked me who would win in a fight between Slade and Cain and I swore I never wanted to find out. *This can't be happening.* Just minutes ago, Slade told me that Cain was like a brother to him. Earlier I saw for myself the trust that Cain placed in Slade.

The whisper in my mind becomes a shout. *Trust is worthless, Hunter. You have to kill Cain before he kills you. Help Slade. Help him kill Cain.*

I slap my hands over my ears. *No.*

This isn't right. None of this is right.

Beyond the fight, Archer drops to her knees in the grass, her hands pressed over her ears as if she, too, is trying to block out... a voice.

The wrong voice.

My heart plummets.

We chose conflict.

Now we're listening to the voice of our fears.

My thoughts speed up while movement around me slows down.

Blood sprays as Slade slams his fist into Cain's stomach, the force of his power doubling Cain over. Slade follows up with an uppercut that crunches Cain's jaw and a boot that sends him sprawling into the grass, Slade's wings giving him height and strength.

Who will win in a fight between Cain and Slade?

Slade will win... because he is angrier, more brutal, and my power flows through him.

I spin from the fight to the creature sliding beneath the roots of the tree. The serpent's dark tongue licks the air, its eyes bright with cruelty and its voice loud in my ears: *Kill Cain.*

My eyes narrow. It's Nihdogg, the Villain.

He's whispering into our minds, drawing out our greatest fears, and trying to make us fight and kill each other.

Cain fears that I will kill Archer.

Slade fears that Cain will kill me.

I dropped my backpack when I landed. Now I scramble for it, crying out as my back protests. *Oh, please, don't let anything be broken...*

I force myself to reach my bag, crawling through the grass to curl my fingertips around the straps, trying to drag it closer. My katana is strapped to it, so close yet so far...

A heavy weight slides over my feet, pinning me to the ground. I twist to find the serpent slithering over my legs, its massive body covering my calves and thighs, its head softly swaying as it glides closer.

Its face rears up over me. "You have seen my true form," it says into my mind. "Now you must die."

CHAPTER THIRTY-THREE

I snarl back at the serpent. "Too shy to show your face, is that it?"

One inch at a time, I draw my backpack closer, hoping the beast is too distracted to notice.

'Only someone who has accepted their own death can see me," it replies. "Someone like that is dangerous."

"Why?"

"Because you know your own strength. You know your own fears. You are willing to die to save the ones you love. You know who you are." Its mouth widens. "Don't bother with your sword. No blade can kill me."

There's a shout beyond us: it's Archer's voice but I can't make out what she screamed.

Nihdogg's head shoots up in her direction. Archer is staring wide-eyed at the snake, but she is only paralyzed for a second.

She launches herself into a run, sprinting around Slade and Cain, her arms pumping.

I've seen this woman kill without mercy and right now, the snake is her target.

Nihdogg hisses, "Golden Wings can see me. She will have to die, too."

The serpent refocuses on me, its jaws opening so wide it could bite my head off, fangs descending, rearing over me. Within its mouth is an entire world, a place of malice, chaos, pain—and everlasting night.

"You first," I say.

I whip my hand from my backpack and launch myself upward, thrusting the contents of my fist into the beast's wide-open mouth and as far down its throat as I can.

The verdan plant disappears inside Nihdogg's mouth, pot and all.

The serpent jolts backward, its mouth snapping shut in reflex. I pull my hand out just in time before it can break my arm in its closing jaws.

It coughs, chokes, and writhes backward, preparing to spit the plant out, but I harness all my strength and slam my fist upward into its jaw, releasing my wings at the same time to give me momentum.

Crunch. The hit smashes the serpent's jaw against its upper lip. It lurches back from me, and at the same time Archer crashes into it from the side, leaping under it at just the right angle to punch the verdan from the outside.

The resounding *crunch* tells me she has shattered the pot.

The beast recoils, releasing my legs, spitting pieces of ceramic smothered in crimson sap. It screams, "What did you do?"

I leap away from it, grabbing Archer and drawing her clear of the verdan poison leaking from the serpent's mouth.

I shout, "Your voice is an instrument of darkness!"

The shield around the verdan only disappears in a place of true darkness—a place where the light never reaches. The serpent's mouth is such a place.

The snake writhes, convulsing in the grass, trying to escape the pain, but it doesn't matter how much it roils and rocks, the poison quickly does its work.

The serpent shudders one last time. Its head drops to the ground, its black eyes dull and lifeless. Its final hiss ripples across the clearing and the hateful voice in my mind finally falls silent.

Archer draws close to me, a disgusted curl on her lips. "Its words were murder."

I nod. "You recognized it."

Worry enters her eyes. "We need to mend the damage now."

Nearby, Cain and Slade back away from each other, their chests heaving, their knuckles bloody. Slade wipes his mouth and Cain tests his jaw. They are both shell-shocked, pacing backward.

Cain stumbles. Archer launches into a sprint, racing toward him.

She arrives in time to grab him as he drops to his knees. She follows him down, supporting his torso while he rests on the grass, his face turned to hers. She strokes the hair out of his eyes, checking his wounds with a worried expression.

I follow closely enough to catch her softly-spoken statement. "You're hurt, Cain."

"I'm an idiot is what I am," he says. "I could have killed Hunter."

His gaze follows me as I hobble across the grass to Slade. I'm much slower than Archer. There's no doubt in my mind that my back is bruised, but thankfully not broken. I'm glad the protective suit covers me. I don't want to see the damage myself, let alone show anyone else.

Slade crosses the distance to reach me first, checking me over with gentle hands—hands that are covered in Cain's blood.

Slade is healing rapidly, his cheekbone knitting back together and his bruises disappearing, but he knows I can't heal myself. His voice is an urgent murmur. "Where are you hurt?"

There's no lying to him. "My back, but I'm moving so that's a good sign, right?"

He unclasps the side of my suit to peel it off my back and check me over. His silence shouts louder than words, his fingertips careful and gentle as he checks each part of my spine.

Returning my suit to its place and clasping it up again, he says, "There's nothing we can do. You need to rest—"

I shake my head. "We have to keep moving."

Slade drops his forehead to mine, taking deep breaths. His arms drop to his sides and his wings droop. The misery on his face kills me. "What the hell happened to us?"

I meet Archer's solemn eyes for a moment, before I say, "We were being manipulated. All of us. The conflict we faced was our own."

Slade asks, "Manipulated by what?"

Archer and Cain remain kneeling in the grass. Archer tips her head back to study the clear sky, the wispy clouds, and the colossal tree branches, its leaves the size of her torso.

"A serpent that lived under the tree," she says. "It was whispering in our ears and playing on our greatest fears."

Slade swivels. "Where is it now?" His gaze passes right over the dead beast.

"We killed it," I say. I take comfort in the fact that Slade has not accepted his own death like I have. I need his hope and determination to balance my need to end Amalia at all costs.

Cain pulls Archer close. "My greatest fear is losing Archer."

Slade nods, his gaze an intense burn as he turns the full force of his fear on me. "I can't lose Hunter."

"You won't," I say. "Neither of you will lose us. We will fight our way through this place. Together."

Cain rises to his feet while Archer supports him. He doesn't appear to have any broken bones, but he's not in good shape.

"I'm sorry, Hunter," he says. "I hope you can believe me."

With a glance at Slade, I stride toward Cain, pausing only to ask Archer, "May I?"

She slides her arm away from Cain with a small smile.

"Cain Carter," I say, wrapping my arms around his big torso and resting my head against his chest. "I believe you."

He freezes for a moment before relaxing into the hug, his big arms rising around me, warm and welcoming, but careful. He knows my back is tender.

Cain murmurs, "When I was pulled from the top of the tree, I fought hard, but I couldn't shake this vision... it seemed so real. You were standing over Archer's dead body holding both feathers. After that, the voice started in my head and I couldn't ignore it."

I shudder. "The only person I will kill is Amalia."

Of all of the people standing in this clearing, Cain's heart is the most open. He allows himself to feel everything there is to feel while the rest of us freeze out our emotions like we've been taught to do. Ruthless. Unemotional.

I close my eyes for a moment before I say, "I never allowed myself to have friends. Allies, sure. But friends… people I care about… we won't always agree on everything but I trust you, Cain."

He drops a gentle kiss on my forehead before he draws back to meet my eyes.

Before he can say anything, I focus on the cut across his temple. "We're going to look after your wounds now. Don't say anything to me about 'help.' This is what friends do."

A smile breaks across his face, then it turns into a grimace. "I won't refuse."

While Slade brings Cain a bottle of water, Archer and I set about cleaning his wounds, after which we're relieved to find he only needs stitches above his eye.

Archer raises an eyebrow at him, making me think they've had a conversation about this before when she says, "I'm no plastic surgeon. This will scar."

He grins. "It's time I had one."

Meanwhile, Slade surveys the horizon. None of us is talking about the rock wall that appeared in the distance when Slade and Cain stopped fighting.

Leaving Archer with Cain, I make my way to Slade, keeping my voice low. "I know the power of your fists, Slade. Cain is still alive, with only one actual wound, which tells me you pulled your punches."

Slade exhales slowly. "What you said about friends applies to me, too. My fear wasn't only for you. My fear was also for Cain… that he would do something he couldn't come back from."

"That he would hurt me?"

"Yes." Slade takes my shoulders. "He would never forgive

himself." His expression changes, becoming fierce. "And I... I did not want to kill my friend."

I lean into Slade. A kiss can't erase what happened, can't make him feel better, but I give him one anyway. He wraps his arms around me with a groan that is as much frustration as fear. "We have to make it through this place."

I whisper against his lips, "Tell me what will happen when this is over?"

He smiles, pressing kisses against my mouth as he speaks. "We will find a way to live together despite mastering separate Factions. We will rebuild the Legion and make its walls safe again." He takes a deep breath. "We could... wear our rings on different fingers and maybe... raise a family together."

There's a question in his voice, vulnerability in his expression that has never been there before. Facing our fears is not only about conquering an obstacle in front of us. It's also about asking for what we want.

"I would love that," I say.

He kisses me again, but this time it feels like a promise. A promise of a future that he wants as much as I do.

CHAPTER THIRTY-FOUR

The next wall is almost identical to the first one.

Gray rock spans the visible distance in both directions, but this time a single entrance forms a break in its center.

The sun is shining out here on the plain, but within the entrance the air is murky, darkness obscuring whatever lies beyond it.

We take a moment to check our weapons, hydrate ourselves, and chew some dried food. We don't know when we'll have the chance to eat again. My katana is firmly strapped to my back this time, within quick reach.

Archer stays at my side while Slade and Cain fan out behind us, watching our backs. We have made it through one gate and one challenge. The rock giant said we would have to get through three of each. I'm hoping this gate will consist of a simple choice again, but we can't count on it.

Growling sounds precede two large wolves that slink out from within the entrance to stand in front of it. They bring the night with them, a dark shadow casting over us even though there isn't a cloud in the sky.

Their heads lower into a hunting position, lips drawn back from their teeth.

One has fur the color of charcoal with a gleaming silver snout. The other is russet, its snout so crimson that it appears to have been dipped in blood.

Their eyes are filled with blue flames and their growls send shivers down my spine. The aura around them is like flames licking across their fur. Somehow, I don't anticipate that this will be a civilized conversation.

"Dinner has finally arrived," says the russet wolf.

The charcoal wolf prowls closer to me. "Such pitiful prey."

"Who are you?" I ask.

The russet wolf fixates on Archer who stands her ground. It says, "I am Hati. This is my brother Skoll. We are Devourers."

I don't particularly want to know what they devour. As Skoll slinks closer, I make out a slash on his snout—a thin line of blood.

"The other Silver Wings already got past you," I say.

Skoll growls, his teeth bared. "You will not be so lucky."

I grimace. Its answer confirms that Amalia is ahead of us. I was worried she might progress through the maze faster than us.

I level my gaze with Skoll. "You will let us pass."

He rounds on me, slinking to the side while Hati begins to circle Archer. "We are hungry for the sun and the moon. It is our destiny to devour them."

Skoll leaps at me, his body awash with flames and his

silver snout wide open, gleaming teeth aimed for my shoulder. Hati springs at Archer at the same time.

We duck and roll beneath the arc of their jumps, causing them to sail over us. They land on the other side, barely avoiding head-butting each other. Slade and Cain step into the fight then, firing two quick gunshots each, but the wolves' hides are thick and the bullets lodge in their skin instead of piercing them.

Skoll and Hati whirl, snarling, preparing to leap at Cain and Slade.

"Go! Get through the gate!" Slade shouts to me. "We'll hold them off."

Archer and I race toward the entrance, pausing as Slade and Cain wrestle with the wolves, muscles straining as they physically restrain them.

I don't want to let them out of my sight—and neither does Archer by the look of things. Slade is trying to give me as much time as possible to rest my back but if I have to run back into the fight, I will. Archer stays with me, not quite passing through the entrance.

Slade releases his wings, dragging Skoll up into the air. The wolf yelps, scrabbling at the ground while Slade swings him around, flinging him off to the side. Skoll tumbles through the grass, skidding and finding his feet, and Slade soars after him, harnessing his killing power in a wash of silver light. He flung Skoll far enough away from Cain that Cain is not in danger.

The charcoal wolf launches itself at Slade, its fangs and claws a rabid blur. Slade shouts as Skoll's fangs sink into his arm, but his killing power explodes, a burst of power that shudders through the beast. Its body falls limp, dragging

Slade down with it. He throws it off and rises into the air again.

Closer to us, Cain grapples with Hati, holding the russet wolf off as it tries to savage at his neck. With a roar, Cain lashes out, kicking the wolf with his boot, leaping at the animal with a dagger in his hand. The dagger hits Hati square in the eye and the wolf howls as blue flame explodes outward, knocking Cain across the field.

Cain tumbles, jumps to his feet and races back, his assassin's magic blazing.

He meets the wolf mid-jump, the two crashing against each other. Cain's powerful fist knocks against the wolf's jaw a second before Slade swoops in, plucks the wolf from Cain's grasp and releases his killing power into it from high above.

The animal falls to the ground, dead at Cain's feet.

Cain looks up with an indignant expression.

Slade shrugs from the air.

Cain grins before he bends over his knees, catching his breath for a second before he rights himself.

Beside me, Archer resumes breathing. "I couldn't leave."

I know exactly how she feels, but I grin. "It looks like they managed okay without us. Let's check out the entrance."

I step into it, craning to see around the corner. "It looks okay."

There's silence behind me.

"Archer?" I turn back to find nothing but a solid rock wall where Archer was standing a second ago. "Archer!"

I spin to a wall that appears on my left and then another on my right. They appear before my eyes, leaving the only openings in front and above me.

Determined to fly over the wall and get back to the

others, I release my wings and rise upward, but I'm not quick enough.

A ceiling of rocks forms above me, stone by stone appearing out of nowhere. I pick up speed, zooming along the rapidly forming corridor, trying to reach the opening but the rocks keep linking together above and around me.

Five seconds later, I shoot from the mouth of the tunnel, finally rising into the air only to find myself in a cave full of diamonds.

Light reflects off the glittering stones into my eyes, blinding me. I throw my arm across my face to shield my eyes and make out a high ceiling soaring above me—high enough that it takes me a couple of seconds to reach it, but there's no exit that way.

Glittering walls rise to the ceiling, forcing me to twist and turn while I fly around them.

I'm getting nowhere.

Or I'm getting lost.

"Slade! Archer!" My shouts echo back at me. "Cain!"

Deciding not to make my situation worse, I glide to the floor, squinting at the reflections in the diamonds opposite me.

Me.

And another woman...

Her silhouette appears behind me, her long hair covering her shoulders, her body clad in warrior's clothing, the edges of a sword in the same shape as mine appearing on either side of her back.

I spin around… but there's nobody there.

A low moan whispers through the cavern, making my skin prickle. I step carefully toward the sound, padding quietly around the next corner, finding the light dull in the next corridor so that I can finally lower my arm.

I am reflected in the diamonds on either side of me, almost as if I am walking with myself for company. From the corner of my eye, the other woman appears as a vague shape, but when I try to focus on her, she disappears.

The moan grows louder, sighing through the corridor.

It makes me shiver, a sense of foreboding settling into the pit of my stomach. It's a sound I know. A sound I've felt. It's the cry of loss and grief, the kind of pain that never goes away.

I emerge into a low cavern with a single opening on the other side. A gentle waterfall flows into a shallow pool on the left.

Amalia kneels on the path at the edge of the water, her head in her hands.

I inhale and hold my breath, reaching for my sword, taking careful steps.

Amalia doesn't give me any indication that she is aware of my presence. She remains curled over her knees, her hair falling across her face.

She cries again, making me pause.

I've finally caught up to her but I can't end her on my own. I need Slade's gun. I need Archer's power. I need Cain's ring. Only together can we end this woman.

"She can't hear you."

I whirl to the woman whose silhouette I saw in the diamonds.

My heart stops.

"Mom?"

A gentle smile lights my mother's eyes as she steps toward me. She's wearing the clothing I last saw her in: her favorite leather jacket, jeans, and high boots—the kind that conceal a long blade. Her katana is strapped to her back. It's the one I carry now.

"I missed you, baby girl." She crosses the distance and wraps me in her arms.

I can't breathe. I don't want to break this moment. Tears spring to my eyes and I'm not ashamed of them. "Mom?"

"I'm here, sweetheart."

She pulls back, her emerald green eyes sparkling with tears, the silver rims around her eyes even more startling to me now than when she was alive.

My voice breaks. "You're not really alive, are you?"

"No, baby," she says softly. "I'm here because I'm your challenge."

CHAPTER THIRTY-FIVE

I jolt a little away from my mother. "I'm not fighting you."

"You couldn't even if you wanted to." She strokes my back, soothing motions, making me realize that my sword is gone. In fact, all of my weapons are gone. I look down to find that I'm wearing the same clothing I was wearing the night she died.

I'm sixteen again and my heart is filled with fear.

She strokes my cheek, a tear spilling down her own. "Your challenge is to let me go."

"No." I pull out of her arms, but she paces after me.

"Hunter… listen to me. Ever since I died, you have made it your mission to do what I wanted you to do. You retrieved the Clave, you kept the feather safe, you found Archer, you saved her life—"

"Tansy did that."

"She never would have if it wasn't for you. You mended Tansy's heart—something I failed to do. She healed Archer because you asked her to. You destroyed Boston's underground and you even killed Gareth…"

"Because he hurt Vlad."

"Because you have friends," she insists, taking my arms in her hands, gently but firm. "You have the chance for a new life now. It's time to live it on your own terms."

Her gaze shifts to Amalia where she kneels behind me. Mom's eyes harden. "If you don't let go of the past… that is what you will become."

I swivel from Amalia, reaching out for Mom as she steps away from me. "I have to go now, Hunter. Remember always: you can overcome the darkness."

She levels her gaze with mine before her focus becomes distant, the light grows brighter and other shapes appear within it—a man standing in an alley.

A trickle of blood slides out of nowhere down Mom's temple, a bruise blossoms before my eyes across her cheek, and a lash whips around her waist, capturing her, yanking her backward.

She spins away from me to the man solidifying behind her, the grimy alley casting shadows across the scene as the diamond walls disappear. They are replaced with the backstreet where Mom died.

Gareth wears a snarl. He shoves her against the wall, her arms pinned to her sides within the lash. "I loved you once, Anna, but you betrayed me."

"That wasn't love. That was lust and envy and… self-preservation. You never felt for me what I felt for you." Her voice lowers to a whisper. "I don't feel anything for you anymore. I discovered what love actually feels like and it is more than you will ever know."

His lips curls. "Who could possibly love you?"

Her eyes shine despite his hatred. "My daughter."

He snarls back at her. "*Our* daughter."

Mom leans into him, her lips an inch from his as she whispers, "Hunter isn't yours."

He recoils as if she slapped him, stumbling away from her, the blood draining from his face.

She breaks free from the lash, snapping it with one powerful upward movement of her arms.

He recovers quickly. "Then I will not show her mercy."

Mom crosses the distance between them, grabs him, and pulls him close, a threat on her lips. "Pray she doesn't come after you, Gareth. Hunter is stronger than me. She's more powerful, more ruthless, more true to herself—"

"She's someone else's daughter," he shouts. "That's what she is!"

Mom's eyes widen as she stares into Gareth's. "I never imagined that the truth would hurt you."

His expression contorts. "I left you alone all these years because I thought she was mine. Now... give me the feather."

"No."

"*Give me the damn feather.*"

"No!"

"Then I will take it." He shoves her against the brick wall again, his assassin's magic glowing.

She strikes out at him with a dagger, a swift warning swipe that forces him to let her go.

He retaliates with a fist, feinting right to avoid the next knife swipe. She dances out of his path and his hand hits the bricks. He gives an angry growl, his gaze narrowing at her weapon.

When she lunges at him again, he grabs her hand, forces

her wrist back and disarms her. It's exactly the same move I taught myself after she died.

He forces her back against the wall, pressing her knife to her throat, swiftly reaching into her jacket, right next to her breasts, to pull out the copper feather.

Her eyes narrow a second before she punches his knife hand away from her, executing the same maneuver to disarm him and take control of the knife again. She lands a hit to his stomach with her knee that doubles him over.

She snatches the feather, closing her fist around it, but he retaliates by barreling forward, not bothering to raise his head, banging her up against the wall. He regains his height, forcing her blade hand down to her side, pinning her with his weight.

She is about to shove him away when he demands, "Tell me what the feather hides."

She sucks in a sharp breath. "N-no… I won't…"

He grinds out, "Why is it so important?"

Mom struggles against him, trying to press her lips together. "It… hides…"

She can't lie to him.

My heart wrenches. This is the moment she chose to die.

Her jaw clenches. Regret passes across her face. There's a sickening tearing sound. Her eyes fill with pain and her blade clatters to the street.

Her eyes close for a moment, before opening again, her face draining pale.

Gareth stares at her, confused. He grabs her bloody hand. "What did you do?"

Mom slides down the wall, her legs crumpling beneath her. He follows her down, clutching her shoulders, running his hands down her side to her thigh. Blood pools across her upper leg.

His eyes widen. "Anna… no… what did you do?" He shakes her "*What did you do?*"

She whispers, "I don't have to answer you anymore."

He leans back on his heels, running his hands through his hair, real emotion passing across his face. He drops his head to her chest, holding her tight.

"Heal yourself," he commands. "Dammit, stop this and heal yourself."

"No."

His hands squeeze her shoulders; his cheek presses into her neck. "Do you really hate me that much?"

A small smile touches her lips as she turns her face away from him. "I don't… have to… answer you…"

Her eyes are becoming glassy, the life fading from her body. He shakes her again, but her body is increasingly lifeless, jolting in his arms, no resistance.

He shouts, "Anna! *Dammit…* Anna… please…"

She doesn't answer him.

He wrenches back from her, anger and anguish flooding his face.

Hatred boils in my heart to see his regret. He isn't allowed to feel sadness. He isn't allowed to cry. Not Gareth. Not the man who caused my mother's death.

I scream into the memory and leap toward him, but my fist slides right through the tears falling down his cheeks. I try again and again, but I have no impact. I can't smash them off his face.

"You're not allowed to care!" I thump my fist against my own chest because it's the only solid thing I can find, and the pain is making me crazy.

All I can do is scream out my rage, my chest heaving as Gareth stares at the feather Mom holds in her lap. It is covered in her blood, more and more of her life flowing from the artery she severed in her groin.

He hovers over the feather—Archer's birth feather—his hand shaking before he descends, snatching it in one swift movement.

The moment he touches it, her blood solidifies around it, his human touch turning her final life-blood into transparent stone.

He curses as he draws backward, rising to his feet, holding it so tight his knuckles turn white. "Why would you die for this?"

A clatter at the end of the alley causes his head to snap up. He whispers, "Hunter."

He immediately vanishes from sight, but I can see his blur this time. He hurries away into the night, carrying the feather with him as my younger self races toward Mom, screaming her name.

I squeeze my eyes shut. I can't watch anymore, can't watch her use her last strength to grab my hands to stop me plucking out a feather to heal her. I can't listen to her final words…

She wants me to let her go, but I can never let go of this moment, can never forget it.

I whirl from the scene in the alley, my focus on the living once more.

My focus is on Amalia.

CHAPTER THIRTY-SIX

I reach for my katana as I creep up on Amalia.

She remains curled forward on her knees at the edge of the glittering pool, her hands covering her face.

Mom told Gareth I was more ruthless than she ever was.

She was right.

I might not be able to kill Amalia right now, but I can hurt her.

I won't do it without facing her.

My hand stretches for her, my sword ready as I grab her shoulder, spinning her toward me. At least... that is my intention.

The moment my hand connects with her shoulder, a scream fills my mind, my surroundings blur and rush around me, and the distant image of a room zooms toward me.

I try to get my bearings as the scene halts abruptly. Sunlight streams into the opulent room, high stone walls reach upward, and a plush chair rests beneath the far window.

I don't know this place. This isn't my memory... but I

know I haven't actually been transported here because the edges are fuzzy just like they were when I saw Mom before.

It must be Amalia's memory…

I wobble, finding myself in the corner of the room, crouching to regain my balance.

A girl leans to one side of the chair, alone, her face very pale. She looks barely twelve years old. She is wearing a long emerald gown that hangs off her thin frame.

Her hands shake as she plants them on the arms of the chair, attempting to stand. Her legs crumple and she sinks back. Tears of frustration fill her eyes, but she grits her teeth and tries again, managing to stand upright, making it two steps before she stumbles and drops to the floor, her dark hair falling over her face.

She thumps the floor with her fist, a cry on her lips. "Where is my strength?"

The door flies open. I'm startled to see Amalia in the doorway, where she pauses before she races into the room, the urgency on her face unmistakable.

She reaches the girl's side and pulls her into her arms. "Elaina! Sweetheart! What happened?"

"Mother…" The girl's voice is weak. "I tried to get up."

"You know you can't do that on your own anymore." Amalia is gentler than I've ever seen her. She leverages her arm around the girl's torso and returns her to the seat, pressing a kiss to Elaina's forehead before she draws back.

Elaina looks up at Amalia in confusion. "You're stronger now. This morning you couldn't lift me at all. How?"

Amalia kneels in front of her, taking her hands. "I found a solution."

Hope lights Elaina's eyes. "A cure?"

Amalia chews her lip. "There is no cure for our lost feathers. We are dying. But I have a remedy."

She carefully spreads her wings, perfect silver feathers shining in the sunlight streaming through the window. A single copper feather rests among them.

Elaina struggles to lean toward it. "Is that a Keres feather?"

"From the Keres Queen herself."

Elaina's forehead puckers. "But she's dying too. Why would she give you a feather? She will only perish faster…"

Amalia closes her wings with a snap.

The furrow in Elaina's brow deepens. "Mother?"

When Amalia doesn't answer, Elaina searches her eyes. The girl's face falls. "You took it."

"She can't save herself—not even with her own feathers. Not with anything."

Elaina gasps. "But—"

Amalia says, "I have one for you, too."

Elaina freezes.

Amalia produces a brilliant copper feather from her pocket and pushes it toward her daughter. Elaina doesn't take it, staring at the golden feather with wide hazel eyes the same color as her mother's.

Amalia leans closer. "Take it, Elaina. Take it and live."

Elaina's jaw clenches. Her eyes jolt up to her mother's. "As what, Mother? As a monster?"

Amalia gasps, but she leans closer, her face setting in hard lines. "You will release your wings and take this feather."

"No!"

Amalia's eyes fly wide. "You would rather die? I won't let that happen. I'm your mother and I will protect you." She grabs her daughter by the shoulders. "Release your wings. Do it now!"

Elaina doesn't resist. She responds by leaning into her mother instead, pressing her cheek to Amalia's neck, her voice quiet. "No, Mother."

Her eyes glisten with tears as she buries her face against her mother before turning her gaze upward again. "I won't."

Amalia's grip tightens, frustration and despair filling her features. "Please…"

Elaina wraps her arms around her mother, shaking her head. "I'm dying. I will do it with my conscience intact. You have to let me go."

Amalia becomes as still as stone, rigid within her daughter's arms. With a sudden cry, she pries herself free, wrenching away from Elaina so fast that her daughter falls forward, slipping to the floor.

Amalia pulls her upright, crying, "I will never let you go! I will never forget what was done to us."

Amalia's face darkens, a snarl appearing on her lips—the Amalia that I know. She is as cold as ice as she says, "I will hunt down Josiah Baines, the ringmakers, the assassins. I will destroy them all. I will take their loved ones from them. I will rip their lives apart like they have broken mine. I will repay my pain a thousand times on the humans that walk this Earth."

Elaina's eyes are wide. She is pale. "When will you rest?"

"Never," Amalia answers.

Elaina whispers, "It won't bring me back."

I jolt as a low scream tears through the memory in front of me. The sound curls around me like a noose, yanking me back into the present.

My eyes are wet. I swipe at them. The waterfall is gentle

and lulling while Amalia stands upright, her deadly gaze very much alert now, her piercing scream of rage heavy with accusation. "That was not yours to see!"

She isn't wrong. I had no right to see the memory that made her what she is today.

I mean it when I say, "I'm sorry about your daughter."

Pain floods her face, but she pushes it away quickly. "I'm not sorry about your mother."

Damn. I nearly felt sorry for her.

My jaw clenches. My sword is still raised, ready to strike.

I lift my free hand—the one I used to wipe my eyes—to grip the weapon with both hands. My tears have well and truly dried up now that reality has returned.

Amalia may have been broken when she lost her daughter, but the woman confronting me now has spent years perfecting her rage and cruelty.

She doesn't wait for me to strike, hitting out with the flat of her hand across my chest to shove me backward. I swing the sword and narrowly miss chopping off her arm.

I readjust my grip and plant my feet when she backs up. "Draw your weapon."

Her eyes narrow at me. "You are so eager to fight and endanger those closest to you."

"You want to destroy everyone, Amalia," I say. "I will do anything to stop you."

"Anything?" Her lip curls. "I could kill you with my Keres power right now."

I challenge her: "Then try."

She folds her arms across her chest, appraising me. "I will give you one last chance to back out of the maze, Hunter. Let me have the feather and I won't kill you…"

A sly smile crosses her face. "I won't kill your child."

I narrow my eyes at her. "I won't live long enough to have children."

She smirks. "You will live long enough to give birth to the baby you carry."

Shock strikes through me. "I'm not pregnant. I can't be."

Amalia scoffs. "Why? Because you went to a human doctor for female contraception? That doesn't work on us, Hunter. Why do you think your mother found herself in a predicament twenty-one years ago? Our daughters are born of the man we love. Often, he is the man we can't have."

She paces up to me and I'm so shocked by what she said that I let her approach. She has to be lying. She is trying to manipulate me, to make me doubt my path. To make me worry about my own safety because my safety… is also my child's safety…

I cast my memory back to the times I was with Slade—the times we didn't take extra precautions.

Is it really possible?

My body is failing me. I've nearly died multiple times. There is no way that any sort of life could have survived inside me throughout all that.

Amalia says, "Leave the maze right now and I will allow you to live in peace for the next eight months. You will live long enough to give Slade a daughter. Birthing her will kill you, but I will let her and Slade live. It's a generous offer, Hunter. You should consider it."

I already know my answer. "A world with you in it is not the one I will leave for my daughter."

My daughter.

I don't believe Amalia that I'm pregnant, not for a second, but with or without a child, my decision is the same.

Her expression darkens, the same cold determination on

her face that she cloaked herself with when she pushed her own daughter away. "No more chances, Hunter."

To my shock, she turns and runs, her body a lithe blur because she's moving so fast. I sheathe my sword and race after her, nearly catching her at the corner but she bursts ahead, twisting and turning through the diamond corridors.

I stay on her heels, my arms pumping, catching sight of the exit, a bright light at the end of the next passageway.

Amalia throws me a final smile as she speeds through it.

We burst from the cavern into a world on fire.

CHAPTER THIRTY-SEVEN

*A*malia releases her wings, turning to face me as she rises into the air and screams, "Welcome to the end, Hunter!"

We stand in the middle of a burning plain. The ground is made of ash, scattered with lumps of coal. Fiery cracks in the ground extend in every direction. Thin threads of molten lava flow around us in fine golden lines.

Hundreds of feet away, the floating island is closer than it's ever been and yet still so far. The rock giant said there would be three gates and three challenges. I'm guessing the meaning of "gate" is metaphorical and this plain is the final one. But it's not the final challenge, that is still ahead of us.

My boots crunch on the dead Earth as I kick up dust. "What is this place?"

"This is the End Land," Amalia cries with a triumphant smile. "The resting place of titans and old gods." She leans toward me with a gleam in her eyes. "And of our ancestors."

"Hunter!" Slade's shout has me spinning. Behind me,

three more diamond tunnels let out, along with the one Amalia and I came from.

Slade runs from the nearest one, followed a moment later by Archer who exits the furthest. They are both pale, tears streaking down their cheeks. They both have pasts that they grapple with, tragedies and death.

Judging by their tense expressions, it wasn't easy making it through the emotional hazards of the diamond maze.

Slade races across the burning ground with Archer on his heels, both of them deftly navigating the fiery threads of flame that crisscross the Earth beneath their feet.

But... where is Cain?

I don't know much about his past. I wish I knew more. Something compelled him to become an assassin. I pray that whatever it is, he is strong enough to let it go...

Mom asked me to let *her* go. I understand now why she wants me to. Amalia refused to let go of her rage about her daughter's death and it has led her down a path of destruction and cruelty. She has become something a Valkyrie Queen should never be: heartless.

Before Slade reaches me, my gaze passes across the tunnel from which Amalia and I ran. Everyone else was faced with their own path, but she and I shared the same one. We are a mirror of each other.

She is a mother who lost her daughter.

I am a daughter who lost my mother.

Before Slade reaches me and lifts me off my feet to hold me in his arms, my eyes meet Amalia's, taking in the cruel snarl on her lips, the darkness in her expression, the smile that lights her eyes because...

She knows.

I have walked the same path that she has, driven by the events of my past.

Well, no more. I'm letting it go. No matter what Mom went through, she fought her battles with her eye on the future.

It's time for me to take my eyes off the past and focus on what could be ahead of me. I asked Slade what we would do when this was all over and he told me we would find a way to live together, we could get married and raise a family.

I want that, and it scares me a lot more than fighting Amalia or facing my own death. But I'm going to fight for it with everything I've got.

"Hunter." Slade's arms tighten around me as if he hasn't held me for years, decades even. "You were gone."

I focus on his pale blue eyes, the shadows under them, and the set of his jaw. I shudder at the pain in his eyes.

I whisper, "What did you see in there?"

For now, Amalia seems content to leave us alone and Slade doesn't pay any attention to her.

He searches my eyes as he says, "I saw the future. I saw a whole life without you. There was a baby and then you died. She grew up without her mother—"

I grip his shoulders. "That won't happen."

His gaze bores into me. "Which part, Hunter?"

I give him a determined smile. "We're going to make it through this."

Archer interrupts us then, skidding to a halt beside us, her dagger already in her hand, keeping it trained on Amalia.

She swipes tears from her face with one determined swoop. Whatever she faced in the cavern, she has got a hold of her emotions, but she can't disguise her fear as she takes anxious glances at the last tunnel. "Where is Cain?"

I shake my head but before I can speak, Amalia floats closer.

She coos at us: "Reunion time is over. It's a shame the other one didn't make it."

"Go to hell, Amalia," Archer shouts, but the tension around her eyes tells me she is seriously worried about Cain. He should have been here by now.

Slade immediately switches into warrior mode, letting me out of his arms and slipping out his Keres gun at the same time, taking aim squarely at Amalia's heart.

She laughs, the delighted sound rippling across the air. "Bullets don't hurt me, Slade."

"These ones will," he says.

Slade's confident statement stops Amalia in her tracks. She pauses her forward flight, eyes narrowed, appearing to reconsider her approach.

I take a quick glance at him. All we need is one clean shot while one of us is touching her. We need the combined Keres and Valkyrie power to end her.

"Well, then," she says. "It's three against one. That seems a little unfair, doesn't it? Let's level the playing field."

She lifts her arms into the air and throws her head back, shouting, "Rise, fallen soldiers!"

She was about to tell me about this place when Slade appeared. I have no idea what to expect as the ground rumbles. I adjust my balance to stay upright as ash and coal shift beneath my feet.

Slade and Archer are tense and on edge beside me. They draw closer to me as the nearest lava threads widen several feet, becoming rivers of molten lava flowing around us.

Heat grows in the air and sweat pools at my throat. The

patch of earth where we stand shrinks until we are forced to huddle back to back to avoid the burning substance.

I'm shocked when the shapes of women rise from within the lava streams, molten flames dripping off their armored forms. Their heads are lowered, their arms held close to their sides, fire streaming from their long hair and muscular torsos as they emerge.

There are at least two hundred of them, rising from molten streams all over the ashen field to form ranks behind Amalia, hovering in the air with her.

"My soldiers!" Amalia shrieks. "Obey your Queen!"

In unison, the women lift their heads and spread their wings, spraying lava off their bodies to finally reveal their faces.

They are each unique with flawless skin and hair of all colors. Their armor is made of black leather with silver buckles and they carry a multitude of weapons—some carry spears, others wield daggers and swords, and yet others hold bows and arrows.

Their wings are silver like mine.

I gasp. "What the hell?"

Amalia gives me a pleased smile. "This is the Valkyrie and Keres End Land. Every warrior who fell in battle rests in this field."

Behind Amalia, two hundred Valkyrie women lower themselves to the ground, folding their wings away while remaining in their rank formations. Now that they have emerged, the lava streams in the ground constrict again, the earth returns to ash, and the burning liquid runs once again in thin threads across the plain.

The Valkyrie army gives a single war cry that echoes around us.

I shudder as I remember the threat Amalia made when I fought her in the sky. She told me she was building her own army to crush everyone I love. I wonder for a moment if she was referring to the warriors now standing behind her, but I don't think so. Not when these women are clearly constrained to an existence within the maze.

Even so, they're a significant threat.

Amalia demonstrates her control over them when she points to two women who stand slightly ahead of the others. They wear different armor, their breastplates colored deep purple, and they carry katanas—just like mine.

Amalia shouts, "Generals! Prepare your warriors. Don't underestimate your opponents." She gives us a haughty smile. "As pathetic as these three intruders may appear."

Now that the earth has reformed under our feet, I have room to turn to Slade and Archer.

My back is still sore but adrenalin masks any pain I feel. I keep my voice low. "I need to go after Amalia. That's the only way this ends. Slade, can you protect Archer and fly her to the island? The Valkyrie have the power to kill her and she isn't able use her power to defend herself against them."

He takes hold of my arm. "They can kill you, too, Hunter."

Archer nods beside him, her violet eyes deeply concerned.

They're both right. I'm vulnerable right now—my body's healing power is nearly exhausted. The Valkyrie killing power could seriously hurt me. Enough strikes could end what is left of my struggling body.

I shake my head, a slow side to side motion. "I need to do this."

Slade's gaze softens. "I know." His thumb brushes across my arm as he searches my eyes. He seems to make a decision.

"Okay. Archer and I will go right. I'll fly us as high and as far as I can. We'll head toward the island. The Valkyrie ranks are less dense toward the back rows so we can fight them more easily there if we have to."

Archer flips a dagger into her other hand and says, "The assassin's code doesn't apply here, so we can kill them, correct?"

I nod and Slade agrees. "They're technically already dead."

Archer continues, "When I fought Amalia after she attacked the Horde, she told me I was stronger than others of my kind. Well, she's about to find out how much stronger." She turns to Slade. "Hold me so I can fight and I'll protect you instead."

He gives her a grin, responding to her declaration with a smile that carries all the rage and violence he keeps constantly in check. "Let's get to it."

He presses the gun containing the Keres bullets into my hand, closing my fingers around it with his big, gentle hands, but he doesn't speak.

There are so many things he isn't saying. The look he gives me tells me he will protect Archer, no matter what she says. The way he glances at the gun reminds me there are two bullets, which means there is a spare if I get into trouble with one of the other Valkyrie.

And last…

He leans into me, not quite pressing his lips to mine. "I love you, Hunter Cassidy."

I kiss him, a fierce kiss, before I slip out of his hold, deftly repositioning the gun in my hand. "I'll see you both on the other side."

My focus is now on Amalia.

CHAPTER THIRTY-EIGHT

I break into a run and spread my wings.

Strength flows through me as I rise into the air above the Valkyrie warriors, drawing on the power that comes from my wings. I'm about to tap into it like never before.

Behind me, Slade releases his wings and plucks Archer from her feet, lifting her high. She adjusts her weapons, giving him a quick nod before he swoops to the side with her, aiming for the edge of the army while I keep the center busy.

I have seconds to get to Amalia before the risen Valkyrie swarm me. Their ranks are far denser at the front, closely packed, the women waiting for the command to attack.

To kill Amalia, I need to hit her with both Keres and Valkyrie power at the same time. If it was as easy as shooting her, I could do it from a distance, but I need to get close to release my killing power.

She doesn't know why she should be afraid of this gun, but she is smart enough to take Slade's declaration seriously.

As soon as I fly over the first row of Valkyrie soldiers, she beats her wings, turns, and soars away from me, her mismatched wings creaking as she flies in the direction of the island.

The soldiers don't make a move yet, but I am their focus. Their faces are upturned, their eyes following me with the precision of an army that knows how to take down a single target with brutal efficiency.

These women were trained for war. They're simply biding their time, giving me a moment of hope to believe that I can reach Amalia before they crush me.

One of the generals shouts a command.

Ten rows back, a row suddenly kneels. The women in the row behind them sprint and springboard off their backs, gaining speed as they spread their wings and spear toward me.

At the same time, Amalia drops to the ground ahead, disappearing from sight among the ranks of women.

No! I've lost her already and there's no way I can fly clear of the oncoming warriors. I can't risk the attacking women disarming me—this gun is priceless—so I quickly slip the gun into my harness while I pull up hard. I take a fighting stance, bracing for impact mid-air. I still have a trick or two up my sleeve.

At the last possible moment, I blur, disappearing from her sight. Amalia knows how to blur but Mom never did. If the other Valkyrie know this trick, then so be it, but if they don't, it will give me an advantage over them.

The warrior shouts, casting wildly around for me. Her surprised reaction tells me that blurring is not a common skill.

I feint right and slam my fist into her, landing a hard hit

on her shoulder, sending her spinning across the field. She crashes into a row to my left, knocking others down as she falls.

My left fist swiftly collides with the next attacker, sending her crashing through the ranks on the other side.

Still blurred, I duck and weave through the oncoming flying warriors, avoiding their wild attacks and landing solid hits on the next five—and the five after that. There are so many of them that I start to lose count.

Even though they can't see me, they don't give up, quickly judging my location based on the position of my attacks.

I fill my hands with killing power every time I make contact, not certain how long I can keep it up, but I'm not about to use half measures right now. Every hit I land has to have enough impact to send my attackers flying—and get me closer to Amalia.

I make it past seven rows. I only have about a twenty more.

Every now and then I catch sight of Amalia flitting between the soldiers, her long hair flying behind her. She remains on the ground, choosing to run along the ashy surface, because she knows I can catch her in the air.

Unlike Gareth, she is shrewd enough to work with her own weaknesses.

The two generals fly at the edges of my vision on either side of me, following the carnage I create as I go. The way they watch my flight makes me worried they can see through my blur. What's more, I won't be able to keep it up much longer. It's draining more of my energy than I have left.

The general who is flying to my left suddenly shouts, and a rank of soldiers rises up far ahead of me.

They don't fly toward me; they hover in the air instead.

The general shouts another order and the soldiers positioned directly ahead of me stay in position, but the ones at each end of the row fly forward with meticulous efficiency, rapidly curving around my position to form a wide ring around me.

They're trying to box me in. I respond by flying higher, intending to sail over their heads, but the general shouts again and the soldiers swiftly rise to the same height.

Dammit, the generals can see through my blur. Blurring is draining too much of my energy now and I need everything to keep fighting.

I crane my neck, frustrated to see Amalia progress through another three rows of women.

I let go of my blur, materializing in the center of the wide ring they have formed around me, taking a moment to scan the right side of the field for Slade and Archer. They've made it much further toward the island—only ten rows from the back—but the general to my right is shouting commands and the Valkyrie soldiers on the right flank have mobilized, swarming toward Slade in a mob. They will try to take him down with sheer force of numbers.

Slade responds by spinning and hoisting Archer into the air.

She's ready, daggers raised, her targeted ascent sending her into the heart of the oncoming swarm.

She makes the most of her air time, deftly slicing through throats and major arteries while avoiding their blades as she descends. As soon as she approaches the ground, she angles toward the nearest Valkyrie, using the woman as an unwilling springboard back into the air.

Archer may not have wings, but her body doesn't seem to

know it. She bounces back toward the sky as if her body knows she should be able to fly.

None of the Valkyrie have used their killing power yet, attacking with weapons instead, which means that they must not realize that Archer is Keres. She doesn't have an aura and she hasn't released her wings so they probably think she's human. I only know she is Keres because Cain told me.

I can't stop the grin that grows on my face. Their ignorance is a small mercy but I'll take any mercies we can get right now.

Slade stays close to Archer's position but, unlike her, he is a major target. He revealed his wings so the Valkyrie women know what he is—and they don't like it. Even from here, I can hear their screams.

"Monster!"

"Aberration!"

They target him with their power, their fingers clawed like vultures.

He strikes back, single hits sending them flying toward the ground, where they don't rise again. They won't stay out forever, but a pile of them builds beneath his location.

In response to his strength, their attacks become more coordinated.

While a group distracts him in front, two others target his back, specifically the vulnerable space between his wings— one of them springboards off the other to approach at rapid speed, timed perfectly between his wing beats.

Her dagger thumps directly into his spine.

Slade roars, swinging to the woman with a ferocious fist that sends her sprawling to the ground with the others.

I remind myself that he will heal, that he is strong, but the fact that his protective suit didn't stop the blade is bad news.

These women dragged their bodies and their weapons up from a place of molten lava. Their steel must be infused with magic. It means my suit won't stop their weapons either.

Archer responds to Slade's shout by leaping up to catch hold of the nearest woman's wing and flying between Slade and his next attacker, who is about to thump a second dagger into his lower spine.

Archer's own knife hits the woman's eye, neatly aimed. I've never known anyone with knife skills like Archer. If anyone can hit a pinpoint target, it's her.

The Valkyrie screams, clutching her face while Archer grabs Slade's arm and shouts, "Down!"

Slade immediately drops to the ground with her, putting away his wings as soon as they touch down.

Once there, Archer yanks the dagger from his back and positions herself so that they stand back to back facing the horde that circles around them.

I don't have time to see more. I return my focus to the soldiers in front of me. I'm not going to wait for them to attack.

I retrieve my sword, the katana's blade glinting in the firelight that emanates from the earth below us.

Even the sunlight here is different, a copper glow that reminds me of Keres wings. If I were running hot like I used to, I would be dripping with sweat by now, but I run so cold that the heat coming off the ground makes me feel more alive than I have for months.

I angle my wings and soar toward the Valkyrie blocking my path directly ahead.

They ready their swords and two of them fly forward to meet me. I spin to deflect the first soldier who tries to dart left and stab me from the side.

Instead of using my sword, my boot meets her chest, propelling her backward. I use her body as leverage to propel myself high enough to fly over the head of the next woman, narrowly avoiding the tip of her blade.

The gap they left in the circle ahead quickly closes, but once again they expect me to fight with my sword. The soldier directly in front of me shouts as I angle backward and my foot connects squarely with her jaw, using her face as a springboard over the others who try to plug the gap.

I don't feel bad about planting my boot in her face. She wouldn't think twice about skewering me.

The general shouts from the side—her voice much closer to my location than I was hoping—and the soldiers on the ground mobilize, but not quite fast enough.

I tuck away my sword and roll mid-air, ducking and weaving as they nock arrows to their bows and fire at me.

My wings are suddenly a liability since they offer a larger target. Arrows can't pierce or damage them but three lodge between my feathers, upsetting my balance.

On the ground, Amalia is only ten rows ahead of me. If I fly fast enough, I can catch her.

Compensating for the arrows protruding from my wings, I angle toward her, but the Valkyrie abandon their orderly approach now.

Thirty soldiers rise into the air immediately in front of me. I fly high to avoid the immediate barrier they pose, but they swarm after me, far too close for comfort.

A dagger slices across the front of my leg; another cuts across my thigh. The steel burns through my protective suit and I scream.

I burst higher, but the nearest woman grabs my left wing and yanks me downward. A quick boot to her face forces her to let me go, but losing control of my wing causes me to lose momentum.

I flounder for a second. It's long enough for another soldier to slice her blade across my other leg. I'm incredibly lucky my attackers haven't cut my tendons, although no doubt that's what they are aiming to do. If they had, I wouldn't still have control of my legs.

Another two soldiers fly in at me from the side. I sacrifice one of my daggers, slamming it into the throat of the woman on the left, ducking and rolling mid-air to fling my other dagger into the second woman's chest.

The swarm closes in, but I'm determined to get to Amalia. She is only three seconds away now.

I reach deep for my power to fuel my flight, spearing toward her while I retrieve the Keres gun and take aim, stretching out my other hand to make contact with her shoulder as I dive toward her.

She glances back, jolting with surprise to see me so close to her position.

I reach for her, squeezing the trigger.

A force like a sledgehammer hits me from the side.

I catch sight of a deep purple breastplate—one of the generals—as I tumble through the air.

The bullet flies wide, buries deep in the ashy ground at the foot of a soldier. The spray of ash is the last thing I see as I crash hard to the ground, barely managing to tuck my head and turn my shoulder to take the impact.

I had counted on Amalia's body cushioning my fall but now...

I hit the ash with a thud, my head connects with a rock, and the world goes dark.

CHAPTER THIRTY-NINE

'm only out for a second.

It's long enough for the general to land on top of me, a knee to my chest, her fist knocking into my cheek before I can get my arms up to defend myself. She is tall, her shoulders broad, her black hair tied back in intricate braids, the sneer on her face cutting through her beauty.

I desperately look for the gun, locating it several paces away.

It's too far away for me to reach it.

My wings spread across the ground, arrows protruding from them. Two warriors step onto my wings, breaking off the arrows to remove them, but they remain positioned on my wings, pinning me with their body weight.

Amalia gloats at the edge of a quickly forming circle of Valkyrie women, hovering over where I lie in the dirt.

I'm expertly immobilized by the fierce general. She hits me again, knocking my head so hard against the uneven ground—into the jagged coal—that my vision spins.

Warm liquid trickles across my forehead.

That is not a good sign.

I don't have breath to scream, gasping for air.

Her gaze is cold and hard. "I am General Griffin. How did you get this sword?"

I squint at my katana as she brandishes it in front of my face.

She must have removed it while I was out. I keep my eye on it. The hard reality is that she could stab me with it right now—kill me with my own sword—and I wouldn't be able to stop her.

I glance sideways at Amalia. She knows all the answers, but for some reason she remains silent.

I swallow, drawing air into my lungs, and take two deep breaths before I can answer. "That sword is mine."

Just then, the other general lands within the circle, dropping neatly to her feet beside Amalia and putting away her wings. She has auburn hair, tied in knots across her head, and is just as fiercely muscled as the one who knocked me from the sky.

She gives Amalia a deep bow, "My Queen, the other two invaders are tiring and will soon be restrained."

Amalia gives her an indulgent smile. "General Glaive, the male Valkyrie is a monster and must be killed. Take that weapon and use it on him."

Amalia points to the Keres gun resting in the ash. Glaive quickly bends to retrieve it.

"No!" I struggle against General Griffin, but she grabs my face with her free hand, her fingers digging into my bruised jaw, making me wince.

She grinds her teeth at me. "I'll ask you once more: how did you get this sword?"

Glaive pauses nearby before she rises with the Keres gun

in her hand, staring at my sword. Surprise shoots across her face before a deep scowl descends over her face.

I growl up at Griffin, "My mother gave it to me."

"You are trying my patience," Griffin snaps. "Who was your mother?"

"Her name was Anna Cassidy."

General Griffon huffs at me as if I'm pathetic. "Not her human name. Her Valkyrie name."

I blink at her. *There's a difference?* Mom was only known by one other name, but it was her assassin's name. Surely that isn't what this woman is asking me for, but it's the only other answer I have.

"They called her the Glass Fox."

General Griffon gasps, recoiling from me. "This is the sword of a traitor."

She pitches it point first into the ash beside my thigh as if she doesn't want to touch it any longer. It barely misses my wings and vibrates from the force of her thrust.

Anger courses through me. To throw someone else's katana into the dirt is to spit on their soul.

I glare up at her, speaking very carefully. "That is a disrespectful way to treat my sword."

Griffin's hand tightens around my jaw. "That sword belonged to our third general: General Glass. She rebelled against our queen after the first ringmaker attacked us. In fact, General Glass tried to kill her, and for that she was banished. Her soul and the souls of her descendants will never rest here with us."

Griffin peers closer at me. "You must be her descendant. You have the same eyes."

I chew on that for a second. I think it means I won't come here when I die. It would mean that Mom didn't come here either. Although Mom was in the diamond maze, so she must be here… somewhere… or at least her soul followed me here…

Not coming here when I die is not something I'll cry about.

I take a glance at Amalia. Ordinarily, I would expect her to be crowing about my capture right about now but she's unusually quiet.

If what Griffin says is true, then my ancestor refused to follow her. There could have been any number of reasons for that, but the one I'm aware of is Amalia's theft of Keres feathers.

It makes me wonder how much truth she told her people about her own actions and to what extent she misled them.

All things considered, the fact that my ancestor fought Amalia makes me incredibly proud.

"She didn't agree with what you were doing, did she?" I shout at Amalia. "She tried to stop you killing Keres—"

Amalia shrieks over the top of me. "The other intruder is a Keres female. You have to kill her. Now!"

My heart sinks. Until now, the Valkyrie have treated Archer like a human. That will change now.

Glaive immediately takes to the sky, her face set with determination to carry out her queen's orders. She takes the gun with her.

The two Valkyrie warriors standing on my wings step off and Griffin pulls me to my feet, but I was waiting for any shift in her weight. I tuck my wings, pull her off balance, and scoop up my sword at the same time.

I swing back, a clean cut that sprays ash and blood through the air.

My blade is whisper quiet. She doesn't have time to react.

Griffin's head hits the ground to screams from the other Valkyrie.

I spin to Amalia, but she is already gone, disappearing into the growing crowd.

I no longer have the gun to end her, and if I go after her, I won't get to Slade and Archer in time to help them. I leap and release my wings, soaring after General Glaive as a barrage of furious women rages after me, ready to beat me to a pulp. I pull my feet up just in time to avoid their grasping hands.

Twenty… maybe thirty… warriors take to the air behind me, a rising swarm as I soar after Glaive. She will carry the message to the Valkyrie on the right flank that they are to kill Archer with their power. I have to beat her to it.

I ignore my bleeding face as I soar after her, the wing-beats of so many women following me that I can't tell them apart. I zigzag to avoid the daggers they throw at me and the arrows they shoot from the ground.

My sword is still in my hands, my most trusted weapon.

In the distance, Archer and Slade have moved further toward the island, but they are surrounded by Valkyrie, still battling them.

Glaive pauses up ahead to shout orders to another rank of Valkyrie below who immediately mobilize in Archer's direction.

Her pause is all I need to catch up, but one of the women shouts from behind me. "General Glaive, watch out!"

The general glances back just in time to see me and avoid the cut of my sword. Dashing forward, she closes in on Archer's location, close enough to shout orders.

With a final burst of power, I hurl myself into her and swing my sword.

Glaive screams, "Kill the Keres woman!"

Too late, my sword meets her neck. I snatch the gun from her falling hand and deposit it safely into my harness, but my heart sinks as quickly as her body drops to the ground below.

The upturned faces of the warriors on the ground tell me that they heard the order. So did Slade and Archer, their exhausted gazes turning my way as I attempt to soar toward them.

Before I can travel more than a few feet, a warrior collides with me. Another three grab me from behind, yanking me backward, while I try to hit and kick my way out of their hold.

On the ground, a silver haze of killing power grows around the women closing in on Slade and Archer.

A wave of iridescent heat sears my skin and forces me backward in a way that a blade can't. They are all harnessing their killing power and pooling its force among themselves.

With a scream of frustration, I curve upward, forced to fly away from it. I can't get in there. I can't help Archer. My damn body is too vulnerable. If I fly through that much death, my heart will stop before I reach the ground.

Slade promised he would protect Archer. The determination on his face is unmistakable as he shouts to her, "Get inside my wings! You'll be safe there."

At the same time, he looks up. His eyes meet mine for a second before Archer dives against his side.

Then he wraps his arms around her, dropping them both to their knees. He ducks his head, releases his wings, and wraps them tightly around her, forming a shield that conceals her completely.

The warriors attack.

Their power hits Slade's wings, rippling across them, silver streaks of light sparking as their killing power collides with the energy in his wings.

I hold my breath as the force crackles and shrieks, but the more they target his wings, the more their power sparks back at them, biting their faces and hands so that they flinch away from him.

They can't get through.

They scream with frustration, their power dying down as they appear to realize that it's futile to try to kill Archer that way. There is no way to get through Slade's strong wings and no gaps in them like there are gaps between feathers.

One of them spits and screams, "A Valkyrie protecting a Keres! You dishonor your people!"

Slade doesn't budge as they continue to hurl insults at him.

In the air, I evade another three Valkyrie who try to grab me. I need to get to Slade and help him, but the remnant haze of killing power still lingers in the air. *Give it two more seconds, just two, for it to clear so I can fly down there...*

I scream as the Valkyrie who spat at Slade drives her dagger into his back.

The only way to get to Archer is to go through Slade's body instead of his wings. The short daggers they used before are nothing like the ones they use now.

They strike between every vertebra in his spine, their attacks vicious and bloody, trying to make him open his wings.

Slade's roar of pain rises above the shelter he created for Archer, above the shouting women. He shakes, jolts. He can't defend himself. All he can do is keep Archer safe.

Rage flows through me.

Nobody hurts my man.

I spear toward them, power filling my hands as I burst forward, knocking the nearest woman to the ground and sacrificing my last dagger into the back of the next one's neck.

I thud to the ground at Slade's back. I don't have time to be gentle, wrenching out the blades that remain along his spine.

"Slade! I'm here!" My voice cracks at the damage the Valkyrie did to him, but I swallow my emotions and pull myself upright. I have to trust that he will heal quickly now that the blades are removed. "I'm here. I'll protect you."

He shudders, the slump of his shoulders telling me he is badly wounded. I take guard at his back. This is the only way the Valkyrie can get to Archer so this is where I will stay. No matter what happens.

I spring at the next warrior who attempts to attack, my sword piercing her body before I kick her back. The next Valkyrie loses a hand. The one after that, a leg. I have no remorse and no sympathy, but neither do they.

I am not one of them. I am their enemy.

They curse and taunt me. "Traitor! Filth!"

I let their taunts roll off me.

Their attacks are relentless. The pain from the wounds in my legs increases and so does the ache in my head. I'm wounded but I can't stop. I have to protect Slade and Archer.

Between the blades and arrows that fly my way, between the ducking and spinning, I catch sight of an endless army. An endless force.

I don't have a chance.

A scream builds inside me.

I won't die here.

I refuse.

The next blade cuts my face. The next fist nearly breaks my jaw. I sense my bones shifting but I turn just before they break. I ignore the pain and strike back as hard as I can but it's not enough…

I don't know where Amalia is. I have the gun, but my hope of stopping her is dying a painful death. My chest heaves and the well of power inside me is nearly sucked dry.

I'm fighting an entire army on my own.

And I'm losing.

CHAPTER FORTY

A roar echoes across the air, so ferocious that the women around me jump, many of them turning to the sound.

I try to place it—a voice maybe—but the reverberation bounces around inside my head.

The Valkyrie women recover and return their attention to me again, their blades blurring as I deflect them. One of them succeeds in swiping my feet out from under me.

I land on my back, expecting a follow-up kick but the woman jolts backward, her head turned.

In fact, they're all looking in the same direction.

I jump to my feet and shoot into the air for a second, keeping my eye on Slade at the same time. I intend to drop right back to the ground once I know what the new threat is, but what I see makes me freeze.

Cain bursts from the entrance to his diamond tunnel, his massive body powering across the field of ash.

His shout echoes around us, amplified by his assassin's

magic. Copper light blazes around him; his protective suit is cut up, and he clutches a gun in each hand.

Even from this distance, I can see that he's angry as hell.

He throws the weapons aside, which tells me that he has used up all his bullets, and charges at the nearest warrior, his Keres power blazing. She screams and drops at his touch, convulsing on the ground.

He leaps over her. Screams fill the air, Valkyrie women drop, and Cain plows through their ranks, his power shrieking ahead of him.

He runs straight for Archer as if she is some kind of beacon. He sprints so fast that he is only moments away from reaching us.

At the same time as incredible relief and gratitude flow through me, fear also rises inside me, making the scene below me crystal clear. Cain's expression is drawn and focused. He wears the look of battle fever that blocks out everything except his target. Whatever happened to him in that tunnel, it made him mad. Real mad. All he wants is to get to Archer.

I have no problem with him cutting through the risen Valkyrie, but neither Slade nor I will survive the Keres power bursting off Cain right now.

The closer he gets to our position, the closer he is to killing us.

I have to get Slade out of the line of fire.

While the Valkyrie women brace, weapons ready for Cain, I drop to the ground, shouting, "Slade! Open your wings. Let go of Archer. *Now!*"

Slade responds immediately. He lurches back and his wings retract, revealing Archer huddled next to him, her arms wrapped around her knees, her head resting on top of them.

She is *glowing*. Her back gleams as if her wings are right beneath the surface, but her expression is blank. She is somewhere else. Whatever she's doing, it's calling Cain and fueling his rage.

I wrap my arms around Slade's waist, pulling him upward, screaming at him to move. "Slade! Hurry!"

He is sluggish, his torso slippery in my arms.

Blood. A lot of blood.

A scream grows inside me. Archer was resting right up against his chest, her Keres power flowing as close to the surface of her skin as it gets. It's like poison to Slade. Meanwhile, the Valkyrie were stabbing him in the back.

Even when I stopped them, he was protecting Archer and wasn't healing the whole time.

Sick to my stomach, I release my wings and pull him into the air, his body limp in my arms, his arms and head dropping forward.

I lift him out of Cain's path just in time.

Cain bashes through the ranks of women, sending them sprawling, and scoops Archer into his arms, running with her, one outstretched arm punching through the Valkyrie ahead of him.

Archer unfurls, her focus snapping back to him. "Cain!"

He roars, "Am I in hell?"

He skids to a halt, far enough away from Slade and me that we're safe from the power raging through him.

The Valkyrie warriors nearest to him drop to the ground, their bodies trembling before the life leaves their eyes. The others back away, rushing to get clear of his power.

Cain's fists clench against Archer's back. "I saw the future. You died and I… was not a good person without you."

I startle to hear that. Slade said he saw the future, too. He said he saw a whole life without me. I wasn't in his version of the future either.

Archer cups her hand to Cain's cheek. She is half curled in his arms, one leg hooked around his hips in a way that appears uncomfortable but she looks right at home there. "I'm here. So are Hunter and Slade. Slade kept me safe."

Cain turns, tilting his head back, a measure of concern passing across his face when he sees Slade and the way I'm holding him up.

With a deep, indrawn breath, Cain dims his power, but he's clearly struggling to reduce it altogether. The battle rage hasn't left him.

In all honesty, I don't want him to calm down. As long as he is glowing, the Valkyrie will keep their distance.

They will take advantage of the break to rally, but we will deal with them when we have to.

I drop to ground, sliding to my knees, keeping a safe distance from Cain that doesn't put us too far away from him that the Valkyrie will be tempted to attack us.

I gently rest Slade's upper torso across my lap, laying him with his chest toward my stomach to avoid putting pressure on his healing back. I support his head in the crook of my arm.

His breathing is shallow and his wounds are healing so slowly that fear grips me.

His body needs to process the Keres power and it's taking far too long. Archer's power is… I shake my head. When she finally gets it back, it will be incredible.

The way Cain fought his way to her, the power flowing

through him, it's as if he was tapping into it somehow. Maybe it's the connection between the Keres rings they wear —the Queen and her daughter—but Cain and Archer are connected like nothing I've seen before.

The impact on Slade was devastating.

I stroke his hair, wishing I had Tansy's power to heal him, tears burning my eyes as I whisper, "You could have been killed."

His eyes flutter open, pale blue slits, the worry in them wrenching my heart around. "Is Archer safe?"

"You protected her just like you promised. Don't talk now. Focus on healing. We won't have long before the dead Valkyrie attack again."

He gives a dry laugh. "It's a Valkyrie apocalypse."

I laugh-cry, tears dropping from my eyes as I press my forehead to his. He exhales and closes his eyes, sliding one arm around my back to hold me close. His nearness affects me like a live wire, bringing me alive, making me painfully conscious of the wounds that my body is desperately trying to heal.

I have to make it through this. We all have to.

I murmur, "I always wanted to know more about my history. I never thought I would be sorry to meet my ancestors."

I take deep breaths, pulling my emotions together for these few seconds of safety. Cain's presence continues to keep the Valkyrie at bay but they won't stay distant for long. We will only have a few moments of peace.

In fact, the Valkyrie are already assembling, forming ranks around us.

I have time now to notice that many of them wear subtly different armor—different ranks and specialties. The soldiers with bows and arrows wear deep red leggings. The ones carrying spears wear a higher number of silver buckles. The generals spoke to me in English, but the soldiers also use a different language—one I don't understand.

I would admire the beauty and ferocity of these women if they weren't trying to kill me.

They are my people, but they follow Amalia. She called them, raised them from the dead to fight on her side.

I don't know if they think or feel for themselves or if they are merely shells. Given that Cain has killed quite a few of them, and I maimed many more, I'm not sure I want to know.

These women were trained for war. They fought the Keres after Amalia started the enmity between our two races. They all died and this is where their souls lie. In this field of ash...

"Wait..." I whisper. "Amalia said that this is the Valkyrie *and Keres* End Land."

Slade's eyes fly wide. His gaze is more focused now, his focus brighter, indicating that his wounds are finally healing. "The Keres rest here too."

My head snaps up. "Archer!" I shout. "Call your people!"

Archer jolts in the process of sliding to the ground as Cain returns her to her feet. "What?"

"We need an army," I say. "Your ancestors rest in this place. You can call them like Amalia called the Valkyrie."

Archer hesitates for a moment before her eyes light up. "You will need to get yourself and Slade clear. They will see you as the enemy."

I attempt a laugh. We will have two armies after us then, but hopefully, they will keep each other occupied while we slip away.

"That's a risk I'm willing to take," I say, helping Slade to his feet.

He leans on me for a brief moment before righting himself. "I'm okay now."

I check him over, relieved beyond belief that his skin has healed across his back where his suit is torn. "You heal faster than I ever did."

He sighs. "I think it's because I'm not *one* of anything. I'm human, Valkyrie, and ringmaker."

I take his face in my hands and kiss him. "You are everything."

He kisses me back, drawing me up against him, easing up to trail a gentle kiss—a bare graze—against my smarting cheekbone where I was hit, his gaze zeroing in on my forehead. Luckily, the blood flow has stopped.

He keeps his voice low. "You're injured, too."

I bite my lip, staying close to him. "There's nothing we can do about it. But I want you to carry this now."

I press the Keres gun into his hands.

A warning tone enters his voice. "Hunter…"

"I'm not giving up, Slade. I will never give up. But I'm not as agile as I want to be right now. Please take the gun and use it the moment you get the chance to end Amalia."

He closes his fingers reluctantly over it. "Okay."

The look in his eyes tells me that the way he protected Archer is how he will protect me now that Cain is back.

I want to kiss Slade, hug him, and tell him how much he means to me, how much I appreciate his care of others, but the way he presses his lips to mine tells me he knows how I feel.

I can't ask for anything more than that he knows how much I love him.

We turn to Archer and Cain, and I say, "We're ready. Do it."

Archer gives Cain a mysterious smile. She says to him, "Before, when you were in the diamond maze, I felt the call of the ring you wear. I sensed your presence and I think you sensed mine." She holds up her left hand on which she wears the Keres ring. "Let me try something, okay?"

He gives her a questioning look when she links their left hands, her arm resting across his stomach so they can face in the same direction.

His focus remains solely on her, his feelings for her stark on his face.

She closes her eyes and my jaw drops when the copper glow around him spreads to her, clouding her silhouette. She is drawing on his power, using it as her own.

The ring on her hand glows in response, adding to the power swirling around her. She never tried to use its power before—or at least, I never saw her try—but now it builds around her.

I'm worried for a moment that her wings will be triggered and hurt her without Tansy here to heal her, but Archer is completely relaxed.

In fact, the only times I've seen her so relaxed are when she is around Cain. They may not have bonded in the technical sense, but they are soulmates.

Even though her eyes are still closed, a smile breaks across her face. "Rise! My people!"

A deep rumble begins in the distance and the ground trembles beneath our feet, causing me to knock against Slade's side.

He catches me and I right myself, staying as close to Archer as I dare.

The approaching Valkyrie back away again, taking to the air and retreating from our position, leaving the field clear on the side closest to the diamond tunnels.

The rivers of lava widen and the earth shifts side to side as women rise from the flames, their heads raised up, not down this time.

They spread their wings as soon as they appear, flinging off the film of lava that covers them, their perfect features drawn into fierce expressions, their bright eyes taking in the army before them. Their armor is also black but with gold buckles, their golden wings catching the light of the copper sun.

With a single ferocious cry, two hundred Keres women form ranks as the fissures in the earth close up again.

The Valkyrie recover, rows of fierce women facing the Keres army.

My heart wrenches that these two races were once friends and allies. Then the Keres Queen betrayed the Valkyrie, trading lives for lives, and Amalia fought for survival by murdering countless Keres women.

Now, they are destined to fight a war without end.

I find Archer's violet eyes on me. She gives me a determined smile, a smile of trust and faith.

I return it.

The war ends with us.

CHAPTER FORTY-ONE

It's time to fly before the fighting starts.

Neither Slade nor I can step within three paces of Cain and Archer right now, so we spread our wings and hover above them, our wing beats ruffling their hair.

"It's time to run," Cain says to Archer, taking wary glances at the two armies as the tension builds between them.

She gives him a grin, her hand sliding from his. "I'm ready. Are you?"

He returns her smile, before he looks up at us. "Lead the way. We will follow your path."

Slade lowers his voice, slipping as close to me as he can while remaining airborne. "Stay in sight, Hunter. I need to be able to see you in case anything happens."

I'm not too proud to agree. It won't do anyone any good if I fall behind.

I nod, beat my wings, and steer right, soaring to the edge of the Valkyrie ranks. It's cooler on this side of the field, away from most of the lava threads. Slade flies close behind me, his wings a glittering force that sears the air.

On the ground, Cain takes off ahead of Archer, following my path, ready to use his power to clear the way for her if he has to. The ferocious scowl he throws at the soldiers as he runs tells me he won't hesitate to kill anyone who looks at Archer the wrong way.

She keeps pace with him, feet flying as they dart around the first row of soldiers.

The floating island is now dead ahead.

Behind us, a battle cry splits the air, both armies raging toward each other, their hatred of each other giving us the space we need to cover ground to the island. I don't look back as we leave the fight behind.

My war is ahead of me.

I can't stop to think about what I'll do if Amalia reaches the feathers before us. The field of ash was a gate. There is still one challenge to go.

The flight to the castle takes longer than expected, every beat of my wings feeling heavier. Slade and I wheel back several times since we can fly faster than Cain and Archer can run, and on the ground Cain and Archer are also tiring.

All the while, the floating island remains on the horizon. Even when I speed up, the distance doesn't decrease. I squint at it, my frustration and confusion increasing.

Eventually, Slade soars toward me and calls out to me. "It has to be a trick." He points at the castle. "It's Realm magic. I can feel it. We'll never reach the island this way."

He points to the ground and I nod my agreement. Exhaustion is flowing through me now. I'm tired, wounded, and more than a little bit hungry.

We land ahead of Cain and Archer, waiting for them to reach us. Cain has dimmed his power so we can stand close to him again. He is the only one who managed to keep hold of his backpack. Mine was cut from me during the fight, and Slade and Archer's are both missing too.

Cain hands around bottles of water and some dried food, while Slade explains, "We've been traveling for over half an hour. We should have reached the floating island by now, but we're no closer to it. I think that the Realm's magic is protecting it by preventing anyone from traveling straight to it."

Archer peers at the castle in the distance as she chews a protein bar. "Then… how do we get to it."

Slade points to the ground. "I could see from the sky that the lava threads are laid out in a pattern. I think it's another maze, but an invisible one. Do you see how the threads are spaced apart? If you imagine walls rising up from them, you can picture pathways and corners. I think we have to follow them."

"But it's so far," she says. "We could wander around for days."

Slade shakes his head with a smile. "If my hunch is right, I think we'll walk straight to it."

Cain says, "We don't have anything to lose. We can take advantage of the walk to eat and catch our breath. If it doesn't pan out, we'll run again."

Archer targets the food. "Eating is good. I need sugar or I'll fall over."

I grimace. "I could use a patch on my leg."

I glance up at the floating island once more before Archer finishes her mouthful and sets about stitching my wounds. I distract myself from the pain by chewing hard on a protein bar.

She tells me that her wounds have healed but a hint of fear enters her voice when she says, "So far, the after-effects of the fight haven't hit me. Normally I would be unconscious by now."

"It must be this place," I say. "Many things are different here. You and Cain, for example, the way your magic called to each other was incredible. His assassin's magic was never that strong outside of the maze."

She gives me a smile that quickly fades. "I don't know how that happened. I sensed Cain's presence so clearly and I think, deep down, I sensed all the Keres power inside the lava beneath us. But… I think I hurt Slade."

Slade and Cain have taken themselves off to the side, arms folded across their chests, absorbed in their own conversation. Every now and then they gesture at the castle. I imagine they are trying to figure out what lies ahead and plan for it.

I clear my throat. "I won't lie to you… he was hurt, but he was never going to let them through."

Archer finishes off the last stitch, but she takes my hand before I can stand up. "Before I met Cain, I never knew what kindness felt like, let alone believed that I deserved it," she says. "You and Slade… you're both ferocious, brutal, and scary as hell but you've given me friendship that I never expected to find. You protected me when I didn't expect to be protected, helped me even when it put you in danger. Thank you, Hunter."

My heart constricts inside my chest. She said she didn't believe she deserved kindness. If any of the rumors were true, then Patrick Ryan's idea of love was a closed fist.

My upbringing was much kinder than that, but I never had friends. The last year of my life changed all that. I found William and Tansy. I found my dad. I found everyone on

Saber Lane. Even Vlad, Cain, and above all... Slade, my fierce, gentle, deadly man.

I return Archer's genuine smile with one of my own. I don't have words right now so I hug her instead. She stiffens a little in surprise, just like I used to when William hugged me, before she relaxes into it.

When we draw apart, Slade and Cain are waiting with more food, handing it to us before we begin the careful trek through the ash. We stop looking up and focus on our feet, remaining within the lava lines and turning the corners when we have to.

A mere five minutes later, Archer turns the corner ahead of me and disappears. I shout and race after her, bumping into her back as soon as I round the same corner, Slade and Cain hot on my heels.

We have entered a solid stone corridor. It is open at the top and leads to a set of stone steps just like the ones at the beginning of the maze.

Finally allowing myself to look up, my heart lifts to see that the stairs lead right up to the floating island.

I breathe a quiet sigh of relief before we embark on the long walk upward.

From a distance, the floating island had appeared to be made of earth with a glass castle resting on it. As we draw closer, it becomes apparent that the base of the island is made of variegated stone, varying colors of brown, fiery orange, and emerald rippling through its surface.

The castle itself is jet black but its surface is speckled with silver that reflects the light around it, making it appear weirdly golden in the sunlight.

An open door waits at the top, leading directly into a large, elongated hall. The hall is made of simple rock, no decorations or vibrant tapestries, only a throne resting at the end of it.

A man sits on the throne, angled forward, elbows on his knees, both hands gripping the hilt of a sword with its tip to the floor. He is dressed in black pants but is bare from the waist up, his broad chest dusted with ash, his hair jet black like the castle. His head is down so it's impossible to make out his face.

The sword he grips burns with a flame that doesn't diminish or flicker, even when the wind whistles through the hall.

A delicate feather floats in the air high up on each side of him—one silver and one copper—the birth feathers of the first Valkyrie and Keres.

I halt in the entrance, drawing a quick breath.

Amalia already stands in front of him.

CHAPTER FORTY-TWO

 lade wraps his arms around me before I can dart forward. "Wait. We don't know what challenge this is. She doesn't have a feather yet, which means she hasn't passed it yet. If we have to fight that man, I want to gauge his strengths first."

Worry spears through me. "We need to get in there."

Archer touches my arm. "But slowly. We've fought a lot of opponents to get this far. We don't know who that guard is and I don't like the look of his sword."

I dig deep into my knowledge of Valkyrie history and beliefs for a man with charred skin and a burning sword...

"It has to be Surt. According to the myths, he is a killer of gods. He brings about the end of the world." I stop tugging against Slade's arms, grateful now that he made me pause. "You're right. Let's go slowly."

I take careful steps forward, Archer prowling beside me while Cain and Slade take up position behind us, keeping watch on either side. From the corner of my eye, I see Slade's fingers twitch across the gun in the harness he wears on his chest. He won't hesitate to take Amalia out if he has the chance.

We stop in our tracks halfway to her position when Surt's voice booms, "Amalia Avery, Valkyrie Queen! If you desire the feather, first you must tell me: who are you?"

Her response is a crisp declaration. "You know who I am."

"That is true, but your answer tells me nothing. Are you nothing, Amalia Avery?"

Her hands twitch and her shoulders tense. Even without seeing her face, I can read the anger in her posture. Amalia is a picture of contradictions but her pride was always guaranteed to fuel her actions.

Her hands clench into fists. Ordinarily, this is the part where I would expect her to attack her opponent and take what she wants. After all, she chose Combat and raised a Valkyrie army in her quest to get to this island.

The fact that she doesn't strike tells me that Surt is not to be trifled with. She might even be afraid of him.

Her head tilts toward the Valkyrie feather hanging in the air on his left. It appears no longer than the length of my forearm, such a delicate object, yet it is her only salvation.

"I am a destroyer," she says. "I will rip and tear and crush the world until it is as crushed as I am."

Surt says, "You speak the truth."

His head remains down, his face obscured. Other than speaking, he hasn't moved a muscle. I have a feeling that when he does, it will be with deadly consequences.

"Make a worthy choice, Destroyer, or my sword will meet your neck."

Amalia spreads her creaking wings, lifts from the ground, and rises cautiously until she is eye-height with the Valkyrie birth feather.

She turns her head slightly, a haughty glance cast back at us, making it clear that she is well aware of our presence—and the fact that she is about to beat us to the feather. Her hazel eyes sparkle with victory, her delicate lips curving into a cruel smile.

A frustrated shout builds in my throat. I can't let her take it…

Before I can move, Slade grabs my arm with a low whisper. "No, Hunter. Look."

Amalia is so absorbed in her triumph over us that she has stopped paying attention to Surt.

The fingers of the ash-dusted man's right hand lift from the handle of his sword one at a time in a quick rippling movement, before he regrips it. It's the first move he has made. I read it as a warning but Amalia isn't taking notice.

Her focus returning to the feather, Amalia tips toward it, her wing beats retaining her height, reaching with outstretched fingers until she is an inch away from taking the feather for herself.

Surt's muscles bunch. He is moving, but why? Has Amalia chosen wrongly? The feather she is reaching for is the Valkyrie feather, the one I would have chosen too…

What is the worthy choice?

Amalia's fingers close around the feather's soft middle. The moment she touches it, a spark of light shoots from the place where she grips it. She stiffens as if she is in shock, her muscles tensing. Her head snaps back and her wings shudder. She sucks in a breath but not with elation. The blood drains from her face, leaving her deathly pale.

In the same moment, Surt stands, rising to his full height. He is as big as Vlad, a wall of muscle and strength. He lifts his blazing sword and swings it in a straight arc toward her exposed neck.

The flames light up her pale face as her attention snaps to him. Without releasing the feather, her free hand whips into the space between them, grabbing his sword mid-air just before it hits her.

Her fingers close around the blade, blood running down her arm. The silver and copper haze glowing around her indicates she is drawing on all her healing strength to stop the blade from slicing through her hand. She pushes back, the cords in her neck straining, her expression stretched thin with pain.

"Why can't I have it?" she screams at him. "It is a worthy choice. It is *my* choice!"

His voice is a booming rumble. "You chose wrong."

"No!" Her shout rises into a high-pitched scream.

The feather sparks again, a sharp, piercing light that makes me wince. It shoots through Amalia, striking her like lightning. Her arms shake as if she is being tossed in a storm, a ripple passing all the way through her body to her toes and wingtips.

Her wings crumple, her head tips back, and her hand unclenches from the feather.

She drops to the floor on top of one of her wings, the other flopping across the ground.

As soon as she lets go of the feather, Surt lowers his sword and steps back, his head bowed once more. He takes two measured paces back to the throne and resumes his seat, leaving Amalia where she lies.

It's impossible to tell from here whether she is still alive but Amalia has survived for so long that it's hard to imagine she could be killed so quickly.

Archer tugs on my arm. "What just happened?"

I feel like I'm stating the obvious when all I have are more questions. "She didn't make the right choice, but I don't understand why. Why was it wrong?"

Archer says, "Surt didn't move to strike her until she held the feather. Maybe she held it the wrong way? Maybe she didn't take it fast enough." Archer grimaces at her own suggestions, quickly saying, "It has to be more than that."

We're clutching at straws. I carefully consider Surt, wondering if there's something we can't see from here.

"All we can do is try," I say.

Archer nods and turns to Cain. He and Slade will come with us, but this is a challenge only Archer and I can face. I give her and Cain as much space as I can while Slade squeezes my hand. "I'll be right behind you." His hand tightens on mine. "I will step between you and that blade if I have to, Hunter."

The determination in his eyes tells me I can't talk him out of it.

"I won't let it come to that," I say.

Surt remains silent and still as we approach. Amalia lies to my right, thrown back a few paces from the Valkyrie feather.

When we are within four paces of him, Surt roars, "Hunter Cassidy, daughter of Glass! If you desire the feather, first you must tell me: who are you?"

Before I entered this maze, in fact only a month ago, I would have struggled to answer that question. Now I lift my voice and reply, believing in the truth of my answer. "I am a hunter. Whether I hunt for answers, truth, or blood, I won't stop until I find what I seek."

I wait for Surt to rebuke me, but he doesn't.

His head remains lowered, his dark hair falling over his face. He roars, "Archer Ryan, you are the last of your kind. If you desire the feather, first you must tell me: who are you?"

Archer gives me a smile before she says, "I am a protector. I won't stop while the ones I love are in danger."

I say to Surt. "We were supposed to be enemies but now we are friends."

Surt is silent for a moment. A small smile lifts the corners of his lips, visible through the hair that obscures his face. "You speak the truth. Only those who know themselves may make a worthy choice."

I take a step toward him. The way the feathers hang in the air reminds me exactly of the illustration in the Coda and Vade that we spent so long trying to decipher—except that this charred man sits between them instead of the woman holding the babies.

I ask, "Who are you?"

There is silence. It stretches so long that I don't think he is going to answer.

His voice lowers. "I am Surt. It is my destiny to destroy the world… but for now, I will make do with devouring the hearts of the unworthy. If you wish to take the feathers, you must make a worthy choice or my sword will meet your necks."

He falls silent.

I eye the flaming sword, the way the fire licks across it. Flecks of ash float around it, settling onto Surt's bare chest and hair. Even when he stood up to strike Amalia, his hair remained over his face, his features obscured.

I'm no closer to understanding where Amalia went wrong.

Maybe it has something to do with knowing our own hearts since he said that only those who know themselves may make a worthy choice, but I don't think that's all it is because Amalia's eventual answer about her inner nature was honest.

I murmur to Archer, "We need to get closer to the feathers, but don't touch them."

"Agreed." She nods and moves to stand beneath the copper feather on Surt's right. There is no chance of her accidentally touching it. It is high enough in the air that she will need help to reach it.

I focus on the silver one.

The moment I stand beneath it, Surt's fingers ripple across the handle of his sword. He gave the same reaction when Amalia reached for the feather, which tells me that we're already making the wrong choice.

Why, why, why?

We've fought so hard to get here, fought together, protected each other. I want Archer to be free of the danger that her wings pose for her. I believe she wants me to heal, too.

Neither one of us is taking power away from the other.

I reach up, focused on the intricate details on the feather, the tiny swirls on every soft tendril. Unlike our permanent feathers, these birth feathers are soft like a duckling's. The closer I get to it, the more Surt stirs.

Making sure to keep my hands away from the feather, I lean in a little, peering at it. It reminds me nearly exactly of the feathers in the illustration with the hidden messages in them...

I gasp, jolting backward, my gaze swiftly passing over the feathers, Surt, Archer, and then back to where I stand. There is something wrong with this picture but it is not Surt or the feathers—it's us.

My hand shoots out. "Archer, stop! Don't touch that feather."

She immediately backs away from the Keres feather. I'm relieved when Surt settles back into his chair, his sword remaining where it is.

I meet Archer's eyes across the short distance between us. "Do you trust me?"

She nods, emphatically. "Without question."

"Then listen... the message hidden in the Coda said: Trust is shared. Only through trust can truth be revealed."

William and I had pored over that picture. He had pointed it out to me more than once—we had both puzzled over the way the picture was drawn—because in the illustration, the feathers were on the wrong side: the Valkyrie feather floated beside the Keres baby, and the Keres feather floated beside the Valkyrie.

"We need to take the other one's feather," I say. "We need to trust each other that much. Can you do that?"

A genuine smile breaks across her face. "Can I trust the woman who nearly killed herself while I huddled inside the wings of the man she loves? Hunter, you don't think of yourself as a protector, but you are. The same way I am also a hunter. Yes, I trust you with my life."

I take a deep breath. My heart is so warm at her complete trust that I don't feel cold anymore. "Then, let's cross the floor."

I take a step just as I sense movement behind me.

Slade shouts my name, his roar echoing around the room.

Sharp pain pierces my back, a burn so sudden and deep that I can't process it.

A bright blade protrudes from my chest. The tip of a sword.

The tip of my own sword.

It retracts, leaving me to topple.

I try to turn. My right hand seeks something to brace against because the world is tipping, the room is sliding to the side.

Amalia's wings creak as she rises up behind me. "Thank you for figuring it out for me."

CHAPTER FORTY-THREE

y knees crumple first and my hip thuds against the stone floor.

Slade throws himself across the distance and slides bodily under me, cushioning my head and shoulders before I crack them against the ground.

"Hunter! No!" Slade's cry reaches me through the scream inside my mind. He presses the wound in my chest, trying to staunch the blood. His other hand cradles my head. "Stay with me!"

I try to speak. "I don't know… how she…"

I didn't hear her creep up on me. It tells me how far gone I was already—how dulled my senses already are. I didn't want to acknowledge that the battle had brought me so much closer to death already.

Slade's determined eyes zero in on me. We both know I only have a few minutes before my healing power dies with me. If I were human, I would be dead already.

His voice vibrates through me like a call to my soul. "I'm carrying you to that feather. I won't lose you, Hunter."

He picks me up, folding me inside his arms where I can see everything that's going on around me.

Amalia is already most of the way to the feather, using her wings to fly toward it. It doesn't look like Surt will stop her this time; she isn't trying to take the wrong feather. The charred man remains as still as stone, the light from his sword flickering across the scene in front of me.

Archer stands her ground beneath the feather, her expression telling me that Amalia will have a fight on her hands if she wants it. Archer doesn't waste breath with screaming, her expression turning hard and cold as she wields a dagger in each fist.

Amalia attempts to fly over her, her hand outstretched, but Archer launches herself into the air, thrusting both daggers into Amalia's exposed chest, hooking them between her ribs and dragging her down.

Amalia screams as she is wrenched away from the feather mere seconds before she would have touched it. She curves her wings and tries to pull herself free from Archer, but Archer follows up with a kick against one of the daggers that forces it hard into Amalia's chest and catapults Amalia back into Cain's waiting arms.

He grabs her wings where they meet her shoulders, pulling them back, his knee rammed into her lower spine. She shouts again, but this time with rage. Cain tips his balance left and they crash to the ground on their sides.

Amalia rolls away from him, snarling with frustration when she jumps to her feet because she is further away from the feather than she was before.

Cain doesn't give her time to recover, filling his next fist with power from his assassin's ring that ripples through Amalia's wings and singes her Valkyrie feathers.

Amalia quickly snaps her wings closed before Archer launches herself across the space, the final bullets in her gun hitting Amalia square in the chest. The barrels click—empty —but she uses them as weapons, striking Amalia hard across the face with them.

Archer and Cain are powerful and coordinated, but even bullets won't stop Amalia.

She will never stop.

Slade hurries with me toward the feather now that the space around it is clear. I lose sight of Archer and Cain as Slade turns toward the feather.

Fear overtakes me when Surt's voice blasts the air. "Slade Baines, son of Josiah Baines, you are not pure Valkyrie. If you try to take the feather, my sword will meet your neck."

Slade pauses only long enough to say, "It is not mine to take. It belongs to Hunter."

As Slade turns to him, I see the corner of Surt's mouth twitch upward. "You speak the truth."

Slade's arms are strong and sure around me as he releases his wings, preparing to rise to the feather. "Nearly there, Hunter. I'll lift you up, but you need to raise your hand. You have to take it for yourself—"

"Look out!" Archer's shout reaches us too late.

An invisible force slams into us, shoving Slade to the side. He bounces against the wall but hangs onto me, rocketing back as another force hits his jaw.

The impact is so rapid that his cheekbone shatters.

My heart stops. I can't process the damage, the way his eyes dim and his wings drop, the seconds slowing as a scream build inside me. "Slade!"

He drops to his knees, his head falling to my shoulder, hunching over me, still gripping me. "*Slade!*"

My heart can't take anymore.

He has taken so many hits for me and Archer.

Too many hits, putting his body on the line every time, heart and soul, fighting for me even when I didn't think I was worth fighting for.

Even when I was so angry that I didn't care how many risks I took, Slade was always there for me.

A new anger burns inside me as Amalia materializes beside us. She must have made it past Archer and Cain by blurring while Slade's back was turned.

She keeps moving at lightning speed. Releasing her wings, Amalia uses Slade's hunched body as a stepping stool, launching herself off his back and up to the feather.

She sails through the air, and despite my rage there is not a damn thing I can do to stop her.

Her hand closes over it. Power ripples through the feather, a bright spark, but this time Amalia smiles, tipping her head back, her hair cascading down her back.

She sighs. "Finally, it's mine."

CHAPTER FORTY-FOUR

Slade's arms tighten around me.

His head is heavy against my shoulder but he pulls me further toward the floor, hunching over me in a protective curl.

I don't know why he's pulling me away from the feather...

Then, a presence rears up over us—a menacing form bearing a blazing sword. With a roar, Surt lifts his sword, swinging it in a terrible, flaming arc toward Amalia's head.

The elation drains from her face a split second before she lets go of the feather and propels herself backward, landing several paces from us. The sword thuds into the wall beneath the feather's position, right at the height where her neck was located moments ago.

Her mouth opens in a soundless scream.

"Why?" she whispers, her murmur turning into a screech of rage. *"Why not?"*

Surt wrenches his sword from the wall and growls, "The

weight of your cruelty tips the scales against you, Amalia Avery, Valkyrie Queen. You are not worthy."

She wrings her hands, her chest heaving, her teeth grinding so hard that I hear them clack above the sound of the hissing sword.

Surt turns his back on her, ambling to the throne where he resumes his seat.

Before he falls silent, he says, "Prepare for your end, Amalia Avery."

Her face contorts. "If I'm going to die, I'm taking you all with me."

Instead of physically attacking us, she throws her hands out, palms up, into the air.

Archer shouts, "She will take our souls!"

I try to see Slade's face, needing to know how badly he is hurt. Neither one of us is functioning right now, but we need both powers to stop Amalia. The Valkyrie power can only come from Slade or me—the Keres power can come from the gun or even Cain's ring. But it has to be done together.

Slade is stirring, healing, but not fast enough. His soul will be Amalia's in the next moment.

He whispers, "Take it… I'll be… right behind you…"

His fist bumps the Keres gun resting against his chest and I know he wants me to use it while I still can.

It's down to me.

I have seconds to get to my feet.

Except that I'm numb. I can't feel my arms or my legs anymore. I've lost my coordination. I should be dead but my power is fighting to keep me alive.

Both Slade and Cain saw a future without Archer and me in it, but I won't let their vision of the future come true.

"Cain!" I scream. I don't know if he understands what I

need, but he's already at my side, pulling me upright. At the same time, Archer reaches for Slade, supporting him.

I grasp at the gun, somehow hooking my finger around the trigger loop so I can pull it out of the harness around Slade's chest. The moment Cain rises to his feet, holding me in his arms, Archer suddenly drops to the floor behind us, clutching her heart. She gasps for air, landing on her side, pressed against Slade's legs.

She rasps, "Hurry, Cain! Amalia is holding my soul."

Cain takes three quick steps with me toward Amalia before he drops too, sending me tumbling across the floor. His hands fist the floor, trying to move, while he gasps for breath.

I hit Amalia's foot.

The gun clatters onto the stone beside me, my hooked finger not strong enough to hold onto it. It stops just beyond my reach.

Amalia stares down at me, her gaze sweeping the room. "Look at all of you, groveling at my feet."

I turn my wrist away from the gun to grip her ankle instead, craning my head back to see her. "What have you done?"

She crouches down to me and laughs. "I'm holding onto Cain and Archer's souls now. I have the power to crush them. I think I'll make it slow and painful."

With one hand still extended toward Cain and Archer, she uses her other to stroke my hair. "Will you finally call me Queen, Hunter Cassidy?"

I consider her lustrous eyes, her sweet smile, her deceptive youth. I wonder if calling her Queen will save my friends, but I doubt it.

That's when a light force tugs at my shoulders, a familiar

sensation that once caused me panic but now fills me with hope. At the same time, the gun rises into the air beside us, seemingly of its own accord, positioning itself so that it points directly at Amalia's heart.

Her focus shifts from me to the weapon in confusion. "How are you—?"

"I'm not," I say. "Slade is."

It's his ringmaker power, his ability to control metal. I don't have the strength to look behind me but I sense his power, the way it tugs at my wings just like his Mom's did. He may not have healed enough to stride across the distance and pull the trigger with his hand, but he can use his mind.

My wings shoot wide and a final wash of my killing power strikes through me, that last of my power, releasing death through my hand into Amalia's ankle where I clench my fist and refuse to let go.

She falls back, grabbing at my fingers, trying to free her ankle, but her legs are her weak point. I feel them now, bony and weak, decimated by the loss of her feather.

Her wings shoot wide, spreading in an attempt to lift herself away from me but my power sizzles through them, attacking the Keres feathers she so artfully attached to herself.

The Keres feathers crackle and burn, peeling and dripping off her wings as she screams, tugs, and wrenches away from me.

Cain and Archer draw deep breaths behind me. I sense their movement as they jump to their feet now that Amalia's power to hold onto their souls is gone.

She twists away from the gun that Slade repositions—remaining aimed perfectly at her heart no matter which way she turns.

I will not let her go. He will not miss.

I whisper, "I will never obey you."

Slade squeezes the trigger.

The bullet hits her heart.

She jolts and gasps a breath. Copper light rips through her, and sears through me too.

My power connects with it, the only shield that saves me from sudden and immediate death.

I'm thrown backward, thudding along the floor, my strength completely gone.

The light fades and Amalia collapses to the floor, her life consumed as quickly as the power that killed her.

CHAPTER FORTY-FIVE

*S*lade's gentle hands turn me over. My wings are still spread, falling across the floor, my silver feathers dull and lifeless.

He picks me up into his arms. "Hold on, Hunter. I've got you."

Archer cries beside him, "Hurry, Slade. She doesn't have long."

Quiet concentration falls over his face. My back prickles, the faintest tug, and very slowly I float up out of his arms, my wings held at just the right angle to keep me upright. My head droops to my chest, but Slade's power elevates me to the height of the feather.

He calls to me, "Take it, Hunter. Please…"

The feather I need is right in front of me, so close, but my arms hang at my sides and not only because I have no strength to lift them.

Amalia wasn't worthy.

I'm not either.

Surt remains where he is, not even a twitch of his fingers.

What gives me the right to take this feather?

I have killed. I am not pure. I have struggled with the darkness inside me. I have hated, I have sought revenge...

...and I have loved, protected, defended, sacrificed...

Mom left me with a message that darkness can be overcome but it doesn't happen in an instant. It is not one act but many, a lifetime of decisions. I have a life ahead of me to fight the darkness.

I am not worthy and never will be, but I am prepared to accept a second chance.

I can't move my fingers, instead, I lean into the feather, its soft tendrils brushing my neck and tickling my cheek.

The moment I touch it, the feather's copper color fades. For a second it turns white before it transforms into silver—a beautiful Valkyrie birth feather hidden beneath the copper facade. The wisps cling to my cheek as if by static, meticulously drawing toward my face. It is as soft as silk as it melts across my cheekbone, down my jaw, along the base of my chin, and into my collarbone.

A wash of energy passes through me, a new warmth that ripples across my torso, making me tingle. The feeling returns to my legs, feet, arms, and hands, and every part of me comes alive.

The gap in my wings where I plucked out my feather begins to fill. A new feather forms to take its place, a perfect silver feather to heal my loss.

As I turn back to Slade, something clicks at the base of my spine, a shift inside me, and all I can think is that the spell that was cast over me when I was a baby, the one that stopped my wings from revealing themselves, must have broken.

I gently lower myself to the floor, folding away my wings,

and step into Slade's open arms. I lower my head to his shoulder, curling into him as he hugs me tight. Tilting my face to his, I press the gentlest kiss to his bruised jaw.

He must still be healing but his response is fierce. "I don't care about the pain. You're alive." He presses his lips to mine and kisses me until I'm breathless, all his fear for me finally leaving his body.

I come up for air to find Archer openly crying, a huge smile on her face as she leans into Cain.

He drops kisses across her cheek, kissing away her tears. "It's your turn now."

She tilts her head back. "I'm going to need a little help."

He gives her a lazy grin before he hoists her up onto his shoulder, where she sits, balancing while he carries her to the feather with the silver facade.

Maintaining her balance on his shoulder, she unclasps her protective suit and peels it off one arm, which she holds upright against the feather. At her touch, it transforms like mine did, revealing its true copper color beneath. She waits patiently for the tendrils to wrap around her forearm. The feather nestles against her skin, softly molding itself to her muscles before it melts into her body.

She gasps, rolls her shoulders, and closes her eyes, inhaling a slow breath. "Oh... so that's what wings are supposed to feel like..."

Cain turns his head to drop a kiss against her thigh, reaching up to clasp her arms and torso securely and swing her down to the floor.

"Try them," he says with a smile.

She steps into a clear space, her forehead crinkling as she rolls her shoulders again. Copper wings gradually unfurl from her back, stretching out wide beside her. They are as brilliant as they were when she opened them to let us into the maze.

Archer's radiant smile makes her glow. She bites her lip as she looks at Cain.

He takes a step toward her but stops himself, appearing uncertain for the first time. He asks, "May I?"

She answers him by catapulting into his arms, wrapping her wings around them both, cocooning them so that they disappear from sight.

My heart lifts. "Archer is finally free from the threat of her wings."

"And you are free to live," Slade murmurs.

I wrap my arms around him and sink into the warmth and acceptance I find there.

"We are both free to live," I say as he strokes my hair.

Except that there might be more than two of us now. In the fight for survival, I pushed aside the possibility that Amalia's claim might be true—that I could be pregnant. It's hard for me to believe anything she said. Her goal was always to manipulate the outcome for her own benefit.

Even so, if it's a possibility, then Slade needs to know.

Before I can speak, a figure appears at the open entrance to the hall—a young girl dressed in an emerald gown. She is a picture of grace, masses of dark brown hair cascading over her shoulders, her eyes a gorgeous hazel color.

For a second I think it's Amalia—that she has somehow been resurrected—and my reflexes kick in.

I pull Slade toward Archer and Cain, calling for them. They are immediately alert, emerging from Archer's wings to face this new challenge.

The girl stops halfway to us, both hands raised in a gesture of peace. "I have come for my mother."

I blink at her before my confusion clears. I finally recognize her from Amalia's memory. "You're Elaina."

She gives me a quick nod. "When my mother called the Valkyrie army back from the dead, she brought me back, too. I don't think she realized it."

Elaina doesn't encroach on our space, remaining where she is. "I didn't take part in the fight just now. I never agreed with my mother's actions. In fact, at the end of my life, General Glass was my only friend. Still, I want to carry my mother to the End Land where she can rest."

I step aside. I don't sense any threat from this girl. Slade gives me a nod of agreement too.

Without another word, Elaina crosses the distance to kneel beside her mother, smoothing out her hair and tucking the remains of Amalia's wings to her sides, before wrapping her arms around her.

She grips her mother's body and spreads her own wings, rising gently into the air before she carries Amalia away.

They disappear through the entrance, leaving a pensive silence. Amalia is finally gone.

All I want now is to leave the maze, to find out if Vlad and Tansy are okay, and to return to Saber Lane and the bookshop.

"Do you think we will have to fight our way out of here?" I ask Slade.

Surt's voice rumbles behind us. "I will show you the way out. But only after I speak with my daughter."

I stumble back in shock as he shifts his sword to the side, driving its tip into a slot in the floor on the left of his throne. He raises himself up out of the chair. At full height, he is as tall as Vlad and just as broad in the chest. He sweeps his thick hair out of his eyes, revealing his face for the first time.

His two violet eyes focus on Archer.

She freezes in shock. "You can't be… How can you be…?"

"Daughter," he says. "You look a little like your mother, but mostly like me."

Archer shakes her head. "This is… not possible…"

He laughs, but it is a gentle sound. "Your mother was rebellious. She was supposed to remain outside the maze, guarding it from the creatures that sought to enter. But not many creatures know about the maze now. Over time, she grew bored. One day, she ventured inside. I didn't meet her that day. Or the next. I didn't meet her until she figured out the shortcut to my castle."

My face falls. I can't believe what he just said. "You're telling us there's a shortcut?"

He tilts his head toward me in a gentle nod. "Do not be dismayed. It took her years to find it. Then… she found me."

Archer waves her hand at Surt in disbelief. "But you… you could have killed her."

He shakes his head. "She never tried to take a feather. All she did was answer my questions. Each day I asked her a new one and she always answered truthfully. Then one day, she started asking me questions."

He falls silent. Then, quietly: "One day, she didn't come back."

Archer approaches him cautiously. "Did you know about me?"

He nods. "You were born here. She wanted to stay in the maze with me, but I am bound to this place until the end of days. What kind of life would it be for a child to be raised in a place filled with monsters?"

Archer gives a cry, her hand flying over her mouth. "But

don't you see? It happened anyway. Human monsters surrounded me, not mythological ones."

He lowers his sad eyes to her. "I am sorry for your pain, daughter. From what I see, you are no longer surrounded by such people."

She stares back at him, brushing the tears from her eyes. "This is a lot to process."

He nods. "You must leave now, because you have already been here for a long time, but you can come back and see me again. You can ask me all the questions you want and I will answer you."

"I…" She turns to Cain. It's a long way for her to travel, but he nods immediately.

"Whatever you need," he says. "We will make it happen."

She turns to the man who claims to be her father, studying his features. "Something tells me you aren't the hugging type."

The corner of his mouth twitches. "I am not."

"Then I will come back with questions."

Surt smiles. "Let me show you the way out."

We follow him to the back of the room and a hidden door that he accesses by touching a sequence of bricks. Outside, a single staircase leads upward into the mist.

Surt says, "These steps will take you back to the entrance. Next time, when you enter the maze, step off the bridge immediately to your left and you will find these stairs again."

Archer and Cain ascend the staircase first while Slade and I follow.

It's a lot for me to take in, let alone for Archer. She moves like she's wading through water, still in shock. When I found out that Ridley was my father, I cried for hours. It took time to think it through. It will take Archer time, too. Probably more so because her father turns out to be a mythological killer of gods.

I peer up at Surt as I pass him, stopping at the last moment. "You said that you are destined to destroy the world. Did you mean that literally?"

He tilts his head as he answers me. "There are many worlds in this place, Hunter Cassidy. There are worlds within worlds. I have already destroyed hundreds of them. Now, go in peace."

I take Slade's hand, drawing free breaths as we climb the stairs.

When I meet Archer halfway up, Slade and Cain go on ahead, giving us space. They glance back every now and then to make sure we are okay. Surt indicated that we would be safe now, but we aren't taking anything for granted until we leave this place.

Archer chews her lip, speaking carefully. "What am I supposed to make of all that?"

I squeeze her hand. "Take your time. Feel what you need to feel."

Her chest rises and falls with a deep breath. "It could explain why I'm stronger than most of my species."

I smile. "Or you could be stronger because you made yourself stronger. I don't think you can give Surt credit for all of it."

She returns my smile and pauses briefly to stare out across the maze.

From here, we can see everything: the floating castle immediately below us, the diamond tunnels that we walked into unawares, and the burning plain stretching out between them.

The armies are gone now, descended back into the ash,

leaving the field quiet. Each way we look, there are different pathways, different choices.

The path we chose was only one.

She points into the far distance to the World Tree whose branches stretch high into the sky. "I didn't realize what I felt, but when we stood on the branches of that tree, I sensed…" She shrugs, visibly grappling with how to describe her feelings. "I sensed other places."

She points to the left of the tree, "Over there is another world—filled with people who look like us and live like us but they heal even faster than Slade does. You'd think they'd be happy but they aren't. There's a war coming to their world."

Then she points to the right of the tree and her forehead creases with a hint of worry. "And in that direction, a titan was buried, more powerful than any other." She shakes her head with wonder. "This maze contains more than we could imagine."

I stare at her. "You can see all that?"

She shrugs. "No matter what you say about my strength being my own, this is definitely something I get from my father." She turns and points in the other direction. "Over there is another world that is so bright, so perfect, that it can't be real, because nothing can be that perfect."

"You are," Cain's voice rumbles behind her.

She gives him a smile that lights up her eyes before she takes his hand again.

Slade reaches for me and I allow myself to feel the peace of this moment, of his hand in mine and the way his expression changes when he looks at me, the quiet heat that makes me wish we were alone right now.

I return his smile as the copper sun sinks below the horizon and we make our way out of the maze.

CHAPTER FORTY-SIX

The clearing outside the maze is peaceful, quiet.

It's strange to see the afternoon sunlight, golden and crisp like it should be, filtering through the leaves overhead. It looks different somehow, brighter, greener, and the air is warmer than I expected.

A lone figure sits on a fold-up chair beneath the spreading branches, a picnic basket at her side with a bunch of flowers spilling from its edge, and her spellbook resting on her lap.

Tansy's head shoots up the moment we step through the entry. She darts out of her chair, dropping her book onto the forest floor as she races toward us. "Hunter! Archer!"

"Tansy!" I hug her as she reaches us, pulling Archer into our hug, tears washing down her cheeks. She smiles through them. "You're back. You're really back."

I return her smile. "We made it. It worked. Archer has her wings and I have my life."

"What about Amalia?" Tansy's expression becomes stern and worried for a moment.

"She's dead," Slade says. "She will never hurt us again."

"But what about Vlad?" I ask Tansy. "Please tell me he's okay."

Tansy speaks in a rush, seeming unable to answer me fast enough. "He's fine. Completely healed. Actually, he's due here any minute. We've been taking it in turns watching for your return. Not just Vlad and me, but the Guardian too. She was here for a few days, and then Ridley. He nearly refused to leave but he had to get back to the Legion. Lutz went south to make sure Parker was okay and—"

"Wait, slow down. I'm confused." I glance at the others, wondering if I heard Tansy correctly.

Cain, Slade, and Archer shuffle around me, wearing identical expressions of confusion.

"You said the Guardian was here for a few days," I say. "But we left yesterday."

She studies me for a moment. "You've been gone for a month."

"A month?"

She nods emphatically. "I nearly lost my mind with worry in that first week. Ridley practically tore up this whole area trying to get inside the maze. But Vlad..." She sighs and bites her lip. "His unemotional nature was a benefit to all of us. He said you were too stubborn to die. We couldn't disagree with him."

Laughter bursts from me, a mix of happy and sad. "Oh, Tansy. I'm so sorry you were worried. It wasn't easy and we almost didn't make it, but we're here."

She smiles, fresh tears spilling down her cheeks. "I'm really happy to see you."

I pull her into a long hug, drawing Archer into it too.

When we finally separate, laughing and wiping our eyes, we find Vlad waiting at the edge of the clearing.

He wears a grin. "Glass Arrow, you're not such a machine after all."

With a cautious smile to Tansy—because I haven't got a vibe from her yet about whether she and Vlad have smoothed over their conflict—I cross the distance to Vlad and hug him.

He hugs me back, dragging me off my feet. "It's good to see you looking so alive, Hunter. You've got color in your cheeks again."

I don't know what I looked like before I went into the maze, but I know I feel much stronger.

"You too, Vlad," I say, arching my eyebrows at him. "You weren't in good shape when we left."

He considers Tansy for a moment. She gives nothing away—a blank slate—as she stands with Archer and Cain.

"Tansy didn't stop until I was healed." He clears his throat, focusing on me and diverting the conversation. "You must want to get home."

"Yes. Please. More than anything."

"The SUV is big enough for all of us." He stoops to pick up the basket, pulling the flowers out and handing them to Tansy, before he heads back along the forest path carrying the basket and the fold-up chair. "Let's go, then. There's food in the vehicle."

I pull Tansy aside before we follow, eyeing the flowers Vlad gave her. "You and Vlad?"

She takes a deep breath. "We're friends. He gives me flowers every day as an apology for what he said. It still hurts, but he can't change what was done to him any more than I can change what happened to me. I have to accept it and move forward."

She draws another deep breath into her chest, exhaling slowly. "I am determined to focus on everything positive in my life. That's what William would have wanted for me. It's what I want for myself."

I ask, gently, "Even if it breaks your heart?"

She whispers, "I'll be okay. I promise." She plasters a smile on her face. "Let's go home. Everyone on Saber Lane will be happy to see you."

She squeezes my arm and goes on ahead, moving past Slade, who pauses at the edge of the clearing for me.

We are all hungry and tired. I would give anything to sink into his arms in a quiet place, eat a meal together, and process everything that happened in the maze, but I can't take another step toward the future without complete honesty.

I hold tight to his big hand as we walk, taking deep breaths, hoping I can say what I need to say. "Slade, there's something I need to tell you, but I don't know how."

He waits for me to continue, carefully picking a path through the trees, staying close to me.

Cain and Archer walk ahead of us, with Tansy and Vlad in front of them.

Slade doesn't ask me questions. He knows that if he does I'll have to answer. Instead, he says, "You can tell me anything. No matter what it is, I'll listen."

I blurt, "It's possible that I'm pregnant."

His expression softens in the dappled light. A smile grows across his face, a gentle one, but he remains serious. "Do you believe you are?"

I shake my head. "Amalia said I was, but she told a lot of lies."

"She did," Slade says. "Except when she spoke with you. She said she had trouble lying to you, remember?"

My jaw drops a little. "You believe her?"

He pulls me to a stop, sinks a tooth into his bottom lip, and drags in a breath. Speaking slowly, he says, "I already knew."

"What?" My shriek stops my friends further ahead on the path. "How can you possibly know when I don't?"

Slade gives me an apologetic smile. "The same way I know that Vlad has an implant where he must have lost a tooth during a boxing match. The same way I know that Archer's feathers are about to make an appearance because she's worried she needs to fly to you right now. Our daughter is already developing wings and a strong spine to support them."

He gives me a very slow shrug, followed by a smile that makes my heart flutter. "It's amazing, Hunter. It's more than I ever could have hoped for—"

I stop him with a kiss—a terrified, joyful, excited, petrified, stunned kiss.

I have no words. I can't speak.

Mom told me to let go of the past and walk my own path. Now I get to do that, not only with Slade by my side, but with a daughter I never thought I'd be privileged to have.

Judging by the look Slade gives me when we pull apart, we might end up with more than one.

A thrill runs through me and I can't wipe the smile off my face, true happiness brimming inside me.

The future isn't certain. There will be other battles, but

right now I have more than I ever dreamed possible, more than I ever thought I would have.

As I leave the maze behind, I take my first steps into a new future.

CHAPTER FORTY-SEVEN

THREE MONTHS LATER

The meeting hall inside the Dominion's Cathedral hushes as soon as we enter, all eyes turned in our direction.

Despite the seemingly unstoppable rain elsewhere in Portland, the air inside the Dominion is warm and comfortable.

It's a far cry from the harsh environment in the Legion, although Slade has made a lot of changes to the Legion's Realm in the last three months, including insulating the cold buildings and adding women's showers. The fresh intake of Novices includes four women who have every potential to make it to their final missions.

Vlad strides toward us with a rare grin on his face. "Welcome to the first official meeting of the Ambassadors."

Behind him, Cain and Archer both wear welcoming smiles as they rise from their seats at the large round table in the center of the room, their hands unashamedly clasped.

In the background, Lutz Logan stands beside a young woman I don't recognize, but the family resemblance with

Cain is striking. She has the same nearly-black hair and green eyes. She takes Lutz's hand as she rises from her seat, her trusting gaze turning from him to us.

I'm a little surprised as I study his clean cut appearance, which is vastly different now that he's living with the Horde. No more unruly mop of hair and crumpled clothing, although a single day's growth shadows his jaw, maintaining his ferocious appearance.

There are about ten other people in the room, including Rowan Robertson who volunteered to be the Legion Ambassador to the Dominion.

The Guardian is also present. She wasn't particularly happy when we presented her with our decision to allow Faction members to cross borders and live in other Factions.

She was also thrown to discover that I already gave Archer an assassin's ring, but the Guardian's discomfort seemed more about protocol being broken than any actual objection on her part. Given that she's the upholder of the Code, I understand her reluctance to bend the rules.

Slade gives me a smile that never fails to make my heart kick inside my chest.

I give him a sultry smile in return that makes him miss a step.

Well, if Cain and Archer can hold hands in this formal setting, I can make eyes at my husband.

With a grin that tells me we'll do something about it later, Slade moves ahead to greet Vlad with the traditional bow before he moves on to Cain and Archer.

After a quick bow to me, Vlad shuffles a little. His question is casual, but the tension in his posture tells me that the answer means more than he lets on. "How is Tansy?"

It's a good thing I don't have to tell him the truth.

Tansy barely rests. When she isn't helping me in the bookshop or using her magic to help clients, she is studying every spellbook she can get her hands on.

She says she's searching for a way to heal her power, but I suspect she's really searching for a way to remove the spell that Mother Serena cast over Vlad.

Despite the passage of time and the distance now between them, she hasn't forgotten him.

One look at him tells me he hasn't forgotten her either.

"She's well," I say. "She's determined to mend her power, but it isn't easy."

He gives me a nod, his expression closed off. "I'm sure she will succeed."

We take our seats and the meeting begins with the Guardian congratulating us on the new peace between Factions. Skirmishes still break out along the borders—I don't think that will ever change—but the enmity between the Masters is long gone.

All I can hope is that it continues into the next generation.

When the meeting is over, I make my way to Archer who gives me a hug and draws me into a quieter spot at the back of the room.

"How is your father?" I ask.

She went back to see him a few weeks ago, but because of the time difference, her visit lasted a week.

"He's as cryptic as he was the first time I met him," she says with a smile. "But I found out a little more about my mother. She was a lot more expressive of her emotions than I am."

Archer's gaze travels to Cain. As if they're connected, he

pauses his conversation with Slade to give her a smile that would make any woman's heart melt.

They don't even have to speak with each other for everyone in this room to know that she and Cain would die to protect each other. Sometimes, words aren't necessary.

I change the subject with a grin. "How are your archery skills coming along?"

She laughs. "Not a hope in hell."

I give her a snide smile. "I thought you said you didn't have any weaknesses?"

She huffs. "Archery doesn't count. Crossbows are more efficient."

"Well, if you want some tips, Dad can give you lessons. He's still trying to teach me. Not that I'm improving."

She leans closer. "And the baby? How are you feeling?"

"Well, since it was only a day for us in the maze, I'm four months along, even though, technically, five months have passed." My forehead crinkles at how mind-boggling that is. "I've let the Guardian know. I'll need to use my judgement to decide when I should pause my missions but for now, I'm taking it a day at a time."

As if I conjured the Guardian by speaking about her, she appears at my elbow, her expression as serene as always. "Hunter, may I have a word?"

"Of course." I give Archer's hand a squeeze before I follow the Guardian from the room.

We make our way to a quiet nook at the end of the corridor outside the meeting hall.

Once there, the Guardian doesn't mince words. "As you know, my time as Guardian will be up in seven months. I have that long to choose a successor, but I already know I would like it to be you."

Cain told me that the Guardian would choose me and I'm prepared to reject her offer. I immediately shake my head. "I'm not the right person for the job."

"Why not?"

"It's too much responsibility," I say. "Deciding who lives or dies is not a weight I want on my shoulders."

I don't tell her that an eagle named *Justice* drove that truth home to me.

"Which is exactly why you should do it," she says.

I grimace. "Guardian, I'm a Rogue Master. I'm a rule-breaker, not a rule-keeper."

She gives me a quiet smile. "Actually, I beg to differ. You could have killed Gareth and avenged your mother at any time, but you chose to show restraint. You could have stepped in and protected Briar, but you trusted the system. I think you're less rogue than you think you are, Hunter."

She takes my hands in a surprising gesture, her palms warm. "If you become the Guardian, your path will change. No more midnight missions. No more putting your life on the line. You can give your child a normal life. They won't have to worry that their mother won't come home one night."

If I were completely human, the Guardian's arguments would be compelling.

The sphere of people who know about me and Slade is very small: Cain, Archer, Tansy, and Vlad. Ridley was the last I told. He took it in his stride, aside from needing several strong drinks afterward. Then a long walk. Then some more drinks. Eventually, he gave me a hug and said it didn't change anything.

Even so, I'm not invincible.

I never expected my own mother to die, and I never want

to leave my daughter that way. What's more, as Guardian, I would control the assassin's rings that were created from my people. I can decide what happens to them.

I can never reverse what was done to the Valkyrie, but I can make sure that only the worthy wear the rings—only those who seek to help the helpless.

Hell, I might even make some rules myself.

This is not the path I saw for myself, it's not the way I expected to spend my life, but I never expected to be married and have a daughter either.

I twist the wedding band around my finger, knowing that this decision will change the course of my life. It's going to be hard. The decisions won't be easy, but neither is life. Neither is love.

I take a deep breath, knowing that my next words will change everything. "I'll do it."

The Guardian exhales. "Oh, thank the saints."

Her soft exclamation is so intense that it gives me pause.

I study the tension around her eyes and mouth, the signs of stress that she was hiding behind a mask of serenity, which has suddenly dropped away. "Guardian?"

"Now that you're my Heir Apparent, there are things I can tell you," she says in a hushed whisper. "Things I can't tell anyone else. About the missing assassin's rings and the Unknowns—"

"Wait, slow down." I continue to search her eyes, startled by the fear I find in them. "Missing rings? Unknowns?" I shake my head. The idea of missing rings is alarming enough, but… "What are Unknowns?"

The Guardian's hand closes over mine as she seems to center herself. "Lady Tirelli's legacy stretches far beyond what we thought. I need your help, Hunter."

Tension rises within me, but I square my shoulders with determination. No matter what happens, no matter what new battles are coming my way, I know that the people I love will stand beside me through it all.

"You have my support," I say to the Guardian. "Now tell me what I need to know."

Find out what happens next, and meet the Unknowns, in Rebels.

REBELS

(ASSASSIN'S MAGIC BOOK 5)

Find out what happens next, and meet the Unknowns, in Rebels.

I am an Unknown. A threat to all around me.

Love is a dream that will never be mine.

My choices have been taken from me.

I've been sent to Bloodwing Academy because I'm one of the magically repressed. I should have magical powers, but I don't. Not yet.

One day, I'll wake up and my powers will be out of my control. I'll be a threat to everyone around me, but that doesn't mean they should lock me up.

Especially with a man like Striker Draven.

He is dangerously fierce. Savagely gorgeous. A fiery piece of hell risen to the surface of the Earth.

As heir to the Draven fortune, he thinks he can have whatever he wants.

He wants to pull me apart, rip out my power, and take my heart with it.

That's if I don't rip his out first.

I'm determined to survive this place and escape it.

Even if the fight for my freedom destroys my heart.

Content information: Rebels is dark urban fantasy romance, the fifth in the Assassin's Magic series.

Recommended reading age is 17+ for sex scenes, mature themes, and violence. Ends on a cliffhanger.

REVENGE

(ASSASSIN'S MAGIC BOOK 6)

I am vengeance. A bringer of fury.

Love is a blade that could tear me apart.

My bond with Striker Draven has been forged in blood.

We fought for our freedom only to discover that our enemies are far more powerful than we thought.

The Assassin's Legion is hunting us like the monsters we are.

But the students are now my family and I would die to protect them.

Just as I would die to protect Striker.

He is strength and fury, a hellish beast whose touch ignites my dark soul.

And yet… the closer I get to him, the greater the danger grows.

Our enemies are weaving a web around us, spun with power and deceit, until I'm left with only one path to freedom.

A path that could break my heart.

Content information: Revenge is dark urban fantasy romance, the sixth in the Assassin's Magic series.

Recommended reading age is 17+ for sex scenes, mature themes, and violence. Ends on a cliffhanger.

ALSO BY EVERLY FROST

ASSASSIN'S MAGIC - COMPLETE

(Dark Urban Fantasy Romance)

1. Assassin's Magic

2. Assassin's Mask

3. Assassin's Menace

4. Assassin's Maze

5. Rebels

6. Revenge

7. Rogue

8. Assassin's Match

SOUL BITTEN SHIFTER - COMPLETE

(Dark Urban Fantasy Romance)

1. This Dark Wolf

2. This Broken Wolf

3. This Caged Wolf

4. This Cruel Blood

SUPERNATURAL LEGACY - COMPLETE

(Angels and Dragon Shifters)

1. Hunt the Night

2. Chase the Shadows

3. Slay the Dawn

4. Claim the Light

DARK MAGIC SHIFTERS

(Dark Urban Fantasy Romance)

1. Wolf of Ashes

2. Bond of Flames

3. Crown of Fate

KINGDOM OF BETRAYAL

(Fantasy Romance)

1. A Sky Like Blood

2. A Sin Like Fire

3. A Storm Like Iron

4. A Soul Like Glass

BRIGHT WICKED - COMPLETE

(Fantasy Romance)

1. Bright Wicked

2. Radiant Fierce

3. Infernal Dark

STORM PRINCESS - COMPLETE

(Fantasy Romance)

1. Book 1

2. Book 2

3. Book 3

DEMON PACK - COMPLETE

(Dark Paranormal Romance)

1. Demon Pack

2. Demon Pack: Elimination

3. Demon Pack: Eternal

MORTALITY - COMPLETE

(Science-Fantasy Romance)

Mortality Complete Set: Books 1 to 4

1. Beyond the Ever Reach

2. Beneath the Guarding Stars

3. By the Icy Wild

4. Before the Raging Lion

<u>**Stand-alone fiction - dark romance**</u>

Corrupt Me: Immortal Vices and Virtues

ABOUT THE AUTHOR

Everly Frost is the USA Today Bestselling author of fantasy romance, urban fantasy and paranormal romance novels. She spent her childhood dreaming of other worlds and scribbling stories on the leftover blank pages at the back of school notebooks. She lives in Brisbane, Australia with her husband and two children.

amazon.com/author/everlyfrost

facebook.com/everlyfrost

instagram.com/everlyfrost

bookbub.com/authors/everly-frost

goodreads.com/everlyfrost